STEEL MAIDEN

DIVIDED REALMS
BOOK I

KIM RICHARDSON

AWARD-WINNING AUTHOR OF *MARKED*

First edition: August 2015

MORE BOOKS BY KIM RICHARDSON

SOUL GUARDIANS SERIES

Marked Book # 1

Elemental Book # 2

Horizon Book # 3

Netherworld Book # 4

Seirs Book # 5

Mortal Book # 6

Reapers # 7

Seals Book # 8

MYSTICS SERIES

The Seventh Sense Book # 1

The Alpha Nation Book # 2

The Nexus Book # 3

DIVIDED REALMS

Steel Maiden Book # 1

For those who dare to dream

STEEL MAIDEN

DIVIDED REALMS BOOK 1

KIM RICHARDSON

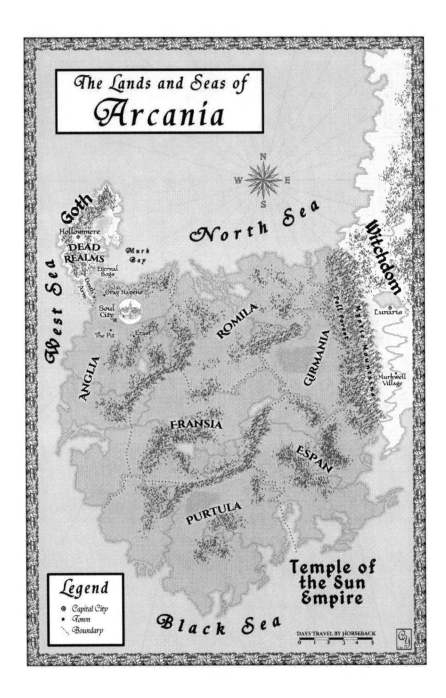

The Lands and Seas of **Arcania**

Goth

West Sea

North Sea

Witchdom

Hollowmere

DEAD REALMS

Murk Gap

Eternal Bogs

Death's River

Gray Havens

Soul City

The Pit

Exrut

Lunaris

ROMILA

Pell Forest

Mystic Mountains

GIRMANIA

Murkwell Village

ANGLIA

FRANSIA

ESPAN

PURTULA

Temple of the Sun Empire

Black Sea

Legend
- ◉ Capital City
- • Town
- ⋯ Boundary

DAYS TRAVEL BY HORSEBACK
0 1 2 3 4 5

CHAPTER 1

THE TEMPLE VAULT WAS completely dark.

I'd been crouched inside a cabinet with my chin resting awkwardly on my knees for about six hours, and now the muscles in my body screamed and burned. Acid from hunger worked away in my empty stomach, and the air was hot and stale. A cold sweat trickled down my back, but I kept my breathing low and steady, held my position, and waited.

I could hear muffled male voices and the shuffling of feet.

Pricks.

If the temple guards discovered me now, they would slit my throat before I could even begin to explain why I was here, hidden in a cupboard in the vault. The truth is there was only one reason why someone would sneak into the temple vault at night—to steal the high priests' treasures.

I bit my lip. This was by far the stupidest and most dangerous stunt I'd ever pulled. But hunger and desperation had brought me farther into Soul City than I'd ever ventured before. And now I'd been foolish enough to seek my quarry inside the vault. I knew the risks.

We'd finished the last of the cabbage soup two days ago, and Byron hadn't any bread to spare this week. I'd sworn last night that I wouldn't spend another night with a hungry belly.

A cramp bit into my leg, but I ignored it. Hiding in cubbyholes for long hours wasn't new to me. I was used to small spaces. Thank the creator I wasn't claustrophobic. My heart thumped loudly in my ears as my hunger was replaced by my anger.

The high priests were the reason we were all starving. There were enough precious stones and jewels in the vault to feed the families in the Pit for generations, and yet we were all starving to death. It was clear that the priests wanted to keep us hungry. We were easier to control.

Bastards.

I remember the stories I had heard when I was a child. Three hundred years ago, after the Great War of the Realms, the Temple of the Sun priests had arrived. No one had known for sure where they came from, but the legends told that the kings and queens of the six kingdoms of Arcania had stepped down, one by one, and relinquished their rule to the high priests. Some legends spoke of a dark spell that had been cast on the kings and queens since they had so willingly given their titles and their kingdoms to the priests. But no one knew for sure.

Not everyone was subject to the priests' will, however, and a great rebellion against them had arisen two hundred years ago. Unfortunately attempts to remove the high priests had been in vain.

12

Most of the men and women from the kingdom of Anglia who had joined the rebellion had been slaughtered like cattle by the temple guards.

But the priests did keep some of the rebels alive. As punishment, and to remind those who might dare to oppose them again that their efforts would be futile, the priests created the Pit. They confined the rebels to the district of Anglia where the rebellion had started. Now ten thousand prisoners were cramped into a muddy, filthy shantytown where they were forced to live out their lives as trash. They would never forget that their ancestors had tried to rebel.

There was a saying amongst our kind. *If you're born in the Pit, you die in the Pit.*

But I wouldn't die here. *I* was going to get out.

I couldn't let my anger cloud my mind. I had a job to do, and I needed to focus. It was risky, but this was finally my chance to get out of the Pit, and I had to take it. I wouldn't mess it up. I couldn't.

After a few minutes of careful listening, I heard the screeching of hinges and then the loud thump of a heavy door. I knew there were only two guards patrolling the vault, and I couldn't risk them discovering me. Although I could hold my own in a fight, even with two grown men, I had to go unnoticed if I wanted my plan to work. That meant no fights.

I had been blessed with a talent for hand-to-hand combat although I had never received any real training. My earliest memories were of throwing a set of knives against the trunk of a tree and hitting the makeshift target every time. I was adept with weapons, especially ones with a blade. I never knew where my skill came from, or why I had it, it just *was*. Rose called it a gift—I called it survival instinct.

My heart thundered as I strained for any more sounds. Only the darkness of my cupboard whispered back. It was now or never.

I held my breath and pressed lightly on the door. I peered through the small crack and blinked at the sudden brightness. A series of flaming torches illuminated the vault in soft yellow light.

I was alone. I let out a shaky breath and then slipped into the vault with the stealth of a cat.

My limbs ached and cracked as I stretched and moaned quietly. I took a calming breath, grateful for the gulps of fresh air, and looked around carefully. Bile burned my throat as I took in the shelves that lined the walls. They were loaded with brilliant gems and precious jewelry.

Sick. All of it. The people from the Pit were starving while this useless chamber sat stuffed with enough jewels to feed a nation. It was probably just a fraction of the high priests' wealth, and it was a wealth that had once belonged to our kings.

One, two, three, I counted in my head. I only had about five minutes before the next rotation of the temple guards would check on the vault.

I clenched my fingers as I stared at a large necklace speckled with rubies and sapphires. I could certainly fill my pockets with necklaces like these—they were practically *begging* for me to steal them. But that would be stupid. I couldn't afford to be stupid. Not now when I was so close...

Even if I did take my fill of precious stones and pearl necklaces, I wouldn't be able to sell them. Women in the Pit didn't own jewelry. Where would we wear it if we did? It would raise questions if I tried to sell it. I'd get caught if I were greedy.

There was only one person in the Pit who *would* and *could* buy such trinkets, and he'd already made a deal with me. I wasn't here for a mere necklace. I had *bigger* plans.

I crossed the chamber to the opposite wall and stood before a tall metal cabinet. Two lions, the royal seal of Anglia, were engraved into the metal. I couldn't see any lock or device that secured the doors.

A trap? Why wasn't it locked?

It felt too easy. A treasure of incredible valuable must have some kind of lock. Even if it were a trap, what choice did I have? I had committed to this, and I would see it through—for my sake and for Rose's.

With my heart in my throat, I pulled open the doors and stifled a gasp as a veil of green fire enveloped me and licked every inch of my exposed skin.

I panicked and stepped back.

The strange wall of green flames could only be magic. What was magic fire doing in the high priests' vault? Priests saw magic as the devil's work. It was forbidden in Arcania, so why was it here? There was not supposed to be any magic on this side of the world. The legends said that magic came from beyond the mystic mountains in the east, from Witchdom. And yet it was right here, in front of me.

I don't know how long I stood there, watching the green flames dance along the edges of the cabinet, but in my moment of panic I had forgotten to count.

Damn, Elena. I cursed to myself. *You can be such a fool sometimes.*

How many seconds had passed? Twenty? Thirty? My cheeks burned at my own stupidity and how easily I had been distracted.

I took a deep breath and braced myself.

"For a better life," I whispered and stepped into the veil of green fire.

I cringed, not knowing what to expect. The flames tickled my skin and warmth spread on my face as though the sun kissed my cheeks. But it didn't burn, and surprisingly my skin didn't melt.

I couldn't hear anything except the pounding of my heart in my ears, but I could see my quarry through the swaying green flame. It was a golden crown set with gems, and it featured two golden lions facing a large red diamond. It was probably the high priests' most valued treasure, and they had gone to the trouble of conjuring magic fire to protect it. It was the crown of the last king of Anglia, and it had been stolen three hundred years ago by the priests of the Temple of the Sun Empire. They had taken it just as they had taken everything else.

Heat flushed my face as my hatred for the priests mixed with the heat of the flames. Many babies had died of the fever last winter, but no healers had been sent to our aid. With all this wealth they could easily have sent healers. But they hadn't. We didn't matter. And it wasn't just the priests, even the nobles and the lords of Anglia pretended we didn't exist.

Although diamonds and precious stone necklaces, rings, bracelets and encrusted weapons hung on the walls of the vault, I knew they were nothing compared to the value of this crown. *This* crown was my ticket out of the Pit. *This* crown would give me a new life.

The crown sat on a plush red cushion, daring me to take it. The thought of Mad Jack's face when I handed him the crown made me smile. I was almost giddy. I had told him I could do it, but he had laughed in my face. And now freedom stared *me* in the face. It was almost too easy.

And he said it was impossible.

Carefully, I picked up the crown, wrapped it in a cloth, and dropped it into the pouch around my belt. I didn't have time to admire it. I knew my five minutes were nearly up. I had to leave now.

As I turned to leave, my vision blurred for a second, and the green fire began to burn my lungs. Smoke coiled from my black wool cloak like a mist, and the smell of burned hair filled my nose. I fought against the dizzy spell that shook my knees. If I passed out now, I'd either burn to ash, or the temple guards would feast on me. The thought was enough to shake me out of my stupor.

I pulled my hood over my head, spun around, leaped out of the flames, and bolted. I was at the vault's door in a few great bounds.

As I reached for the handle I looked back at all those gleaming diamonds and pearls. It was the richest sight I'd ever beheld. Part of me wanted to reach out and fill my pockets with treasure for the others in the Pit, especially for the little ones, to fill their aching bellies. But I knew it was too risky. I couldn't chance anything going wrong when I was so close.

The only thing left for me to do was to run.

CHAPTER 2

THE RISING SUN WAS a glowing yellow disk by the time I exited the vault. My knees shook and my stomach twisted in hunger and excitement. I was exhausted from the lack of sleep, but it wasn't anything I hadn't felt before, and it was worth it. The thought of starting a new life sent a jolt of adrenaline through my veins and pushed me forward.

Luck was with me today. The temple guards didn't even notice me slip through the front vault doors and into the safety of nearby shrubbery. The world was overflowing in hues of yellows and orange as though the sky itself was painted in liquid gold. The warm light of the rising sun announced the coming of a new day, the beginning of my new life.

I didn't have time to marvel at the great stone buildings with their manicured lawns or the blooming flowers that draped their balconies. Soon the next rotation of the temple guards would arrive, and Soul City would wake up. I had to get out now.

Dizzy from hunger, I rushed towards the southwest wall of the city. Voices rustled across the clearing, and I kneeled behind a large bougainvillea with my dagger in my hand. I peered through the leaves, and my breath caught.

Two temple guards stood at the gate. The gaudy yellow Temple of the Sun emblem stood out against their black uniforms. From their relaxed disposition, the slump in their shoulders, and their laughing voices, they hadn't heard me. Twenty feet to their left was my escape—a split in the stone wall.

My blood turned to ice as my throat went dry. The fear that pulsed through me turned to anger. I hadn't come this far only to be caught by these damn fools. But I didn't have the cover of darkness to cloak me anymore; I only had my wits and my stealth. It *had* to be enough. I wasn't sure if I believed in a higher power, but still I prayed to the Creator.

Keep me safe. Keep me hidden. Please don't let them see me.

If I made a wrong move, my life wouldn't be the only one lost. I couldn't let that happen.

A guard put a flask to his lips and drank his fill, then handed it to the other guard. I gripped my lucky dagger, an Espanian blade I had won in a fight, and ignoring the trembling in my fingers I held my breath and ran.

I ran wildly, second-guessing myself with every desperate stride. My thighs burned as I neared the wall, and my heart battered painfully against my chest. I winced as my feet crunched on the gravel. The sound was like thunder in the still of dawn. For a second I feared that I had been discovered, but the guards hadn't moved, and their attention was still locked on their drink.

I slipped through the small fissure in the stone, and the cold, sharp rock cut my skin. But I ignored it and pulled myself out to the other side. Once my footing was secure on the soft grass, I let out my breath. But I didn't stop. I rocketed over the grounds outside the wall, still propelled by the fear of being discovered. Although I was running without food or rest, I felt like I was flying.

The Anglian crown hit my hip as I ran down the small rise, as though it was trying to tell me to put it back. But it was too late. There was no turning back now.

Even before I saw the Pit, the smell of unwashed bodies, vomit, piss and desperation hit me like a slap in the face. And yet, I couldn't help but smile. No one in the Pit smiled very often, but I met this early morning with a hop in my step and a smile.

I slowed my run to a walk. My throat burned as I took in the ramshackle scenery of home.

The Pit.

I walked through the muddy streets, and the toxic, dank air pressed heavily around me. I never did get used to the smell. It choked me like tight invisible hands that squeezed the air out of my lungs to keep me from leaving. It was a constant reminder that I was a prisoner, that this was really a giant prison, and that I would eventually die here.

Those who are born in the Pit, die in the Pit.

Damn them all. Damn this place.

I had always looked for a way to escape. I wouldn't let the Pit's icy hands keep me under for much longer. Today was my lucky day. I could feel it.

Most of the buildings were made of the wood and scrap metal that Soul City had discarded. We used their garbage to build our homes. Most of them were little more than huts with mud-thatched roofs. We used anything we could get our hands on. We built our homes with trash because we were trash.

Soft yellow lights spilled through some of the makeshift holes in the walls that we used for windows. It was always dark and damp, and lighting was necessary even during daylight hours. The layout of the village was haphazard, and the houses were skinny and wretched, like me.

A crumpled lump lay in a dark and narrow alley surrounded by vomit and waste. He moaned stupidly as I carefully walked around his vomit. I covered my mouth as the bile rose in my throat. I ventured deeper into the village and passed the night owls on their way home from the underground taverns and rundown inns of Bleak Town. This part of the Pit was a breeding ground for crime, drug addiction, alcoholism, and prostitution.

I kept my head low and my hood up as I passed through Bleak Town. I held my bag securely and quickened my pace. Finally I trudged up the path to a small camp with rotten wood planks and a crooked tin roof. I stepped up to the front and opened the wooden door as quietly as I could.

"Where have you been?"

I froze mid-step in the doorway.

Rose jumped from her chair surprisingly quickly for someone her age.

"I've been worried sick. I haven't slept a wink. You never came home after the curfew…I thought…I thought the priests had taken you."

Her concern had become too common in recent weeks. Her eyes automatically went to the small area carpet with the trap door underneath.

"They didn't," I said finally, a little more harshly than I had anticipated, and I immediately felt my cheeks burn with guilt.

Her lack of faith in my abilities was getting to me. I knew she loved me like a daughter and that her worries were out of kindness. She had devoted her life to keeping me safe, and the guilt I felt at her sacrifices was taking its toll on me. The only way I could ever pay her back for everything would be to rescue her from the nightmare of the Pit and to give her the real home she deserved.

Her face was paler than usual, her skin too thin and pulled tightly around her cheekbones. The dark circles under her eyes stood out even though the light of the cottage was dim. Wisps of gray hair fell around her thin face from her chignon, and her brown linen dress hung loosely on her skinny frame. She looked years older than she actually was. The Pit had done this to her. She should have been plump with rosy cheeks, not skin and bones.

I had hoped for the smell of food or even bread to calm my aching stomach, and I did my best to hide my disappointment. Rose had taught me to stitch and sew years ago, but even between the two of us, there wasn't much work for seamstresses in the Pit, and there was even less coin. For a woman in the Pit there was no real trade except for farming if you were one of the lucky ones with land. Otherwise it was sewing or prostitution. And that was only if you escaped the clutches of the priests.

Our entire cottage comprised of a single room. We had a kitchenette with a small round dining table, and two beat-up chairs were angled next to the hearth. We shared the small cot tucked in the corner near the hearth. The only thing of value in our cottage was the small bookcase that contained Rose's collection of history books, atlases, and three books of children's fairy tales. Books were a rare commodity in the Pit, but if you could find them they were worth every coin. Any price was worth the sight of Rose's face lighting up when she held a new book. I traded for them every chance I got, and now we had a pretty impressive collection.

"I don't know what I would have done if they'd taken you—" Rose wheezed in a fit of coughing.

I rushed over and handed her a cup of cold tea.

"Here," I said and brought the cup to her lips. She took a sip and sat back down. I frowned at the state of her.

"Your cold isn't getting better. We need a healer."

"Healers only come if you have the coin to give them."

A shadow passed in front of Rose's brown eyes. They used to be so full of light, but now they were dull, and it frightened me.

I swallowed hard. "I told you to rest. Why didn't you listen to me?"

Rose raised an eyebrow. "And *I* told you to stay out of trouble." She took another sip of her cold tea. "You're just as stubborn as your mother. Hardheaded mules, the both of you. Never listening to reason."

I knew she was trying to scold me, but I took it as a compliment.

"I'm a grown woman, Rose. Stop treating me like a child."

"Then stop acting like one."

For a sick old woman, her voice was fierce. "I made a promise to your mother. I promised to keep you safe, to keep you hidden from the priests. They must never find you. Do you understand? They must never ever know of your existence. Don't make me a liar, Elena."

Tears welled in her eyes, and I struggled to keep my own eyes dry. I cupped her gnarled fingers into my own and knelt beside her.

"I won't. I promise. They'll never find me. I swear it."

She changed the subject.

"Philip came around earlier looking for you," she said, and she gave me that knowing stare that would have made me blush if I had been a girl of sixteen.

"I could see it in his eyes," she said. "He'll never make a decent woman out of you."

I rolled my eyes.

"Oh, Rose, not that again. Phil's just a friend, nothing more."

It wasn't a secret that Phil and I met regularly in the woods. It wasn't love. It was just two lonely people who needed each other's comfort. To feel a warm body sometimes made the nightmares go away. Sometimes.

I brushed her off and said, "I'll talk to him when I get back from my meeting."

I looked in her eyes and could see that there was no judgment in them, only sadness. I didn't want her pity.

I could feel the weight of my bag against my hip. I smiled and said, "I have news, news that will change our lives."

Rose looked at me with that worried look she always gave me when I had been away from our miserable cottage. "What are you talking about? What is that *smile* all about?"

"We won't be hiding from the priests for much longer. Our luck has changed."

I pulled open the bag on my waist and placed the crown on our small wooden table. Her eyes went wide.

"Elena," she whispered, her mouth a tight line. "What have you done?"

Her lips trembled. "Where did you get this?"

"Soul City," I replied proudly. "The temple vault."

"The high priests' vault?" Rose had gone even paler. Her gaze traveled over the golden crown and then back to me. I could see the whites of her eyes.

"You must take it back. Quickly, before they know it's missing!"

"No," I said sharply.

I crossed my arms. I didn't want to fight with her today. I was too tired.

"It's too late for that. If I tried to take it back now, I'd be caught for sure. I'd be facing the noose. Stop looking at me like that. You don't understand, I did it for—"

"How could you, Elena?" Her eyes turned damp. "How could you jeopardize us like that? The risk…"

I sighed. "Because I did it for *us*."

She stared at me in shock.

"For you and for me. Don't you get it? This is our chance to get out of this hell once and for all—to start a new life. Aren't you tired of starving? Don't you want better clothes? Shoes without holes?"

My voice came out louder and more angrily than I'd expected.

"Don't you want a fire to keep you warm instead of this black hole?"

I pointed to the useless, cold hearth and then to the crown. "With this crown we can buy new lives for ourselves. I'm tired living like this. I'm tired of being hungry all the time, of living in this filth. We could go east to Romila or even Girmania—somewhere where there are no more priests, and where no one knows who we are."

"The priests are everywhere. Even in Girmania."

Rose looked down at her cup of tea. "I know you mean well, Elena, truly I do. But this is madness. Even if you wanted to sell that…that gold *crown*…no one would buy it. No one in the Pit or even in all of Anglia has enough coin for such a treasure."

I jerked my chin at the crown, unable to keep the smugness from my voice as I said, "I already have a buyer."

I saw the fear in Rose's eyes.

"Who?" she said after a while, her eyes narrowed.

"Mad Jack."

Rose's teacup crashed to the ground as she stood up. "Mad Jack! That murderous, wretched man. Do you know what he does to young women like you? Do you?"

I had heard the rumors about human trafficking. People said that his gang stole ten-year-old girls and forced them into prostitution and slavery. Most of the time, their parents didn't even bother to look for them—one less mouth to feed. But they were just rumors, and I'd never seen any proof of it.

I sighed and shrugged. "I don't care about those rumors."

"Rumors!"

"Yes, *rumors.*" I braced my hands on the table as Rose shook her head.

"Right now, all I care about is making the trade so that *we* can get the hell out of here."

"How can you trust him?" said Rose. "The man's vile. Don't go. I beg you."

Mad Jack was lord of Bleak Town. He was a thug, a murderer, and a psychopath. But he was the law in the Pit, and he was the only one who could pay good coin for the crown. We'd already made the deal. All I had to do was bring it to him, and Rose and I were free.

"It's too late for that," I said and avoided her eyes. "I've already made the deal. He's waiting for me. I'm to bring it to him today."

Rose was silent for a while. Her brows narrowed. "I promised your mother I'd look after you. She was like a sister to me. If something were to happen to you now after everything we've done, after all the years we've been so careful to hide you from them—"

"And you did. Now it's time for me to take care of you. I'm not the scared little girl anymore, Rose. Let me do this. Let me do this for us. For our new home on the beach in the south of Espan."

I smiled at her. "A little color and heat would do us some good, you know. We both look dreadful."

"Elena," she said, and I could see the darkness in her eyes shift as she shook her head. "This is crazy. Even if you do manage to sell it, I won't go with you."

"I won't," she added stubbornly, as though that would stop me.

"I'll carry you if I have to, old woman."

Just for a second I saw a smile on her face. "It's too dangerous, Elena. I can't let you risk your life."

"It's done. There's nothing left to say."

"They will come for you now," Rose whispered. "They'll take you away. They will trace this crown back to you, back here, back to us. Everything we've done, everything we've sacrificed for will be destroyed by this foolishness."

I clenched my teeth. "It's not foolish."

I rubbed my temples as a giant headache pounded against my skull. I didn't want to argue with her. Rose was frightened. She was born and raised in the Pit, and I knew that leaving it would terrify her.

"I was careful. No one saw me enter or leave the vault—"

A bell rang in the distance.

Rose's eyes widened with fear as we looked at each other. "The priests!"

CHAPTER 3

ROSE ONLY NEEDED TO give me a look. I snatched up the crown, hit the table back with my hip, kicked the carpet over, and pulled open the trap door.

But as I stood there, ready to jump in, something inside me stirred.

I glanced at Rose. "No."

I took a step back. "I don't want to hide anymore. What's the point? I'm too old for them to pick anyway. They're looking for adolescent girls who won't fight back. They want girls who will submit to their perverted desires. They're not looking for a grown woman. Let them come."

Rose's pale eyes hardened. "In. Think of your mother's sacrifice. Stop being so stubborn."

I frowned. I hated when she played that card. "This is ridiculous. Besides, you know as well as I do that they won't even bother with us. They hardly ever do anymore—"

The gravel just outside our cottage crunched.

Rose's face blanched, and she took hold of my arm and tugged.

"Don't be foolish, girl," she hissed. "The priests mustn't find you. Ever. Now, get it!"

She pulled, but I yanked my arm out of her grip. Apparently I was as stubborn as my mother.

Rose's mouth opened as if she were about to say something else. I could see it in her eyes for a second, but then it was gone. Whatever it was, she'd decided not to tell me. She straightened and said. "Please, Elena. I'm too tired to argue."

Deep down I knew she was right. If I had been followed, I didn't want Rose to get hurt. Her fragile bones were no match for the priests' wrath.

As I settled into my crouched position, I looked up at Rose one last time before she dropped the heavy door, and I was submerged in darkness again.

I heard the scraping of our table being pulled over me, then the chairs. My heart hammered in my ears and made it difficult to hear. We hadn't had a priest visit in years, and I couldn't help but wonder if somehow I'd been discovered. No. I knew I had been careful. But there was still that lingering feeling that maybe someone *did* see me, and that the priests were coming for me.

I heard Rose sigh heavily, and the light tapping over my head suggested that she was bouncing her leg up and down nervously. I was covered in sweat, and I let out a shaky breath. Minutes passed. My breathing stilled, and I began to relax a little. Maybe we'd been lucky again. I couldn't hear Rose's foot tapping anymore, so I knew she was feeling calmer now. We were going to be fine. I opened my mouth to call out to Rose—

A knock came from our front door.

I heard Rose gasp as I hit my head on the trap door in a panic. I would not give in to it. Despite my heart's wild pounding in my ears, I strained to listen. I heard Rose's feet patter softly across the floor and then the click of the lock. Finally the door screeched open.

"Good morning," said a man's voice.

It was a deep, emotionless voice and sounded more like a command than a greeting. My stomach tightened, and I suppressed the tiny gasp that threatened to escape. My heart hammered against my chest. I was having a panic attack.

"Priest," I heard Rose mutter in a near hiss. I had to quash a nervous giggle.

Heavy footfalls moved around our little cottage, and I knew the priest had let himself in. I felt a small sense of ease because it was a priest and not the temple guards. Perhaps they still didn't know I had stolen the crown. Still, a priest showing up at your front door wasn't much better. What was he doing here? Would they have sent a priest instead? There was only one reason why they came around, and I preferred not to think about it.

I could feel the crown pressed against my side. I had fixed an appointment with Mad Jack for this morning. If the priest lingered for much longer, I was going to be late. I knew Mad Jack didn't tolerate tardiness. He would see my lateness as an insult and perhaps as a setup. If I didn't make it on time I probably wouldn't make the trade, and I would lose everything.

"How can I help you, priest," came Rose's voice from above.

"There's been talk about a beautiful woman, a beautiful *young* woman, who comes and goes from this…this…*dwelling*, if you can even call it that."

The priest's voice echoed above my head, full of contempt and arrogance.

"I have come to see if the rumors are true." He clicked his tongue. "Obviously it is *not* you."

"Obviously," said Rose, and I imagined her face as she tried to control her fury. She was a master of disguise when it came to her face.

"I haven't been a young woman for over forty years." Her voice sounded as though she was giving the priest a slight smile.

"I am sorry you wasted your time, but as you can see there is no young woman here. Only an old one."

I had to applaud her. She lied so effortlessly. I wished I could be as sly as she was.

The floorboards creaked under the weight of the priest as he crossed the room.

"Mmm. Yes. And yet I have heard these rumors for three years now. I wonder why that is…if there is *no* other woman than yourself here, why the stories?"

"There isn't." Rose's voice was final. "Perhaps they meant my clients. I cater to many young women with my sewing business. Perhaps that's what *they* saw." Rose knew that spies lived in the Pit with us. Too many times we'd seen temple guards appear at neighbors' doors and take them away. They never returned.

"Perhaps," said the priest, but I heard no agreement in his voice.

There was a pause.

"We keep accounts on all the females in the Pit. Our records show that you are barren. There were never any children born at this address."

"That's right. I'm barren. I could never have children," said Rose quietly.

I heard the hurt in her voice, and I felt my own throat squeeze at her sadness. It was a subject she never wanted to talk about. As a child I had asked her many times why she didn't have children of her own, not fully understanding what *barren* meant. I could always see the tears welling in her eyes. I loved Rose like a mother, and I knew I was the closest thing she'd ever had to a daughter. She'd protected me all these years and put her own life in danger because of me. But Rose was sixty-five now, which was ancient for those living in the Pit. It was my turn to take care of her. Not the other way around.

And yet, here I was, hiding in my cupboard again, like a frightened little mouse.

"Hmm." I heard the priest move about the room.

"Even in your haggard state, I can tell you were never one of the beautiful ones. Your nose is too big. Your lips too fine. Your features are uneven, and there is nothing interesting about your eyes. You lack the refined bone structure of natural beauty. If you had been lovely, we could have used you. Even a barren concubine can find ways to please us."

I could feel the wicked smile on his face. I wanted to claw out his eyes.

"Had you been born a beauty," continued the priest, in love with the sound of his own voice, "you could have been saved by the priests of the temple. We would have fed you and clothed you in glorious gowns. You would have gone to parties and been the envy of all the women in Anglia...*if* only you had been beautiful. But the ugly ones are left behind, left in this God forsaken slum, where you belong."

I cursed a million curses in my head, and a cold, icy feeling welled inside me. I wanted to be with Rose, to stand next to her while this wretched man tore her apart. I wanted to spit in his face. How dare he speak to Rose like that? I wanted to tell him that most women, particularly the prettiest ones, would rather die than become a priest's concubine.

"Well," said Rosy, almost cheerfully, "I guess those woman have all the luck in the world then, don't they. I wasn't born beautiful, and at my age I don't really care anymore. If there's nothing else, I really should be getting back to my sewing..."

"And what of your husband? I do remembering reading that you had been married."

"Died of the fever ten years ago."

I couldn't detect any anger in Rose's voice. She was a true champion. I loved her for it. I heard the soft patter of Rose's feet move towards the door.

36

The priest continued, and I had to concentrate to hear his voice over the squeaking of the floorboards. He was right on top of me, right next to the table. If I made any sound, he would hear me. I held my breath, as sweat trickled down my forehead, and my bowels turned watery. "If I find out that you're lying—"

"I'm not," came Rose's voice, but the priest continued as though he hadn't heard her.

"Even in your state … your age … underneath all that filth, you are still a woman. And I have different needs than the other priests. My pleasures are of the *inflicting* kind. I find screaming delightfully arousing."

I cringed as I listened to this sadistic priest. The horrors, the brutal, twisted tortures that the priests inflicted upon women were legend. The mangled, twisted bodies of prostitutes were commonly found in the ditches that divided Soul City from the Pit. The priests felt it was their right to do whatever they wished to women who weren't beautiful enough to be concubines. "Make no mistake, *peasant*. If I find out that you are lying—if you are hiding a woman here—there are worse things than death."

"As I said. I'm *not* lying," said Rose. Her voice rose, and I prayed the priest wouldn't hurt her. Not my Rose.

"You can tear this place apart, and all you will find is little old me. Nothing else."

After an uncomfortable silence the floorboards squeaked above my head, and I heard the heavy tread of the priest's feet to my left. I knew he had moved towards the door.

"I find no claim to these rumors, for now," said the priest.

His voice became a little more muffled as he moved a little farther away.

"I will continue my inquiries on this matter. Pray that you do not see my face again because if you do," I sensed the evil smile on his lips, "it will be the last face you will ever see."

I strained to listen. My insides twisted. I was about to be sick with an empty stomach.

With a screech and thud, I knew that Rose had closed the door. But I still held on to my breath. What if the priest had killed her silently? What if this was a trick? What if he knew where I was all this time, and this was just a ruse to get me to come out. I was so panicked that I didn't hear the table being moved until a whoosh of cool air slapped my face.

I blinked up into Rose's flushed face.

"You can come out now. He's gone."

I let out my breath and clambered out of my private dungeon. Only then did I realize that the crown had gouged into my side and left an angry red mark.

As I opened my mouth to thank her, she grabbed ahold of my wrists.

"Elena. They're on to us. I don't know who told, but someone did. Next time we won't be so lucky."

I stared into the brown eyes I'd grown to love so much and nodded.

"I know." I swallowed. "But there won't be a next time."

Rose frowned. "Elena, please! Don't do this."

Ignoring her, I ran to our single north-facing window. I could see that the shadow on the sundial outside was on the number seven.

"It's already past seven in the morning. Damn these priests to hell if they make me miss this chance."

"This is a bad idea, Elena," came Rose's voice behind me. "I beg you not to go."

"Can't. I've already made the deal."

I turned back to Rose, grabbed her by the shoulders, and kissed her forehead.

Rose shot daggers at me with her eyes.

"Even after this, with what happened with the priest, you're still going out? They know about you, Elena. I don't know how, but they do. And now they'll be looking for you, take my word for it. You must see that. You must see how stupid and selfish you're being."

She shook her head. Her eyes were filled with disappointment.

I felt a pang in my chest. But I was doing this for us, to save us from this hell. She didn't get it. She would just have to trust me.

"It's because of the damn priests that I'm doing this," I said quickly and held her gaze.

"I'm doing this for *us*. I know you can't see that now, but it's the truth."

Rose's eyes reddened as they welled with tears. I felt my own eyes burn with the sadness that lingered between us. I blinked my tears away and released her.

"I know you love me. You've been a mother to me for all these years. It's my turn to take care of us."

She opened her mouth to protest, but I cut her off and kissed her on the cheek.

"I'll be back later with the supper of your dreams."

Before Rose could stop me, I dashed out the front door.

CHAPTER 4

I RAN FUELED BY the fear of what Mad Jack would do to me if I didn't make our appointment. I ran on exhaustion and an empty stomach. Blood pounded through my veins, and yet I felt numb with dread.

I had seen the tears in Rose's eyes, but I hadn't said anything. I would see her smile again when my pockets were filled with coin. She had sacrificed her life to keep me safe. It was my time to pay her back. She deserved a good life, and I was going to give it to her.

I pulled my hood down and kept to the shadows as I ran through the mud in our ramshackle village. I passed the small square in the center of town. People were already setting up for the day's market. Some looked up as I ran past, but most were preoccupied with displaying the paltry goods they were hoping to sell. There were no stone houses here like in Soul City. Our homes were a cluster of scrap metal and wood planks. They looked particularly grim in the bleak light of the early morning. It wasn't the scent of spices, sugar, and roasting meat that I smelled, but rather the stink of horse manure, vomit, ale, and human waste… I did my best not to take it in, but the hot, toxic air always seemed to find a way into my skin.

My lungs burned, and I ran desperately to make that appointment. I just had to. I had nothing left but a fool's hope that Rose and I might finally get out of the Pit.

With the town square behind me, I made for Bleak Town, the deepest and most crowded area of the Pit. The deeper I ventured, the worse the smell got. The buildings were worse here, too. The crude structures toppled over one another dangerously and looked as if they would fall apart in a gust of wind. Barefoot children with worn-down clothes hanging on their skinny bodies played backgammon in the street. They were coated with grime and looked like they'd never bathed once in their entire lives. The air was hot, and my clothes stuck to my body. The taverns that lined the road were busy.

I made for Mad Jack's lair, the Dirty Habit. It was the only inn in the Pit, and the only two-story building in the village. It stood out among the other buildings, but not in a good way. The second floor had burned in a fire three years ago, and it had never been replaced. Now, the top of the building looked like a skeleton of a dead animal.

There was no front door to the building either, so I stepped up quickly and made my way inside.

A few harlots raised their brows at me, their cleavage spilling out of their barely-there outfits. Their eyes were lined with black kohl and their lips were swollen and red. All the sofas and chairs were occupied by clients. A plain but curvaceous woman winked at me as she passed by, completely naked.

Although I blushed a little, it wasn't new to me. I'd been here before. I moved as quickly as I could as I negotiated my way past the tables, the half-naked women, and the many hands of men that tried to grab me as I headed towards the back.

I could see the small office area behind two bodyguards, and I caught a glimpse of Mad Jack sitting at his desk. I felt my knees give way. Thank the Creator! He was still there.

The guards looked at me, but before they could stop me I blurted, "I have an appointment with Mad Jack."

At the mention of his name he looked up.

He was young for a street lord, older than me, but no more than thirty. His black hair was oiled and neatly pulled back into a ponytail. His white shirt was opened at the collar and revealed his strong muscles underneath. I wondered what it would be like to touch his golden skin, to trace my hands along those powerful shoulders. Although most of the women in my area said he was a vile and ugly man, I'd always thought he was handsome, striking really. If it weren't for the long scar on his right cheek, he would have been gorgeous. No doubt that scar saved him from the clutches of the priests who did not discriminate between the sexes when selecting the beautiful ones for themselves.

His eyes were dark, with the thickest lashes I'd ever seen on a man. They were the kinds of eyes that held you paralyzed just by their beauty, like they could see into your soul. There was no doubt in my mind that Mad Jack had broken many, many hearts.

When his eyes met mine, I couldn't help but blush. He did that to me. But I didn't have time to bat my lashes at him, even if I was that kind of woman, which I wasn't. I was here on business.

I smiled as I lowered my hood. My heart raced as I imagined the surprise he would feel when he saw that I had stolen the object he had told me no one could ever take. I was very pleased with myself.

Taking his silence as an invitation to enter, I pushed past his guards, rushed into his office, and plunked the crown his desk.

"And you said it was impossible," I purred. "What do you think now, eh?"

Mad Jack stared at the golden crown with disbelief. My smile faded when I met his eyes again. He wasn't looking at me with the shock and envy I had expected. He was looking at me with a mix of fear and regret, like he hadn't expected me to hand it to him, like he didn't *want* me to. I got the sense that he didn't want me here either.

His eyes darted behind my shoulder, but I didn't turn around. I looked at him and then raised my hands.

"I know I'm late but I can explain. See, there was a priest who came around looking for me, and I had to hide and wait till he was gone before I could—"

"You won't be hiding no more. It's over."

The rest of my excuse died in my throat.

I turned to look at the man who had just spoken. Two temple guards stood behind me. I hadn't even thought to look and hadn't noticed them, even though their black and yellow uniforms were a dead giveaway. But there they were. They had been waiting for me with their hands on their swords.

I felt the blood drain from my face as I took in their confident smiles and the wicked intent in their eyes.

But the betrayal, Mad Jack's betrayal, pierced my heart and shattered it.

I felt the angry tears run down my face before I even realized I was crying. In a fit of rage I whirled around.

"How could you? You bastard!" I spat. "How could you betray me like that? To *them*? How could you do this to your own people? You double-crossing son of a bitch!"

I knew it was crazy and foolish to scream my head off at someone who could just as easily cut it off, but he just sat in his chair looking uncomfortable. For a second his face and eyes showed pain and regret. It was fast, but I saw it. And I also noticed how fast his expression hardened when he noticed the men watching him. He composed himself, straightening, but I had seen it.

"I'm sorry, Elena," said Mad Jack, his voice stripped of emotion. He avoided my eyes.

I squeezed my fists hard. My nails bit into my flesh.

"Why would you do this? Look at me. Look at me, *traitor*."

His eyes snapped to mine. His expression darkened, and I could see his anger as clearly as I could see his betrayal. So many emotions went through me as I stood there shaking. I was losing myself. For a moment I thought I'd gone too far and braced myself for the assault that was coming. He was going to hit me.

Mad Jack's dark eyes pinned me on the spot. He didn't move, and I didn't understand the struggle I saw on his face.

"Because, like you, I'll do anything to get out of this dump."

He opened his mouth and then closed it again. "I saw an opportunity and I took it."

"By betraying your own people." My lips trembled, and the room started to spin.

I felt the temple guards move behind me before I saw them. They stood on either side of me.

I kept my focus on the traitor.

"…by giving me up to the very people who put us in this cage," I hissed.

He looked down at his desk. I leaned forward, my voice quivering with anger and fear. "You know what they'll do me," I breathed. "You know. And still, you're handing me over to them, like you own me, like you had the *right*. You had no right. Nobody owns me."

Mad Jack clenched his jaw and breathed loudly through his nose. His eyes darted from me to the guards. He grabbed the edge of his desk with his fingers. His knuckles turned white as he said softly, "There's nothing I can do."

I frowned. "You've been working for the priests all along, haven't you? You're one of their spies."

My eyes burned as the exhaustion and the hunger of the day spilled out of me through my tears. I thought of Rose, and it was all I could do to keep standing.

Mad Jack pressed his lips in a hard line, but said nothing.

Everything became clear to me. "You're the one who snitched. You told the priests where to find me. You traitorous piece of shit!"

He shook his head. "No. I promise you, Elena. I didn't betray you."

"No?" I spat out a laugh. "What the hell do you call this? You've just killed me. You've just killed Rose. You bastard!"

I spat in his face.

"May the devil curse you. May you rot in the hell with him—"

Mad Jack's eyes widened. It was my only warning.

Something hard collided with the back of my head. I fell sideways to my knees and tried to blink the black spots from my eyes.

"Don't hurt her!"

Through my blurred vision I saw Mad Jack move from his desk.

"Don't even think about it."

A guard held a sword to Mad Jack's neck. "A deal's a deal. The whore is ours now. Get her weapons."

"Bastards," I managed to say and was immediately recompensed with a brutal kick to the stomach. I screamed in pain as I fell forward, clutching my stomach. I couldn't get enough air into my lungs, and the searing pain told me that I had broken a rib. Cradling my ribcage, I stood up and looked my attackers in the eyes.

"Why does a whore need so many weapons, eh?"

One of the guards held my lucky dagger and my short sword. "Well, it doesn't matter. It's not like they were any use."

He tossed them on the ground.

"Go to hell," I wheezed.

Another brutal blow crunched the bones in my face, and I screamed in agony. My knees buckled and I fell. I tried to keep from passing out, but the pain was too much.

The room spun, and my world darkened around me. I heard Mad Jack yell something angrily at the temple guards. Someone was calling my name. A shadow passed in front of me, and I saw the traitor's face, masked with worry, hovering above me. Then I slipped into the darkness.

CHAPTER 5

I WOKE UP TO the sound of gravel crunching. I felt a searing pain in my lower legs and wetness against my skin. My eyelids were heavy and stinging, but I forced them open. As my world slowly came into focus, the ground moved beneath me. I blinked the heaviness from my head. I was being dragged by my armpits.

The same two temple guards that had knocked me unconscious were dragging me like a corpse. My lower body bounced on the hard ground as rocks and dirt tore into my clothes and into my flesh. The more aware I became, the more I felt the pain, and the more I wished I could be unconscious again. I moaned as the wounds on my legs ripped open again and again.

As soon as they heard me, they dropped me.

My chin hit the ground hard, and I tasted blood in my mouth. I winced at the pain. Then I remembered what they'd done to me, to my face, and I was surprised I wasn't in *more* pain. Maybe I'd been wrong. Maybe they hadn't hit me as hard as I had first thought. Technically, I should still be unconscious.

I was too hot. Was it a fever from infection? I'd never felt like this before. I'd never been sick a day in my life.

"The peasant bitch is awake," said one of the guards. "Get up and walk. We're tired of dragging your sorry ass around. Up."

Somehow I pulled myself up and stood. Anything was better than being dragged. My head felt heavy and light at the same time, and my legs burned in protest. I looked down and gasped. My breeches and part of my tunic were shredded and covered in dirt and blood. My exposed flesh was torn and raw. I swallowed my panic and looked around.

I blinked in the brightness of the sun. Immediately I recognized where we were. The tall stone walls, the manicured, glorious gardens, the radiant stone buildings, the clean air, and the spotless and nearly sparkling streets all told me I was back in Soul City. The only thing out of place was the long trail of blood that marked the road behind me—my blood.

A waft of roasting meat nearly sent me to my knees again. My mouth watered and my stomach ached. My throat burned nearly as bad as my legs. I needed water more than I needed food. I didn't know how long I'd been unconscious. The short shadows along the buildings showed that it wasn't midday yet. They probably dragged me out of the Pit as soon as they had finished beating me.

Something hard hit me in the lower back, and I went sprawling. I used my hands to break my fall, and I cursed as my hands became as torn and bloodied as my legs.

"Better get used to the beatings, whore. This is nothing to what's coming to ya."

I whirled around angrily, but froze when the tip of a sword was pointed at my face.

I could blame Mad Jack all I wanted, but deep down, I knew this was *my* fault. Sure he had deceived me, but I had had been reckless. I knew that I had made the mistake of stealing the crown.

"How does a whore from the Pit get her hands on a kingly crown, eh? Thought you'd give up whoring and try your hand at thieving?" said the same guard. His imp-like face was hard and unforgiving. Years of battle showed in his cold and beady eyes. He shared a look with his comrade, and they both smiled.

I studied the guard's finely crafted sword. Its shimmering pommel was engraved with a sun, a mark of the high priests' temple guard. When he noticed that I was staring at his sword, his troll-like features hardened in a smile.

"Thought you'd get away, did ya? Thought you could take what don't belong to ya and not suffer the consequences?"

He pulled my hood back with the edge of his sword. My long dark hair fell around my shoulders.

I saw the feral look the guardsmen get when they see a pretty face. I shivered inside, but I wouldn't show them fear. Like a trapped animal, I hid the anxiety that filled me. The priest's guards were notoriously ruthless and loved to abuse their power, especially with women from the Pit.

Slowly, I moved my hands towards my belt, but didn't find the hilt of my daggers. I had forgotten that they had taken my weapons.

"Pretty little thing, aren't you?" said the younger guard with an oily voice that matched his oily face. He looked about my age. The front of his uniform was soiled and wet.

"A little too skinny—I like my women with meat on their bones. But you're still a woman. Maybe, I'll just have a little fun before we bring you to the high priest?"

I frowned at his mention of fun. My hands trembled in fury.

"*I'm* the senior guard, Garth," said the older man.

"Never said you weren't, Baul." Garth rolled his eyes.

"If anyone gets to do anything, it'll be me first." Baul looked at me and grinned.

"We'd be within our rights to do with you what we will, seeing as you broke the law, and being from the Pit and all. We can do what we want with you."

Rape would be worse than a death sentence. If I had a choice, I'd pick the noose. I had witnessed horrible things when I was growing up in the Pit. I'd discovered women's bodies left to rot in the sun. Girls and women who'd once been full of life had been tossed away like garbage. I knew what was coming, and death would be better. Could I outrun them? I wouldn't get very far. I was completely useless. I was a damn fool.

The tip of a sword brushed my neck, and I felt warm liquid trickle down to my collarbone.

"But the high priest said unspoiled, and he was *very* specific," said Baul. "Too bad, I think you would have enjoyed me. I guess it's your lucky day." He laughed without humor.

"I guess it is." I spat, feeling like the unluckiest person in all of Arcania.

"But don't thank the Creator just yet. The priest has plans for ya. Mark my words, you're going to pay for what you did."

His expression became suspicious, and he leaned forward. His hot breath tickled my ear, but the smell of rotten eggs and ale stung my face.

"How *did* you do it? How could a *woman* walk through the sorcerer's fire?"

There was trace of fear in his voice, and I took comfort in that.

Good, let them be scared. But the truth was I hadn't really thought about it much. Why *was* I able to pass through the green fire when everyone seemed to think that it was impossible? I knew it was magic, I just didn't know it was sorcerer's magic. Maybe the sorcerer had made a mistake with his magic? Did Mad Jack know that I'd be faced with magic? He had acted so strange, so surprised when he saw the crown. What had he not told me?

"How did you get past the fire?"

My attention snapped back to the guards.

"How is it that you're still alive? You should be dead. No one can survive the fire." He paused. "Unless…"

"She's a demon." Garth turned pale.

"I'm not a demon." I scrambled to my feet.

I would look them straight in the eye. I would not cower on the ground like an animal any longer. Their demeanor changed for an instant, and I saw the nervous fear in their eyes.

Something about me made them nervous. It filled me with new hope.

Baul tapped the pouch at his side, my pouch, where the crown lay hidden. He stared at me curiously, and for a moment he said nothing.

"How'd you do it then? What kind of trickster are you?"

I smiled wickedly. "Give me back my weapons, and I'll show you."

"She's got magic, that's what," said Garth. His eyes widened in recognition.

"She's one of the cursed, a magic bearer. Only a witch could get through the sorcerer's fire, or a sorceress."

I flinched. No one had ever accused me of being a witch or of possessing magic. It was absurd. If I weren't in so much pain, I would have laughed out loud.

"If I *had* magic, do you think I'd still be living in the Pit? Don't you think I would have magicked myself out of this hell?"

I could see they were thinking…

Baul raised his brows. "She's got a point."

He smiled maliciously. "Unless you're a stupid witch."

Both guards started laughing, and I wished I could kick the laughter out of them.

I knew I wasn't a witch. Witches could cast spells and enchantments, raise the dead, and even shape-shift into other creatures. I would have found that useful to hide from the priest, if I were a witch—which I wasn't.

I knew that witches called their powers out of the Earth itself. Even if all those tales about witches were true, I still didn't understand how *I* managed to get my hands on the crown.

I knew things would get a lot worse if I were to do anything stupid. The priest had said I should be delivered to him *unspoiled*, and yet they had beaten me unconscious. I wasn't ready for another beating.

I had already ruined Rose's life. Perhaps my dumb luck would grant me another chance to make up for my impetuousness. If only I could get back to Rose...

Baul laughed under his breath.

"It don't matter what she is. Magic is forbidden in the Empire. Magic is treason and is punishable by death. You steal our high priests' treasure? It'll be fire for you. That's right. We *know* how to kill witches. I'll enjoy seeing you die."

Before I could protest, Baul grabbed me by the arm and yanked me hard around. "Tie her up."

My arms snapped back forcefully as Garth bound my wrists together with rope.

Baul snapped me around again to face him.

"You're going to wish for death before he's done with ya."

He rolled his eyes over every inch of my body, and as I recoiled he raised his sword and pointed. "Let's go. Try anything, and you'll die."

We moved in silence. Garth was at the front while Baul walked behind me. His nearness made my skin crawl.

We made our way deeper into Soul City. The city was surrounded by a ring of thirty-foot stone walls with gateways leading out into the rest of Anglia. I had always wondered why they bothered with the walls. Maybe they feared the other realms, and the walls would keep them protected in case of a rebellion. The thought of crumbling walls made me smile.

Soul City lay in the northwest region of Anglia, the western realm of Arcania, which bordered the West Sea. The city was the heart of the Temple of the Sun Empire. It was a new regime, and by the looks of it, it was blossoming.

Traders were busy with carts topped with fresh meat, vegetables, and rice. The city bustled with sounds of wagons and merchants organizing the day's market. A plainly dressed and weatherworn mother and daughter arranged handmade jewels and silks scarfs on their small table. When I got closer, I saw that the material was embroidered with the symbol of the temple, a brilliant sun etched in gold. They looked up at me curiously as I passed them, but they quickly looked away in fear when the guards caught their eyes.

Women dressed in fine silk gowns and men in refined tailored coats busied the streets. It was common knowledge that after the priests had come into power, most of the noble and wealthy families had still been allowed to reside in the six kingdoms. They kept their lavish villas and their pockets filled with gold. All they had to do was yield to the priests' rule and abolish the monarchy. They got to keep living as if nothing had changed. They made sure the folk from the Pit stayed in the Pit. There was no mingling with our kind of people. The noble families never stood up for us and never cared about us, even though we were Anglians just like them.

If Soul City was the pride and joy of Anglia, we were its shame. The rejects, the crippled, the poor, and the old were relegated to the Pit.

I caught a few vicious glares from some noble women in ridiculous tall hats. I wondered if they'd ever laid eyes on someone from the Pit before. Their disdainful expressions led me to believe that they had not. One gave me a nasty smile like she was glad I was going to die. Bile rose in my throat. I hated these people almost as much as I hated the priests.

I heard laughter and turned to see children playing together. Their fine happy smiles matched their fine happy clothes. I envied their innocence.

But as I passed the children, a cry caught my attention. In the middle of the street, in full view, a young man was tied to a post. His naked body was caked with dried blood, and red, angry lesions covered his skin. He looked barely human. A sun symbol was branded on the side of his cheek. He wouldn't last the day in the hot sun. Women in long elaborate gowns looked on as if the poor man disgusted them. Others laughed. He was on show for the wealthy.

Heat rose to my face. If I had the use of my arms I would have punched them.

Garth caught me looking, and he smiled.

"That's nothing to what's gonna happen to you, witch." He laughed.

But I couldn't look away from the young man's sad eyes. What had he done to deserve this? Angry tears welled in my eyes as Baul hit me in the back and propelled me forward.

Two men wearing robes tied in the middle with gold sashes strolled in the street. Their pale skin stood out against the deep black silk of their robes. I could see intricate designs in gold trim woven around their sleeves. The backs of their shaved heads were tattooed with the image of the sun.

Priests of the Temple of the Sun.

But what I saw next made my knees go weak.

Two young women and a young man wearing only see-through white tunics walked behind the priests. Their heads were down, and their nipples and genitals showed through the thin fabric. They wore thick leather collars around their necks like tethered dogs. They were young. So young.

I felt ill, but I couldn't look away. Rose and my mother had tried to save me from a life of sadistic torment and sexual slavery, but now I stared unblinking at my future. My blood chilled. If the high priest didn't kill me for stealing the crown, this was the life that awaited me.

CHAPTER 6

EVERY STEP FORWARD SENT a jarring pain through me. My legs were cement blocks, too heavy, and I dragged them along, taking my time. We were moving too fast towards whatever torment and misery awaited me. I didn't dare look at the guards. The misery and tears in my own puffed-up face were a dead giveaway that I was already miserable. No doubt the guards were smiling.

I felt detached from my body like I was having a waking dream. I tried not to think of the bleak sadness I saw in the faces of the concubines we had passed. I couldn't imagine what it would be like to be paraded around town naked and with a collar around my neck, to be a sexual pet.

Mad Jack's betrayal still hurt more than I expected. I didn't want to admit it, but I had thought that he'd been sweet on me. His dark eyes stared at me for a little too long and a little too often when I saw him in the Pit or traded with him for food or for another book for Rose. I'd picked up on it years ago. And I had welcomed it. But now I realized how wrong I'd been. I had fooled myself into thinking he cared.

It wasn't the first time I'd been wrong about men. I'd had my adolescent heart broken a few times. I'd had a few casual lovers, but I'd always been careful not to let my guard down, not to let myself care, or give my heart away. Once you did, you couldn't get it back. Affairs usually ended up hurting anyway, but for some reason, Mad Jack's betrayal ached more than I cared to admit.

The puzzled look on Mad Jack's face still haunted me. I couldn't figure out why he had looked so sorry, when he had basically handed me over to the guards.

I was so caught up in my own anger that I hadn't noticed the temple until it was right in front of me.

It was a pyramidal structure, approximately forty-five meters in height and was surrounded by smaller pyramids that looked like pointy hats. It was made of gold, to represent the sun, but it also represented wealth and power. I was amazed at its size and beauty. The wealth of the temple was obvious, but this went beyond anything I could have imagined. It was wrong.

"Move!"

I hadn't realized I had stopped to admire the temple. But I wasn't really admiring it. I feared it, and the fear choked me. My legs stiffened, and I couldn't move. I took a long shuddering breath.

"I said move!"

Something rock hard hit me in the back again, and I stumbled forward, surprised that I actually caught myself before I fell on the stone path.

"We don't have all day. We've got more important things to do than to parade a witch around the grounds."

Baul shoved me through an archway, and I could see the grand entrance to the golden temple. Garth ran forward and threw open two massive walnut doors. I tensed as I walked through the doorway and into a foyer that was two stories tall and emptied into a large hallway. My heart thudded painfully.

It was a plush space. Walls of gold surrounded plate glass windows that looked out over the city. The white and gold banners of the Temple of the Sun hung from the walls. Our feet echoed on the black marble floors. And somewhere within the temple I could hear the distant sound of voices chanting. Gold columns lined the grand hall on each side and supported the second floor above.

Priests scurried around the temple in a blur of ebony robes that billowed behind them as they moved about with important expressions on their faces. I had never seen so many priests at once. I saw the unmistakable look of lust in the eyes of those who stared at me, but most of them ignored me completely.

Adolescent boys followed some of the priests like eager puppies. Their dreary, linen robes stood out against the silky black robes of the priests. Apprentices, I realized. I also spotted temple servants in brown tunics. Everyone was male. All boys. All men.

I broke into a cold sweat. Was I the only female in the entire temple?

As I made my way forward, I caught glimpses of rooms on each side of the hall. The hall eventually opened up into a large chamber with an altar in the middle. I frowned at the altar. This was where they performed their temple ceremonies, where they intimidated and converted unbelievers.

I committed the interior of the temple to memory, just in case I survived. I would need to know the layout if I were to escape.

We walked around the altar and came to a chamber on the left where a man sat behind a large mahogany desk with a stack of documents in front of him. He scribbled in a large ledger and did not look up. He wore a heavy-looking white robe made of silk. It was embroidered with jewels and golden thread around the cuffs and neck, and a large sun symbol was stitched in lavish jewels on the front. He wore a pyramid-shaped white hat, and I suspected he was the high priest.

A shadow appeared behind him, but as I tried to get a better look, Baul grabbed me and held me steady in front of the desk. Garth looked nervous, which only made me feel worse. Blood pounded in my ears as I tried to steady my breathing. I looked around the chamber for a means of escape if things turned sour.

Baul cleared his throat. "I beg your pardon, Your Grace, but as you requested we have brought you the thief."

"Which thief?" said the high priest without looking up from his ledger. I saw a shadow behind the high priest again but it disappeared before I could get a good look.

"The thief who stole the Anglian crown, Your Grace." Baul stepped forward, placed the golden crown on the desk, stepped back, and folded his arms behind his back.

The high priest dropped his pen and looked up. The dark purple shadow under his eyes made his pale gray eyes stand out.

With a stone-cold expression on his thin face, the high priest took the crown and inspected it as though he was making sure it was the real Anglian crown. As he placed it back on the desk, his eyes found me, and my breath caught in my throat. I shuddered under his unnatural stare.

The high priest looked particularly interested in me. "*She* passed *through* the sorcerer's fire?"

I cringed under the priest's piercing stare. There was something wrong with the way he looked at me. It was almost like he was *happy* to see me, thrilled that I'd *survived* the fire. But why would he be?

"Yes, Your Grace. She must have some kind of magic. Shall we bring her down to the prison cells or would you rather we take her to your chambers—"

"No."

The high priest pushed his chair back and stood up. In a single swift move he made his way around his desk and stood before me. His white robes billowed behind him like great big wings. He was taller than the two guards, and he looked like he spent more time scribbling in his ledgers than he did eating. His pale eyes bored into mine. I felt my heart rate accelerate, but I wouldn't look away. His face showed intrigue, contempt, and even victory. He was the creepiest man I'd ever seen.

But when the shadow emerged beside him, I flinched and stepped back.

The shadow wasn't a shadow at all but a horribly deformed creature with long gnarled fingers and toes. It seemed to be made of mist. Its body had a see-through quality, as though it was a specter, as though it wasn't really there. Its dark gray skin was barely covered in what appeared to be a ragged old pair of trousers and a shirt. When it turned its large, protuberant eyes onto me, it took all my self-control not to bolt.

What kind of priest would keep company with such a creature? My eyes flew to Baul and Garth, but neither of them seemed to take any notice of the vile thing. They were both watching the priest. The smell of wet dog and rotten flesh emanated from it, and it looked straight at me with large, wet eyes.

The high priest frowned, but then he followed my gaze to the creature. When he turned back to look at me, he looked satisfied.

The creature moved towards me, but the priest shot it a look and the beast cowered behind him and nearly disappeared altogether behind his robes.

The high priest circled around me, inspecting every inch of me. I saw his brows furrow when he examined my singed cloak, but then his brows rose when he inspected my hands and face.

"Fascinating," said the high priest. "Not even a single burnt mark on her at all. It's quite remarkable."

He smiled. There was something ominous about the way he watched me, and I felt a chill in my bones. His long hooked nose gave him the appearance of a bird. My heart raced as I stood helplessly while he examined me like I was his new prize. I recognized the hunger and lust in his eyes.

My world was crumbling around me. The floor appeared to shift, and I struggled to keep it together. I didn't want to show him fear.

"I won't be your concubine," I blurted.

My voice trembled with fear and rage. I pulled at my restraints. "I'd rather die than become a priest's love toy. You should kill me. I promise I'll find a way to kill myself if you don't."

Baul and Garth fought back smiles, but I saw their shoulders move up and down. I glowered at them.

The high priest smiled casually.

"If I want you to become one of my—as you put it—love toys, then you will, my dear woman. And there is nothing you can do about it. It is a great honor to share the high priest's bed."

He moved towards me, and I grimaced.

"You have a pretty face, high cheekbones and unusual almond-shaped eyes, very pleasing." His eyes didn't leave my face. "Yes. Very pretty. But you are incredibly skinny and sickly looking. Your skin has none of the qualities and softness of my other concubines."

"Try starving for most of your life. It does wonders to the skin."

He raised an eyebrow. "How old are you."

I didn't feel like answering, but I didn't feel like getting another beating. "Nineteen."

"Hmm. The signs of aging have already plagued you. And there's no shine to your hair. I prefer my women with curves, no doubt something that time and food can repair."

He leaned forward, and the next thing I knew he began licking my face with his wet gray tongue. I whimpered in disgust and fear. I held my breath as I smelled his hot, putrid breath. He licked my cheeks, the corner of my mouth, and down my jaw.

I trembled and stifled a scream.

This is it. He's going to rape me right here while the other two watch. My spirit was shattered, but then he stepped back.

"You smell like you've slept with the pigs."

My face burned with shame. I probably did smell. I couldn't remember the last time I'd had a real bath. It seemed my unsavory smell had saved me. I almost smiled.

"No," the priest shook his head, but his smile returned. "Definitely, *not* a concubine."

The guards shared a look, and then Garth said, "Your Grace, do you wish us to *dispose* of the witch for you? We'd thought we could—"

The high priest whirled on Garth.

"She's not *just* a witch, you idiots. Don't you know what she is? Can't you recognize it?"

The high priest paused briefly to give the guards a chance to reply.

"No? No, of course *you* wouldn't. An ordinary witch would have burned in the sorcerer's fire. But she's no ordinary witch. What you have here before you is something extremely rare. Something extraordinary."

My stomach tightened into a giant knot.

"I'm not a witch," I said quietly.

I braced myself as beads of sweat trickled down my temples. My heart was beating so fast I could barely hear. What was this priest talking about?

Baul frowned. He was clearly as confused as I was, and he looked from me to the priest.

"I don't understand, Your Grace? What *is* she then? A demon? Djinni?"

The high priest chuckled at that. But before I had time to react, before I even knew what was happening, in a blur of white, the high priest reached out and grabbed Garth's sword.

With an ugly smile and eagerness in his eyes, he rammed the sword through my stomach.

CHAPTER 7

I STUMBLED FORWARD, and blood gushed from my throat and spilled down my front. I looked down and saw the pommel of Garth's sword sticking out just below my left ribcage. My breath came in rapid wheezes, and there didn't seem to be enough air in the chamber. I was cold, and I couldn't stop trembling.

Tears spilled down my face from the pain. I'd never been stabbed before, especially not with a giant sword. The blood didn't stop pouring out of my mouth, out of me. I knew what that meant. I blinked the black spots from my eyes, barely aware that a crowd had gathered around me. I grimaced at the throng of priests and their apprentices. I was dying, and I had an audience.

"And now for the great revelation."

I looked up. The high priest looked as if he were crazed. His hot breath tickled my face. He smiled wickedly, and then with one great heave he pulled out the sword.

I staggered from the force of the pull and immediately felt the wetness gush from my left side.

I stood in a pool of my own blood. I wished I'd left Rose on better terms, and I cursed Mad Jack as I felt myself slip away.

The high priest raised his voice. "And now, my brothers, watch as a miracle appears before your eyes."

I recoiled as the high priest put his hands on my body. Was he going to stab me a second time?

He drew my cloak to the side and lifted my tunic, exposing my chest. I wanted to protest. I wanted to hit him, but my hands were still tied behind my back. The loss of blood had made me so dizzy that I could barely keep standing. I felt myself drifting away. Soon I wouldn't care anymore. Soon I would be dead.

I heard a gasp from the crowd. The high priest's smile widened.

And I wasn't dying.

It felt like a hundred needles pricking my skin, and then my body was blanketed in warmth. My vision cleared, and my dizzy spell all but vanished. I felt better. But that was impossible. I should be dying. I didn't understand what was happening. I followed the high priest's stare down to my exposed chest, to my wound.

A golden light glowed from inside my body and spilled through the bloody gash. I blinked. The blood stopped spilling as though the light from inside me had cauterized the wound and stopped the bleeding. I felt a pull, and then a tug, inside. I stared as the pink flesh and damaged organs deep inside the gash sewed themselves up again. Slowly, the skin around the cut gathered and sealed itself. In seconds nothing of the ghastly wound was left but a thin scar.

I was still standing. How was this even possible? Maybe the guards were right. Maybe I *was* a witch.

"Spectacular!" The high priest's voice was full of praise. "Utterly spellbinding."

"But…how can this be?" asked a voice behind me, as though he were reading my thoughts.

"She healed herself? Is this magic? Is this witchcraft?"

The high priest pulled down my tunic and I felt easier. I felt my strength returning, like I was slowly waking up. He turned to face the gathered crowd of priests.

"Brothers, this woman is not a mere witch, but something far more valuable," he paused, capitalizing on the moment. "She's a creature who will never get sick or catch a cold. She is immune to sorcerer's fire and has a natural resistance to magic. And as you can see, she even has the ability to heal herself from a fatal wound."

I met the high priest's eyes. He held my gaze for a long moment and sneered at my confusion. He looked satisfied. He had known I wouldn't die before he ran me through with the sword. It had all been just for show. He knew I could *heal* myself. Apparently he knew more about me than I did.

The wicked gleam in his eyes sent a chill cascading down my spine. And then it hit me. I remembered what Rose had said to me.

They must never find you. Never. Do you understand? They must never ever know of your existence.

What if Rose hadn't simply been hiding me from the priests' search for concubines? What if she had known what I was all along? Did she know I could heal myself? Had my mother known? Had

70

she protected me for an entirely different reason? Rose had always spoken of the oath she'd sworn to my mother. It was her duty to keep me safe. But now, seeing how I had healed myself, I wasn't sure what she had been trying to protect me from.

The high priest watched me curiously. He knew I was struggling with the truth of what had happened. His lazy, vicious grin all but confirmed my suspicions. He had other plans for me.

"Her kind were undefeated once," he proclaimed. "I thought they had been wiped out in all the worlds…until now. She is a gift. A thing of myth and legend, a real treasure."

Baul and Garth stared at me intently, but I refused to look at them.

I braced myself. If I had magic in me, was I a witch or something else? If I could heal myself from a fatal wound, what else could I do?

My fears were gradually replaced by self-assurance. If swords couldn't stop me, then maybe I could still find a way to escape. I needed food. But I felt stronger and more confident.

I tightened my hands into fists behind my back and felt the rope tear into the flesh of my wrists. The skin around my wrists was warm. Was I healing? The high priest had guessed correctly that I'd never been sick. The sword in my chest had been painful, but I had survived. I could do it again.

I'd promised Rose that we could get out of the Pit. It was a promise that I wanted to keep. I was filled with hope that we might escape.

Healing magic certainly seemed to brew inside me. And by the way the high priest was watching me, something told me there was much, much more he wasn't telling me.

He raised his hands. "Brothers of the Temple of the Sun. I believe the Creator has handed us a unique gift."

He smiled. "Is she a witch? Perhaps, but she is much more than a mere witch. This woman is a—"

"Demon spawn," called a voice behind me.

Even before I turned around, I recognized the voice. Where had I heard it before? The voice belonged to a middle-aged priest. He must have been handsome once, but the years had not been good to him. With his head held high he stared down at his brethren with a scowl. He had my dark eyes.

I knew that face. I *knew* him.

The high priest didn't hide his surprise. "Brother Edgar, do you know this young woman?"

The priest, Brother Edgar, stared at me. "This unholy monstrosity is my daughter."

I flinched. Blood pounded in my ears as the pain of recognition overwhelmed me. I thought I had managed to forget his face, to forget what he had done. My mouth opened, but I just stood there stiffly. This wasn't how I had envisioned my reunion with my father.

In my head I had killed him—many, many times over.

The high priest raised his hand for silence.

"I will not pass judgment on our fellow brother here for having had a past before he joined the Temple of the Sun. Many of you here have had a life before the temple."

His pale eyes moved across the many guilty faces in the crowd of priests and came to rest upon Brother Edgar.

"Thank you, Your Eminence." Brother Edgar bowed from the middle, but his eyes never left mine.

The high priest smiled briefly. "Interesting."

He looked back at me before he continued. "Although, I don't quite see the resemblance. She must take after her mother."

He paused for a moment. "Her mother must have been very beautiful. Where is she?"

The high priest asked the question with some urgency, even though his face was expressionless.

"Where is her mother?"

I suddenly felt cold.

Brother Edgar's mouth curled into an ugly snarl. "I killed her, Your Eminence."

CHAPTER 8

I TREMBLED AS I fought the tears. I bit down on my tongue to keep from screaming.

It was as though it was happening all over again. I had long ago suppressed the memories of my mother's execution at the hands of her own husband, and now they came back to me like a blow to the stomach. My mother's neck, her stomach, even her hands had been pierced by swords, arrows, and daggers. I remembered my mother on her knees shouting for me to run. And I remembered my father lifting a great axe and bringing it down brutally against the back of her neck. Nine years later and the memory of my mother's head thudding to the floor still haunted me.

I hated this man more than anything. He had robbed me of my childhood. He had destroyed any chance of my understanding the powers that I had just discovered I possessed when he had killed my mother. When I thought of the Devil, it was his face that danced before my eyes.

I fought against my restraints, but they wouldn't break. I glared at him with as much hatred and malice as I could muster. He was not my father. He was a murderer. I would avenge my mother. I *would* kill him.

Brother Edgar only smiled. He appeared to enjoy the pain that I was suffering. His black eyes bored into mine and burned with a fury and hatred that matched my own. I raised my chin and stared at him. I wouldn't look away.

The high priest looked disappointed that my mother had been killed. "Pity. I could have used her. Two would have been better, but one is still all I need."

My eyes fell on the high priest. "Need me for what, exactly?" I snapped.

Before the high priest could answer me, Brother Edgar cut in.

"She got was she deserved. *She* wasn't a woman. She *wasn't* natural. I found out what she was when I saw her using magic to heal. I was appalled. The creature had tricked me into thinking she was a natural woman when she was really a demon."

He straightened and looked at the high priest.

"I should have known, I should have seen the signs, but I was a fool in love. Fooled by her flesh. Fooled by her beauty. But once I discovered her secret, I killed her."

He looked at me in disgust. He smiled. "I should have killed this one too."

"Maybe you should have because *I'm* going to kill you," I said, my voice as cold as ice.

I knew he was trying to break my spirit just as he had broken my mother's. But I wouldn't let him. He wouldn't break me.

Brother Edgar's eyes widened, shocked that I should have the gall to threaten him. He moved towards me, so close I could smell his wretched breath.

"How dare you speak to me! Demon! You will suffer the same fate as your whore mother. I will send you back to your master. Accursed creature. Whore of hell!"

My head jerked back as he backhanded me across the face. Blood flew from my lips, and I tasted blood in my mouth again. Whatever healing ability I had, it did nothing to reduce the pain I felt.

"I should have killed you, demon, just like I killed your mother."

I bared my teeth. "I'll speak to you any way I damn well please, *priest*. I'm not afraid of you."

I barked out a laugh. "You think you can scare me? Break me with your pathetic words? I'm not the one who hides behind a black robe to feel important. You are weak. Not I."

I straightened up and spit blood into his face.

Brother Edgar faltered, and I knew I had struck a nerve. He wiped his hand across his face, and his eyes narrowed.

"Why you little bitch."

He punched me hard, and I crashed onto the ground. I curled up into a protective ball and waited for the next blow. But it never came.

The high priest held Edgar by the arm and looked as if he were disgusted with him.

"Enough, Brother Edgar," he said as he let him go. "You've proved your point. But I'm curious. If you had the chance to kill her, as you say, then why didn't you?"

I rolled back onto my feet and spit some more blood onto the perfectly clean and polished floors.

"She escaped. No doubt she used some demon trick, Your Eminence. I looked for her for years after that, but I couldn't find her. I couldn't fix my mistake. Someone hid her well."

He smiled wickedly, and the thought that Rose might now be in danger sent a cramp into my chest.

"But now I see that my patience has rewarded me. I can finally finish what I had started."

He turned around and addressed the other priests.

"Do not be fooled, brothers. Do not be fooled by this creature's beauty because *she* is *no* woman."

He pointed a finger at me, and I glowered. "This abomination is a demon, a girl sorceress. And we need to rid the earth of these demon women once and for all!"

A murmur of agreement ran around the chamber, and my heart began to race, faster than before.

"The creature should die." An old priest with a thin wrinkled face pointed his walking stick at me. "She will only poison our minds with her lies. We will go mad if we let her live. I have seen it. I have seen the wicked ways of the magic bearers. Kill the creature. Kill her!"

"Yes, kill her!"

"Kill her!"

"Kill the beast!"

My mind raced, and I focused on the high priest. I would have welcomed a quick execution over the life of a courtesan, but I could see that Brother Edgar wanted to make me suffer. A chill settled deep into my bones.

"Perhaps she is destined to die." The high priest turned to me, his lips pulled back into a sly smile.

I could barely breathe.

"But," he said slowly. I could sense the guards and the priests looming behind me. "Perhaps the Creator has other plans for her."

There was something so evil in the look in his eyes that I began to shake.

"What's your name?" the high priest asked after a moment.

I could hardly hear him over the roar in my ears. I hesitated and then raised my chin proudly, "Elena. Elena Milegard from the Pit."

One of the guards smashed me in the back with some kind of club, and I stumbled forward...

"Your *Grace*," Baul instructed me. "Show some respect, witch."

"Elena Milegard, Your Grace."

I was proud to use my mother's maiden name. Brother Edgar and I stared at each other with equal hatred.

"Well now, Elena Milegard, from the Pit," the high priest said. "I do not want you as a concubine. But there is something I want you to do for me—"

"She needs to die!" bellowed the hateful Brother Edgar.

"My lord," he added quickly.

The high priest scowled at him.

"I will do it. Let me take her down to the cells and beat the demon out of her. It would be my pleasure. This is, after all, the result of my own folly. It will give me great pleasure to *rectify* my mistake."

His black, soulless eyes fell on me again and even though I hated this man, I watched him without feeling. He would not break me. I didn't fear him, and I wouldn't go down without a fight.

"Under different circumstances I would have to agree with you, Brother Edgar," said the high priest. He strolled around the chamber, but then his eyes fixed on me again.

"But as it turns out—this *is* different."

Brother Edgar looked shocked. "Your Eminence?"

The high priest turned around and faced me.

"I don't believe in luck or chances. I believe that she was brought to us by the Creator, and that he has a plan for her."

A murmur of disagreement ran around the chamber, but no one seemed to want to voice his discontent.

I was just as confused as the other priests. The high priest's sly smile was not reassuring, and I shifted uncomfortably. What could be worse than being a concubine? My mind was in overdrive. I braced myself for what was to come.

The high priest looked at me through keen eyes. "Elena, have you ever heard of the Heart of Arcania?"

I fidgeted under his icy stare.

"The stone?" I shrugged. "It's a myth, a fairy tale. I've read about it in a children's book."

The high priest seemed pleased with my answer.

"You can read? How marvelous. I can assure you that the precious stone is no myth. The Heart of Arcania exists. The kings and queens of old desired it, too, but no one has been able to recover it."

He raised his voice. "As you are well aware, my brothers, the Great Race will start in two weeks."

I stole a look at the guards. Both Baul and Garth looked as perplexed as I was. I wasn't the only one left in the dark. Brother Edgar glared at me, and I met his eyes with vengeful fierceness and kept glaring at him until he looked away.

"Every hundred years," began the high priest, "representatives from the kingdoms of Arcania participate in a Great Race on the anniversary of the Day of Reckoning, when the Temple of the Sun came into power."

I watched the other priests. The only ones that looked slightly confused were the apprentices. The hateful, self-important priests looked on knowingly. Whatever this race was, it was clear they knew about it.

Still, something in the high priest's attitude unsettled me. He had never appeared to be enraged that I had stolen the Anglian crown—not by a long shot. He had looked joyous.

"For the last three hundred years," the high priest continued, "we have maintained this tradition."

I watched as heads shook in the chamber.

"So what does that have to do with me?"

"Everything," said the high priest.

I noticed Brother Edgar's face darken.

"You see, Elena. This is no ordinary race. The champions from each kingdom must travel to dangerous lands and undertake quests in which they must face both monsters and the undead. Anyone, regardless of their station, can enter the race if they dare. Most will never return. Only the strong can survive...only the *gifted*."

I scowled.

"A race? You want me to participate in a race?"

The high priest's white robes swung in a great arc around him.

"As I am the one who must chose the champion who will represent the Temple of the Sun Empire, who better could I select than a *thief* who also happens to be gifted. It is clear, the Creator himself has chosen her."

Brother Edgar stepped forward.

"Your Eminence. You cannot be serious. You cannot trust this creature. It would be madness," he growled.

I could see a large vein throb on his forehead.

"She will betray you. You cannot allow this. She must die!"

A consensus of agreement sounded through the chamber.

The high priest looked at Brother Edgar dismissively.

"I am high priest here. Not you, Brother Edgar."

The high priest seemed to grow taller, and the chamber darkened as though the torchlights had been dimmed.

"I will take your opinion under advisement. But make no mistake, Brother Edgar, I will not hear another word from you. Is that clear?"

Brother Edgar's eyes met mine for a long charged moment. Then his face went from red to a deep shade of purple, but he pressed his lips together and was quiet.

Once the high priest was satisfied, he turned to me.

"Elena Milegard. You were caught stealing the Anglian crown, a crime punishable by death. Moreover, you are a magic bearer, a crime also punishable by death.

I swallowed hard.

"As such, my brothers want your death."

He paused.

"And under normal circumstances I would not hesitate to see your head on a silver plate. In my opinion, any magic bearer is an enemy of the Empire, of all things natural, and of the Creator himself."

The high priest sighed and straightened his sleeves. I found it odd that while he claimed magic was evil, he chose to use it himself.

"But I find myself with a tool of opportunity. Therefore, I'm giving you two options, Elena. You can choose death, or you can choose to redeem yourself as my champion for the Great Race. What will you choose?"

I raised my brows. He already knew what my answer would be.

If I agreed to be his champion, I might be able to escape with Rose to Girmania or Espan. I did my best to keep my expression blank although I smiled on the inside.

"And if you think of escaping," said the high priest as though he had read my mind, "think again. I will send other champions along with you, and if you leave I *will* hear of it."

He paused and turned to Baul with a cold smile on his face.

"What was the name of the person who hid her?"

"Rose Fairfax, Your Grace," said Baul.

I wanted to cut out his tongue.

"Rose," purred the high priest. "Hear me now, Elena. If you try to leave or if you try to escape, I will torture Rose until she begs me to end her life."

My lips trembled, but I couldn't find my voice.

"There's more. If you do not win this race, if you do not return with the stone, my red monks will hunt you down and kill you. Not only will they will hunt and kill your beloved Rose, but after that we will kill every miserable soul in the Pit, even the children. I will spare no one. The stone is important to me. I will not accept failure."

The high priest watched me and seemed to be greatly entertained.

I set my jaw. The red monks were ruthless assassins. There was no hiding from them. They would sniff you out like attack dogs and kill you in the blink of an eye.

His eyes narrowed.

"And if you try to save your village by warning them, I will know, and I will destroy them. And it will be *your* fault. So think on that before you do anything foolish."

I wanted to spit in the high priest's face. It was always about them. Everyone else was dispensable.

"The race will start in Soul City, and the champions will head west to Goth, in the Heart of Arcania, inside the Hollowmere. Should you agree to race, then your task will be to recover the stone and bring it back to *me*."

I had heard of Goth. It was another continent, west of Anglia. It was the realm of the dead.

"If I win this race and retrieve your stone, do I get a full pardon?"

I knew this was a long shot, but it was worth asking. I would keep my promise to Rose.

"Yes."

I knew he was lying. There was no way he'd let anyone with magic survive. They'd hunt me down and kill me. But I had no other choice.

For a long moment, nobody moved or said anything. I hated these self-proclaimed Gods, but when I saw the shock and outrage on Brother Edgar's face, I felt new courage.

I looked the high priest in the eye and smiled.

"I'll do it."

CHAPTER 9

TWO WEEKS HAD PASSED since I'd met with the high priest in all his horrible glory. I had been thrown into the temple's prison until the day of the race.

At first I wasn't sure what I'd expected, maybe a room in one of the priests' temple houses? It became quite clear that although I was their champion, I was to be treated like a condemned prisoner. I *was* a prisoner. Any which way I looked at it, it all came back to the same thing—I was a pawn in the high priest's game.

But players have the potential to alter the overall outcome. Players can always break the rules of the game. And for the past two weeks, all I could do was make plans on how to break them. I would turn the tables on the high priest. I would.

I was fed cold stew of unknown meat once a day, just enough to keep me from starving, and a bucket of water for drinking and washing. I didn't use much. I didn't know how long I'd be stuck in here. The almighty high priest could easily change his mind.

I closed my eyes and rested my head against the cold stone of my cell. Darkness had been my closest friend for the past days. My bed was a pile of filthy blankets on the stone floor. My only company was these four walls and the guard that slid my meal through the slot in the door once a day. The stale air stank of urine, blood, and despair.

Every waking hour in this sewer infested cell, I thought of Rose. She had kept me safe all this time, only to have her efforts wasted by my stupidity. Perhaps she had known about my healing abilities. I wished that she had trusted me enough to tell me if she had. Maybe if I'd known, I wouldn't have gone to such lengths to steal from the very people from whom I should have been hiding. Had my mother and Rose feared that I'd be forced into a game? A race?

The truth was I was terrified to possess these healing magic powers. How could I have not known all these years? I had never been sick, but had I ever broken a bone or cut myself? I racked my brain but I could not remember any broken bones, or anything that would have revealed my secret early on. So many questions died with my mother. Only Rose knew. I was sure of it. And I would ask her as soon as I'd finished with this race.

I shoved Rose out of my mind and replaced her with the other person who occupied my mind. I thought of Mad Jack. I thought of the muscular tanned skin under his shirt, his straight nose, his haunting dark eyes, and his full lips. I thought about how they would feel on my own lips, and how his rough calloused hands would feel on my skin. There was nothing else to do in this shit hole but think. I thought about how he would look without his clothes, and I wondered if he'd be a gentle lover. Would he be as rough and wild as the reputation that preceded him? I didn't know why I thought about him so much. He *had* betrayed me after all. It was his fault I was here in the first place. As the days passed, I would think of him often. At first bitterly, but then my tears would come, and I'd remember the look of pain that flashed in his eyes before the guards beat me, and I couldn't stay mad. It was almost as if he had tried to tell me something…but what?

"You're such a fool, Elena," I whispered to myself and suppressed my yearning for Mad Jack. I had enough to deal with without getting emotional over a street thug. I deserved better. Rose deserved better.

I heard the rustling of keys and then a click. I pulled myself together, and the creaking metal door swung open.

"Get up. It's time," grumbled the stinking prison guard.

Just seeing sunlight would be a major improvement. I jumped to my feet, stretched, and didn't bother hiding my hopeful smile.

"You won't be smiling for long, witch."

I wasn't sure what he meant. Just because I had some kind of magic didn't necessarily make me a witch. Or did it?

"So the race is today?" I managed.

"It is."

I followed him through the dreary stone corridors of the dungeons. My boots shuffled through puddles of unidentifiable muck as we passed several cells along the way. They echoed with moans and smelled of rotting corpses. I knew that the stories I'd heard growing up were true when I had first stepped down into the dungeons. The priests had destroyed the king of Anglia's castle but had kept the foundations. They had kept the dungeons and had built their golden temple above them. It was creepy and disturbing.

After a few moments of tedious silence, we finally climbed up the staircase that led to the main floor of the golden temple. I shielded my eyes from the flickering light as I heard and smelled the guard disappear back down into the bowels of the temple.

As my eyes slowly adjusted to the brightness, I gasped. Four women stood in front of me and with the indifferent stares they gave me, I knew instantly they didn't like me. Or at least they didn't want me there.

They appeared to be concubines. They were all dressed in the same see-through garb but in multiple colors. They wore their leather collars proudly, like expensive trinkets, as though they were wearing jewelry, and not the priests' tethers. I did my best not to stare at their glorious womanly curves. They had bodies I could only dream of. I stared at their faces instead. And even in their individuality, the shapes of their faces, lips, hair and skin color, they all shared one trait—they were all beautiful.

They frowned disapprovingly at me. I knew I must look and smell worse than the sewer itself. My face burned with shame. I looked like a complete fool next to these goddesses.

My spirits lifted at the smell of rose water and vanilla, however. These women looked and smelled delicious. It seemed that only the rich, or concubines, could afford perfumes.

"This way," said a concubine with golden hair that cascaded in waves of liquid gold behind her back. I knew she must be the head concubine because she held her head high and looked serious.

I might have smelled like the piss I was forced to sleep in, but I wasn't afraid of these women. I knew they weren't here to beat me. They looked too fragile and clean. I didn't argue and I followed her. The others fell into step behind me.

I followed the head concubine down corridors and hallways until I was dizzy. We passed a few priests who smiled at the women but glowered when they passed me. I glowered back. Finally we arrived at a bath area where four large square baths steamed with water so clean, it didn't look real.

"Take your clothes off," ordered the head concubine.

Who was I to argue? At this point, I didn't care about undressing in front of these women. We were the only ones in the bath area, so I felt even more at ease. My clothes were stiff with sweat and grime, and I was dreadfully embarrassed at my filth. The water looked divine. They didn't have to tell me twice.

I peeled off my clothes and dropped into the steaming bath. The hot water soothed my skin. I'd never been in a bath this large, this glorious, and this hot. It was heaven.

The concubines held me, rubbed my skin with hard bristle brushes, and washed my hair.

"Ouch! That hurt!" I yelled.

The red-headed one *tsked*. "You are as filthy as the wild children, miss. We *will* scrub you clean, no matter how much you fuss."

She pursed her large red lips and began to clean my fingernails with a hard brush. The women ignored my many requests to be gentler and scrubbed me until my skin sparkled red.

As they fussed over me, I examined the concubines more closely. One was blonde, one was a redhead, and the other two were brunettes. The one rubbing a bar of soap along my right arm had her hair piled on top of her head in braids. The other concubines wore red ribbons braided into their long locks. The girl who scrubbed my legs had tanned skin that stood out sensually against her see-through yellow robe. They all seemed to know what to do without communicating, and I wondered if they had bathed prisoners often. Every now and again, I caught questioning looks between them. They didn't have to say anything, but I could tell they were mystified about me. There was also a hardness in their eyes that I couldn't explain.

I couldn't suppress the feeling of dread that shook me. I could easily have been one of them, a priest's love toy. Any of them could have been *me*.

Once they were satisfied that I was clean enough, they dried me with plush white towels that smelled of lavender.

"You're *very* skinny. Do you know that we can count your ribs?"

The head concubine was watching me. The scorn on her face had disappeared, and there was pity in her large blue eyes.

I was embarrassed. They had seen *every* inch of me, every imperfection. I wrapped my arms around myself.

"I don't need your pity," I said rather harshly, but I felt like I was being judged, like they wanted to make sure I knew that I didn't belong with them. What did they know about me? Did they ever starve?

"There's not much food in the Pit. We do our best." I glared at the blonde until she looked away, but not before I saw the pink that stained her cheeks.

"She is skinny, but you can't hide the fact that she's beautiful," said the redhead. A frown wrinkled her silky, milky skin. Her emerald eyes widened.

"Skin and bones and still stunning. How did you manage to escape the priests looking like *that?*"

"Helen! Hold your tongue," the blonde looked over her shoulder. "We were told not to make conversation with her."

"There's no one here but us, Kayla." Helen shrugged and turned back to me

"You're tall and fit. You have the most beautiful raven hair I've ever seen. It's a little dry, but I'm sure if you rubbed in a little oil and ate *proper* meals for a month it would be glorious. You have cheekbones to die for, and your dark almond-shaped eyes give you a real exotic look. You're really quite stunning."

Her face became serious. "Even as a child, you would have been beautiful. They would have discovered you. How is it that you're a grown woman? How did they not find you?"

I could see a flash of painful memory spread across her delicate features.

"Maybe she's highborn?" said the one with the tanned skin. Her coffee-colored eyes sparkled, and a tiny smirk made its way to her face.

"Don't be ridiculous, Triss. She's *not* highborn," said Kayla, before I could reply.

I was pretty sure she was about my age, but she looked down at me like she was about to scold a child.

"The state of your nails and your clothes, and the way you carry yourself more like a soldier than a lady—you might look highborn, but you can't fool me."

I hid my anger and smiled. "Never said that I was."

"She's a witch, didn't you hear?" Triss' white teeth glistened as she smiled.

"Witches can change their appearance. My mom told me that. It's the only explanation that makes sense. There's no way she could have hidden for so long. She shape-changed into a cat. Didn't you?"

I rolled my eyes. "I'm *not* a witch."

"What then?" pressed Helen. Her cheeks reddened, and she put her delicate hands on her hips. "How did you do it?"

Although it was Helen who had asked, I could tell that all the women were dying to hear how I'd escaped the clutches of the priests for so long. They had stopped moving, and their eyes fixed on me. While they were obviously intrigued, I could also see that they were angry with me. It was unfair that I had escaped for so long while they had been trapped.

I didn't want to lie to them, and somewhere I felt that I owed them the truth. They had been here for years, probably since they were eleven or twelve years old. My stomach twisted at the thought of the priests soiling their innocence.

I tugged on my towel.

"After my mother died when I was ten," I began, not wanting to tell them that she had been murdered by my father, "I was placed in the care of a barren woman. There was a trap door under our living area, and I'd hide there when we had unwelcome company. The priests knew she could never have children, so they seldom came by. But sometimes they did. They had heard rumors over the years, and they would come and check periodically, just to make sure. I was lucky."

"Until now," said Helen.

It was almost as if she were glad that I had finally been discovered. It was plain that they all felt that it hadn't been fair that I'd escaped the clutches of the priests for so long. I saw a hint of envy in their faces. And even if I wanted to hate them for it, I couldn't. If I'd been one of them, I'd hate me too.

"It doesn't matter anymore," said Kayla, and we all looked at her. "They own you now."

Even if I knew this, it still stung when she said it. She shook her head disapprovingly.

"This is a fool's race. You're going to get yourself killed."

"So I've been told."

She was right. I was a fool participating in a fool's race for a group of men I detested. I almost trusted them enough to explain why I was really entering the race, but I couldn't risk Rose's life by telling them that the high priest was blackmailing me.

Although they resented me, I could see that they were also sympathetic. Maybe because they thought I'd be dead soon. Maybe they were right. A life as a priest's concubine was better than no life. I couldn't believe I was thinking this, when just two weeks ago I'd sworn that I'd take my own life rather than become a concubine.

They dressed me in silence, and it only made me feel worse. But I brightened at the sight of my new clothes: a long-sleeved green linen tunic with a leather bodice, a pair of soft leather leggings, knee high leather boots, and a black cloak made of the finest wool I'd ever touched. All my life I'd had hand-me-downs, and most of the time I'd made my own clothes from rags that even the people of the Pit considered trash.

I stood there gaping like a lovesick girl. I was immediately struck with a profound sense of guilt because, for a moment, I'd forgotten where the clothes had come from.

When they were finished dressing me, Triss stood behind me and weaved my hair into one long braid.

"There," said Triss. She held me by the shoulders and faced me.

"You look beautiful."

I envied her perfect smile and her sparkling white teeth.

I smiled in spite of myself. "Thank you."

I had never really thought of myself as beautiful. Rose had said it often enough, but with the priests always on the lookout for me, I wore it like a shadow. My good looks were a curse, just as they were for these women.

"That's enough, Triss. She's had enough pampering."

94

Kayla was all business now. She straightened to her full height, at least two inches more than the rest of us. "Come along now. This way."

We all filed behind Kayla as she took us out of the bath area and down another corridor. The only sounds were the soft soles of my boots padding on the polished stone.

The blood pulsed in my ears. I feared the priests, and I feared the race that I knew nothing about.

And after what felt like an eternity, Kayla pushed open the doors to the front entrance.

When the fresh air first hit me, I nearly laughed out loud. The clamor of voices in the distance was stirring and exciting, and it burst our silence.

We passed through the holy district where priests' houses lined the streets. Their limestone walls sparkled in the early sun, and I was disgusted at their beauty. As soon as we entered the merchant district, the voices grew louder.

Crowds surged between the trees that lined the broad avenues, and music bellowed around us. We made our way down the cobblestone streets, and I could see black flags with gold suns flapping above grand buildings and villas. Noblemen, women, and children in colorful gowns of the richest silks waved small temple flags and paraded in the streets.

I was shocked at the display of sparkling jewels. Just one of their trinkets would have fed Rose and me for years.

Merchants stood by kiosks filled with exotic meats, and servant girls filled the goblets of the wealthy with wine. Although the smell of roasting meat and spices was almost overwhelming, it couldn't suppress the fear that twisted my insides.

This is it. This is how it starts.

I followed the line of courtesans through the streets of Soul City, but no one paid any attention to the gorgeous, nearly naked women who walked by with their heads held high and their shoulders back. I couldn't help but admire their courage. I wasn't entirely sure I *could* do what they did. They were by far the most beautiful women in the city, and I'm sure they pulled courage from that. But even then, they were still the priests' property. It didn't matter how beautiful they were—they were still slaves.

The people of Anglia were more interested in the clothed woman who strolled between the concubines. *Me.* A few men looked on, curious, but the women caught my attention. Their leering, cruel faces surprised me, and I couldn't look away. When they saw that I had become self-conscious because of their stares, they burst out laughing. The blood rushed to my face before I could stop it. Everyone could see my face and ears turn red. They laughed harder because they knew they had struck a nerve.

The courtesans didn't flinch. I guess they were used to this sort of thing. I wasn't.

I did my best to ignore the laughter behind me and searched for any signs of the other competitors. But there were only merchants and the wealthy here. Where were they taking me?

With every step closer to the race, my breathing became more rapid. I knew I was having a panic attack, and I clamped my trembling fingers into fists. I wouldn't show fear.

I was distracted from my panic when the concubines suddenly stopped in front of a large wooden building. A giant man stood just inside a set of double doors. He wore a stain-covered gray apron over his uniform, but it did nothing to hide his bulging muscles. A symbol of the sun was stitched over his right breast. Although most of his face was covered with a thick brown beard, I could still see lines around his eyes that revealed years of hard labor.

"Follow me," he said, his voice deep and without feeling. He turned and made his way inside the building.

"Um…" I whirled around. "Am I supposed to follow him?"

The concubines were gone.

CHAPTER 10

I WAITED FOR A moment, searching the streets for the women who had scrubbed me clean, but they had vanished like specters. Slightly annoyed at being abandoned without a goodbye or even a *good luck*, I turned and walked into the building.

It was blazing hot and smelled of burning coal, wood, metal, and sweat. A sheen of sweat quickly covered my body. The building was an armory, and the walls were lined with shelves that overflowed with swords, daggers, spears, regular bows, crossbows and longbows, battle-axes, maces, bludgeons, picks, and an assortment of deadly looking weapons I'd never seen before. Long wooden tables were piled with shields, metal helmets, mail hauberks, and hundreds of leather and metal gauntlets. And through a small opening at the back was a blacksmith shop.

Fire blazed in a giant stone forge at the back, and an anvil sat in the middle of the shop. Tongs, bellows and a variety of hammers varying in size for shaping and finishing weapons were piled on top of worktables. The mystery man was no doubt a blacksmith.

"Take what you like," said the strapping man without a glance in my direction.

I walked over to the nearest table, but I didn't take anything. I had hoped my own weapons would be returned. I missed my lucky dagger. But I was fooling myself. I didn't *know* what I needed.

The priest had said that this race was deadly, and that most of the competitors never made it back. But what did I need? I was skilled with a blade and a short sword, but I wasn't trained in combat. It just came naturally to me. Worse, I didn't know how to use most of these weapons. If I was meant to weapon up, it confirmed my suspicions that the race was going to get ugly very quickly. What kind of weapons would the others bring with them? I was probably the only inexperienced peasant in the damn race. I had to be smart and stick with what I knew.

I swallowed hard. "What should I take?"

I hoped I'd hidden the tremor in my voice.

The blacksmith turned and watched me for a moment.

"Nothing fancy. Go for something that you can easily draw and use, like a dagger or a short sword. You're too thin to wield a regular sword. And anything else you can carry, nothing too heavy, you need speed."

I smiled. He hadn't insulted me and had made a truthful and helpful judgment call.

I strapped a leather weapons belt around my waist and selected two daggers, a large hunting knife, and a silver short sword. I bound my forearms with thick leather bracers.

I spun around and grinned. "Done."

The blacksmith raised his eyebrows in approval, but before I could ask if I should use a leg strap, a temple guard appeared.

"I'm here to escort you to the race." He stood with his hand on the hilt of his sword. The hard expression on his face made it clear that I should expect no charity from him.

"Yes, sir," I murmured under my breath.

"The high priest instructed me to give you this."

He handed me an oval-shaped cage made of gold. It was the size of my hand and looked like a small birdcage with an opening and a lock.

"If you get the stone," he raised his brows, obviously questioning my abilities, "you're to put the stone inside. Understood?"

He was very specific.

"Got it." I tested the weight of the cage. It wasn't too heavy, but the gold would feed a thousand hungry bellies.

"Why do I have to put the stone in this?"

The guard ignored my question completely and turned to leave. After I'd mumbled my thanks to the blacksmith, I followed the guard back through the streets.

"Excuse me, but is there any food for the racers? I've hadn't had much since I was locked up and I was wondering…"

The guard kept walking without answering.

"Guess not," I said grumpily.

We merged onto the main street, moving west towards Soul City's west gate. We rounded a corner between the tall limestone buildings that towered beside us, and the gate came into view.

It looked and sounded as though the entire population of the six kingdoms of Arcania had come to see the start of the race. Thousands of nobles and highborn folks crowded around the west gate and stood on the ramparts. Musicians played a melody I had never heard before, and I let the music cheer me for a moment. The unmistakable white robes of the six high priests glimmered on a raised platform. Like great kings, one for each of the six kingdoms, they sat on thrones and looked down on us all. While they all differed physically, they all shared the same cold, evil look in their eyes.

The high priest of Anglia's pale skin and eyes were lost in the brilliance of his silk white robe. He looked godlike and surreal, which was probably what he was going for. He held a jeweled staff with a yellow diamond and a sun symbol on the top. His cold, self-important smile made my stomach churn. He hadn't seen me yet.

As I looked more carefully I could see that the priests were accompanied by grotesque, shadowy figures that hovered next to them. No one else seemed to notice these small, gnarled beasts that knelt beside each priest. I suspected that I might be the only one who could see them. While they were grotesque, their wet eyes told a story of pain, and I immediately felt sorry for them. They were probably slaves, like the rest of us.

I searched the crowds for Brother Edgar, but I couldn't find him. I had the unmistakable feeling that he was watching me from somewhere.

We finally came to a stop at the entrance to the west gate, and I saw the other champions, my competition.

There was no mistaking them. Representatives from all of the conquered nations were lined up on their steeds facing the west wall.

I recognized the blue and white flag of Fransia, and the orange and yellow flag with the eagle and snake emblem of Romila.

Even atop their great horses the Girmanians were huge. They were broad-shouldered men and women whose muscles bulged underneath their thick leather clothes and steel armor. They looked like fairy tale characters as their horses chomped at their bits under their green, black, and yellow colors. I could see the intricate designs that had been shaved into their heads.

The riders from Purtula were dark-skinned, and the fierceness of their appearance was matched in the intensity of their eyes. Their purple and green flag was emblazoned with two snakes coiled around a sword.

The Espanians' emblem depicted a red dragon on a blue shield, and their red and blue uniforms shone in the sunlight.

I had the sudden impression that I was being watched.

A woman with a red dragon stitched to her cloak was staring at me. She was Espanian with coffee-colored skin and dark glossy hair. She looked like she'd been in the sun a while. Her expression was curious and intense. Was this an intimidation? There was something strange about the way she was looking at me.

She turned away, and I continued to survey the other champions.

I spotted the Anglians. I knew their heraldic badge all too well. The red and gold lions embroidered on their tunics were the royal seal of Anglia.

I thought it strange that the priests had allowed the representatives and supporters from the different realms to wear the royal colors of their countries. I would have thought that everyone would have been obliged to wear the simple black and gold emblem of the Empire. Perhaps the priests had reached some agreement with the states they had conquered regarding the display of colors.

My eyes rested on a man with his back to me. When he turned around, his appearance took my breath away.

His white tunic was cut low and revealed his broad, muscular chest. His face was flawless, as though the Creator himself had molded him. His thick dark blond hair fell in soft curls around his square jaw, and I could see his ocean-blue eyes staring back at me. He smiled a cheeky confident smile. I turned my head away quickly, but I knew he'd seen the flush on my cheeks.

New movement caught my eyes, and I spotted a plainer looking group of men and women on horseback. Their mounts were regular carthorses, and they wore thick linen tunics and cloaks like the one I had worn the day I'd been caught thieving. Their clothes were travel-stained, and they looked weary. Although their weapons and clothes were not on a par with those of the nobles from the other realms, there was a fierce pride in the folk from the Pit.

I should have been representing them, not the priests.

I counted quickly. These were at least a dozen racers from each realm, and that meant more than seventy in the race. I turned to make a comment to the guard next to me, but he had vanished.

And then the last person I'd expected to see here stepped up to me.

"Are you all right?" asked Mad Jack.

It was more of a statement than a question. I recognized the two cronies who stood next to him. The tall freckled redhead was Leo, and the shorter one, whose hair was shaved to the scalp and who stank of ale, was Will. They said nothing, but watched me nonetheless.

Mad Jack sighed in relief and then smiled at me. It was a smile that would have sent me to my knees weeks earlier, but now all I did was stiffen.

"Thank the Creator. I was afraid..."

He didn't finish but looked surprised at himself for what he was about to reveal.

I didn't care how genuinely concerned he seemed. My feelings of betrayal and hurt cascaded down on me until I could hardly breathe. I could feel my angry tears well up, but I suppressed them and glared at him. I clenched my hands into fists.

"What are *you* doing here?" I hissed.

I didn't try to hide the anger in my voice or how loudly I spoke.

"I thought by now you'd be in your new manor, spending all the coin you got from the priests for turning me in. I do hope I was worth it."

Mad Jack's jaw tightened, and something dark flashed in his eyes. He leaned forward, and his lips brushed my ear.

"You weren't supposed to *get* the crown," he whispered.

I broke out with goose bumps.

"You were supposed to fail like everyone else before you."

He leaned back just slightly. I looked at him. We were so close, too close. My pulsed raced. I inhaled his musty smell, and something warm came alive inside my body. I couldn't trust myself to speak, and I was tempted to kiss him. I hated that he had that effect on me. I shouldn't be thinking about kissing him. I should be bludgeoning him.

"What do you mean?" I asked.

"When I first told you about the crown, it had been a joke," he said. "I never thought you'd go through with it."

I crossed my arms. "Well I did."

"Someone close to the priests must have overheard our conversation because the next thing I know a priest showed up with a bag full of gold and told me that I'd get five times that much if I could arrange to have a thief try to steal the crown."

He shrugged.

"Well, I've been in the vault, and I know about the sorcerer's fire. I knew it was impossible, and I never thought you'd go through with it. It would be the easiest money I'd ever made, so I played along. I thought they were damn fools until you showed up with the bloody crown."

He raked his hand over his dark hair and shook his head.

"I couldn't believe that you'd done it," he said with a low incredulous laugh.

"How did you, Elena? How'd you do it?"

"I'm not telling you anything," I said tightly. I wasn't about to reveal my secret to the man who had ruined my life.

But it did strike me as odd that the priests should have offered to pay someone to steal their own treasure. It was almost like they suspected that someone like me existed. It was as if they'd been waiting for me.

"What's that in your hand?" Mad Jack had spotted the gold cage that I carried.

"Nothing," I said. I slipped the cage inside the pouch tied to my belt and pulled the string tight with a knot. I didn't feel like sharing anything with him at the moment.

When I looked back at Mad Jack, his eyes were lingering on my lips. He looked up casually, and our eyes met. I strained to keep my face expressionless. But he didn't look bothered at all that I had seen him staring at my lips. He smiled slightly before he became more serious.

"I came here to tell you not to worry about Rose," he said.

I whirled on him with tears in my eyes.

"Don't you hurt her! I swear, if you hurt her I'll kill you," I snarled.

I threw myself at him in a wild rage. I wanted to gouge out his eyes, but his loyal bodyguards held me back while I kicked and thrashed.

"Let her go." Mad Jack snapped his fingers, and Will and Leo let me go.

He looked up and met my eyes. "I'm sorry you have such a low opinion of me. I would never, *ever* hurt Rose."

There was pain in his eyes, but I didn't care. It was his fault I was in this mess.

"Ha! Are you kidding me? You *betrayed* me. Remember? How do I know you won't hurt her? How can I believe you? You broke my trust. I'll never trust you again."

Mad Jack's eyes narrowed slightly. "I suppose you have every reason to say that."

"I do."

The muscles in his shoulders tensed.

He examined my clothes and my weapons.

"So it's true. You're the priests' champion."

"That's right." My voice was bitter, and I clenched my teeth and forced the bile back down my throat.

Mad Jack's face went cold and his eyes hard.

"Shit, Elena. Do you know how dangerous this race is? Do you know what you'll face? What's out there?"

I stared at him blankly. The truth was I had no idea what obstacles I'd face. It was the card the Creator dealt me, and I would see it through, for Rose's sake and for everyone in the Pit.

"Is this what they're *making* you do?" his voice was hard. "For the stealing? They're forcing you to race, aren't they?"

It stunned me that he hadn't figured it out before. I thought he had made this deal with priests. In any case, they owned me now. I'd be free after the race.

I couldn't confirm his suspicions, especially with so many people around. The high priest had warned me of the consequences if I told anyone that I was being blackmailed. I was pretty sure the high priest had ears and eyes everywhere in the city.

"I'll take your silence as a yes," he said, his voice a near whisper.

"They're going to get you killed. You're not experienced enough for this. Look around you, Elena. All these people are warriors. They've been trained to wield a sword and to fight since they were children. They're the best their countries have. You're just a…"

"A what?" I growled. "A woman?"

Mad Jack clenched his jaw and gave me a long look.

"This is madness. You won't know what to do—"

"I can manage. I always have."

I was getting tired of him telling me how useless I would be in a fight, but I knew he was right. I couldn't entirely shake off the terror I felt at what I was about to do, and for whom I was doing it.

I might not be a warrior, but I did have a secret healing ability. And that at least gave me the comfort not to bolt.

I can do this.

"Elena…"

"Stop being such a prick!"

I didn't care anymore. I really wanted to scream again that it was his fault. My face and ears burned, and I knew he could see I was flushed with anger and frustration.

"Why don't you go back to your *Dirty Habit* and leave me alone."

I didn't want him to see me break down. I wouldn't lose it.

He looked at me sympathetically.

"I came here to tell you that Rose will be looked after. She'll have food, plenty of it, and I have my men watching out for her. So you needn't worry."

I raised my hands. "Why do you even care what happens to Rose?"

He stared at me in silence. The color faded from his sun-kissed skin. He looked beautiful.

He dragged a hand through his hair again.

"I'm sorry, Elena. I never meant for any of this to happen. I hope one day you'll find it in your heart to forgive me."

With that, he turned on his heel, and he and his cronies left.

I bit my tongue. I hated that he had just left me here. I wanted to scream at him again.

I watched him move around, speaking with the others from the Pit. The hammering of my heart and the flush on my cheeks betrayed me. I didn't know why I cared so much, but I did. Or at least my body did.

It was then that I noticed he was wearing riding clothes and had more weapons strapped on him than I'd ever seen him with before. There was a confidence in his stride that I hadn't noticed before either. I watched him mount a beautiful white mare. Will and Leo pulled themselves up onto tawny-colored horses beside him.

The blood left my face. Mad Jack had entered the race.

CHAPTER 11

MY PULSE RACED. *Why would Mad Jack join the race?* I felt foolish. Of course he would enter. He was a street thug. If there was a prize to win, he'd want dibs on it. That's all he was. A thug. Just a really, really good looking one.

A loud neighing caught my attention, and I whirled around.

The guard that had escorted me through the city held the reins of a giant black warhorse and led him up behind me. The majestic creature towered above all the other horses. Its gleaming black body shone in the sunlight, and it wore a black saddle blanket embroidered with temple sun symbols. With breechings on its haunches, a chest piece, and rein covers, the horse was equipped for battle. The guard brought the horse next to me, and I jumped back.

The horse raised its head at the sudden movement. It stared at me with round brown eyes, and I wondered who more frightened, the horse or me. Probably a little of both.

"What's the matter, Miss. Don't you ride?" the guard looked puzzled.

I tore my eyes from the horse and shook my head.

"Of course I *don't* ride. You need coin to keep horses, and I'd barely had enough coin to eat. So no, I don't ride. Never have, actually."

My heart dropped. Most of the horses in the Pit were the large strapping work kind, with legs and hooves as big as my head. Horses were too expensive for Rose and me.

My competition all sat skillfully on their mounts. They all looked as if they had had years of experience. My heart sank even lower. I don't know why I was so shocked. It wasn't like we'd *walk* to Goth. It would probably take two months. Of course we'd be riding horses. I just wished I had practiced a little beforehand. Clearly this was a disadvantage. Already I had one strike against me, and we hadn't even started...

The guard threw me the reins. "See if I care, witch."

He turned and left.

I stood staring at the giant beast.

I felt eyes on me again and scanned the crowd.

The high priest from Anglia was staring at me, and I could see that he was angry. Obviously he'd seen what had transpired between the guard and me. Anyone standing nearby would have recognized the fear in my eyes, too. I knew he had anticipated that I would know how to ride. It was stupid on his part. He should have known I couldn't keep a horse. Even from a distance, I could see the high priest's face turn from red to an ugly shade of purple. *Blood of Arcania.* I was not getting off to a good start.

"Excuse me."

I jumped at the sound of a voice behind me. I turned to see the handsome young man I spotted before.

"You look like you might need a little help with the horse."

He moved towards the black beast and took the reins in his hands. I noticed that he casually glanced over my shoulder to the podium. He looked troubled for an instant, but then his concern was gone by the time his eyes met mine again. He smiled at me again, and it sparked something hot in my chest.

He looked about my age, maybe a few years older, with a goatee. He held himself gracefully, like the noble man he probably was, and wore the red and gold colors of Anglia proudly. He patted the horse's neck gently.

"He's a magnificent animal. Strong, but calm, with an even temperament and quiet nature. Perfect for someone who's never ridden. He'll take good care of you."

"Is it that obvious I've never ridden?" I said.

It was hard not to stare at the skin that peered through the neck of his tunic.

He laughed softly, and my heart did a somersault. "It is."

I could listen to that laugh all day.

"So you know about horses?" I mumbled stupidly.

My stomach was full of butterflies, and I felt like an adolescent girl. *What was wrong with me?*

"I do," he said, and I wished he'd stop smiling like that. "You could say I'm a seasoned rider. I've been riding since I was five."

I sighed. "Of course you have."

I stared at the soft curls that brushed against his jaw. He hadn't shaved for a few days, and that was just fine with me.

"I'm probably the only one here who's never actually been on a horse." The words came out more desperately than I had wanted. I didn't want him to think I was scared, even though I was terrified.

He gave me a lazy smile, and his eyes met mine. "Well, you're going to have to learn quick," he said and steadied the horse.

"Can you climb onto this fellow's back on your own?"

I don't know why, but I looked over to the podium. The high priest was watching me with a frown, clearly aggravated that I hadn't climbed up on the giant beast yet. We were the only two not saddled up.

I might be poor, but I had my pride. I was going to do this. I had to do it.

"Of course I can."

I moved beside the great beast. I'd seen riders mount their horses before. I knew I had to put my left foot in first. I grabbed hold of the saddle, stuck my left foot in the stirrup, hauled myself up, and swung my right leg over the beast's back.

I felt a mixture of fear and excitement as I sat on my new companion. I smiled as I felt the enormous beast stir beneath me. It was gentle, even though I could tell that it sensed my fear. The smell of horse filled my nose, and I reached out and patted the great creature on the neck. I think I was soothing myself as much as the horse.

"You steer the horse with the reins." The handsome stranger handed me the reins.

"Hold them just above the pommel of the saddle. Keep your hands steady at all times, too much movement, and you'll jab your horse in the mouth with the bit. Urge the horse forward by gently squeezing your calves into the horse's sides. His name is Torak."

He gently stroked the horse's neck. "He'll take good care of you."

I raised my brows. "You know this horse?"

He nodded and continued to stroke the horse's neck. "I do. He used to belong to my family."

Something sad appeared in his eyes. "We sold him to the temple, along with many other great black beauties."

I wanted to ask him why his family had sold their horses. Clearly he cared about them, but it wasn't my place to ask. And it felt too personal.

He moved towards the back of the horse. "You've got provisions here."

He motioned to the large leather saddlebag and peered inside.

I opened my mouth to stop him, but thought better of it. I didn't think he was trying to sabotage me; it was more like he *wanted* to help me. But I just couldn't understand why. It wasn't because he thought I had a pretty face, or was a damsel in distress…it was something else.

"There's not much in here," he continued and closed the flap. "But it'll keep you for at least two weeks. Then you'll need to find food on your own."

He watched me, and when I said nothing he added, "Do you know where you're going at least?"

I nodded. "I'm heading west to Goth. The stone is somewhere in that realm. I'm guessing that's not a secret."

I didn't add that the high priest had told me about the stone being inside the Hollowmere. I had a feeling that information was only for my ears. I felt guilty about not saying anything since he had helped me, but I couldn't risk it.

The stranger nodded.

"There's a map tucked in the side pocket and a compass. But for now, follow the main road till you get to the end of Anglia that borders the West Sea. That'll take you about two days. Keep to the road till you hit the long narrow passage called Death's Arm. Goth is a three day ride from there."

"Thank you," I nodded.

Our eyes met, and I blushed from my neck to the top of my head. "Why are you helping me?"

He looked at the priests behind me.

"Don't thank me just yet. You might regret it when you see what we'll be facing."

He was quiet for long enough that I thought he wouldn't add anything else. But then he added, "You looked like you needed it more than the others. I just didn't feel right having you go off on this race without a little assistance. It wouldn't be fair. I don't want to offend you…but you're the least experienced here."

We stared at each other in an awkward silence. I opened my mouth but closed it again. He started to turn away.

"I'm Elena," I blurted as I held out my hand. "Elena Milegard."

It was the least I could do, but I also wanted to know his name.

He took my hand and smiled. His perfect teeth and perfect smile made me weak. His callused hand, strong and sturdy, was gentle. He lifted my hand to his mouth and kissed it. His lips were smooth, his breath hot, and it tickled my skin. I almost fell out of the saddle. Thank the Creator I was sitting.

"It's nice to meet you, Elena. Landon Battenberg, at your service."

His blue eyes pierced mine, and I could see by his smug smile that he knew the effect he had on women, on me. The name Battenberg seemed familiar to me, but I couldn't think past the way his lips had brushed my hand. I wondered how soft they would feel against my own lips.

"Well, thank you again, Landon."

I straightened, and it took all of my self-control not to show how much I'd enjoyed his gentle kiss.

"Good luck, Elena." Landon's face turned serious. "You're going to need it."

He walked away. His broad shoulders swayed back and forth, and I could still feel the warmth on my skin where he had kissed it.

I bit my lip and said softly, "I'm sure I will."

Despite myself, I smiled as I watched him mount his own warhorse. It was a great bronze-colored steed, powerful yet graceful, just like Landon. I couldn't tear my eyes from him. But I couldn't let his good looks and his five minutes of kindness distract me. This was a race after all. And I was in it to win it.

As Landon turned my way, I pretended to look elsewhere. That's when I met Mad Jack's glare.

I was shocked to see fierce anger in his eyes. It was like a silent accusation. And although I wasn't sure what was going on, I couldn't help but feel the guilt that spread through me. But why? What hold did he have on me?

Shrugging, I opened my mouth and mouthed *what?* But he just steered his horse to the opposite side of the line from the Pit folk, like he was trying to put as much distance as he could between us.

I hadn't realized that I'd been holding my breath. I was stunned and a little hurt by his gesture. He didn't own me. I could speak to whomever I chose.

Suddenly, bells chimed.

The crowd hushed and an uncomfortable silence spread across the grounds. As the crowd drew in a collective breath, I suddenly felt nauseated. I tried not to think about Mad Jack and why he made me feel so miserable inside. I focused on the race. If I wanted to win this thing, I'd have to keep my feelings in check. I sat still on my mount, my eyes on the platform, and I waited like everyone else.

I wasn't surprised when I saw the high priest of Anglia stand up. He raised his arms and with a superior smile on his face, he began to speak.

"Welcome to the anniversary of the Day of Reckoning," his voice boomed.

"After the world had been devastated by war, the Temple of the Sun united the six kingdoms under one rule, and we have lived in peace for over three hundred years. We celebrate this day by inviting all the kingdoms to participate in the Great Race for the glory of the Heart of Arcania."

I glanced over at my competitors, to remind me again what I was up against. The fact that there were a handful of women cheered me somewhat, but they looked as fierce as the men. Some of them actually *looked* like men.

"The rules are simple," said the high priest.

His smiled widened. "There are no rules."

Laughter erupted from the crowds and the guards, but the competitors sat straight-faced, as I did. I studied the other high priests. They watched their leader with stony faces.

"The Creator be with you all," said the high priest. "May the best man or *woman* win."

His eyes rested on me, and I stifled an icy shiver. But before I had time to gather my thoughts, he walked casually to the giant bronze gong and hit it with a great swing of his jeweled staff.

Immediately, the sounds of hooves tore the ground like a great thunderstorm. The ground shook as the riders and their mounts galloped through the west gates.

All except for me.

Rattled, and with my face burning in humiliation, I took control of Torak's reins and hit his sides with my legs. I could see the disappointment in the high priest's face without looking.

Torak galloped forward with a great bound, and I lost control of the reins. I pulled myself straight with the pommel, and as I fumbled with the reins Torak dashed towards the west gate.

As we thundered out the west gate, I caught a glimpse of Brother Edgar standing next to the wall. He was smiling. A chill rippled down my back. I guess he assumed that this race would be my death sentence.

I swallowed hard as I was thrown around on the horse's back. I cursed into the wind and felt like a fool.

The Great Race had begun, and I was last.

CHAPTER 12

I DISCOVERED VERY QUICKLY that riding did *not* come naturally to me.

After the first few hours of riding, I had chafed my inner thighs against the saddle. And if it weren't for my supernatural healing abilities, I probably wouldn't have had any ass to sit on at all.

I kept sliding off to the side of my saddle, cursing into the wind and pulling myself back up. At first my pride had been hurt. How many people had seen my disastrous beginning? I wondered if Landon had seen and had regretted helping me. I was truly the worst prepared competitor. But instead of feeling sorry for myself, I got angry.

I had been left behind and was breathing the others' damn dust. It didn't seem to bother Torak, but I couldn't breathe without coughing up a lung. I made a temporary mask with my cloak in order to breathe, but the dust tapered off, and I could breathe again without it. I wiped my eyes and peered down the road before me.

It was empty. The dust had disappeared and so had the other racers. They were gone.

It wasn't that Torak lacked speed; his strong, lean legs were like a great machine. But I had felt him slow down a few minutes into the race. I realized after a while that he was trying his best not to throw me off. He was trying to keep me on his back. I liked him immediately after that.

I hadn't seen any of the others for at least two hours now. I was already trailing behind.

"Why did I have to steal that damn crown!"

I had to believe that there was still a chance to save Rose and my village. I had never doubted for one second that the high priest would murder thousands of peasants, farmers, and children if I didn't bring back that stone.

Damn him. Damn the Temple of the Sun Empire. Damn them all to hell.

I rode on with a heavy heart. How was I going to catch up now? Let alone win?

Even though riding didn't come easily for me, I figured every day would get a little better. I felt a little progress as we galloped on through Anglia. I thrust my body forward and tried to ride with the rhythms of horse. The wind in my face and my hair overwhelmed me with a feeling of freedom. I felt like a bird in flight. I felt the beast's great power under me, and it became my power as we started to move as one.

Torak's thick, black mane flowed around my hands, and eventually I began to enjoy myself a little more and even to take in the scenery.

In the beginning I'd passed tall stone buildings and cross streets, large villas and acres of beautiful manicured lands. I'd never ventured farther than Soul City, and I'd never thought I'd ever be going west. East was where I'd set my sights. East was where I wanted to start a new life with Rose.

My chest tightened at the thought of something happening to Rose. Mad Jack had promised that he would care for her, that he would see to it that she had food and protection. He had obviously felt guilty about handing me over to the priests we hated.

Did he think I'd forgive him? No. I didn't think so. His betrayal still made me furious.

Going west wasn't as bad as I thought it would be. Anglia was beautiful country. And as time went on, the buildings decreased in size, lots became smaller, and the great stone buildings were replaced by smaller dwellings with colored roofs and smaller windows. They were still mansions compared to the thatched huts in the Pit. Even the worst areas of Anglia were characterized by beautiful homes and lavish gardens. The inequality made me furious.

Passersby looked a little baffled as we galloped by, so far behind the rest of the pack.

"You're last!" a stupid fat man with no neck shouted. I couldn't place his accent.

"Thanks for the tip," I yelled back, fuming. Like I didn't know. I ignored the pig-like man as I passed him in a blur.

Golden fields and farms with large ponds dominated the countryside for another few miles and then ended abruptly at the edge of a forest.

Without breaking stride, we plunged into a stand of pine and spruce and hemlock trees. The road narrowed, and tall evergreen trees surrounded us on both sides. As soon as we entered the forest, the cool air brushed my face, and I was glad for it. The trees offered us welcome shade.

Torak's back was covered in sweat. He needed a well-deserved break. And I knew the other competitors would eventually need to rest their animals as well. It would be dark soon, and I wouldn't chance breaking the horse's legs in the dark. It wasn't fair to him. The tall trees on all sides would most probably hide most of the light from the moon. It was stupid to travel at night, especially in a strange land.

"Whoa, big guy," I said and pulled gently on the reins.

Torak slowed to a stop, and I swung my legs over and dismounted, grateful to be on solid ground once again. My thighs burned as I shook my legs and tried to get the blood flowing again. Although my legs felt like wood planks, I thought I'd be in worse condition than I was. My healing abilities were still effective.

I straightened up and sighed.

"Right. You need water. You're thirsty aren't you, Torak?"

Torak watched me with big brown eyes. I thought I saw his eyes widen at the mention of water, so I took that as a yes.

"I saw a creek next to the road. Come on. Let's get you some water."

I took the reins and led Torak along the edge of the road where I'd spotted a creek and hoped I hadn't dreamed it. I heard the sound of trickling water and eased Torak towards the sparkling creek. He went to the water and began drinking. After I had helped myself to some deliciously cold water, I figured this was a good time to have a look inside the large saddlebag. I moved next to Torak and peered inside.

It was packed. I had dried meats, breads, cheese, a container of water, and apples. I even had spare clothes and undergarments. I pulled out an apple.

Torak stopped drinking and turned his big eyes to the apple in my hand.

I cut the apple in half with my hunting knife and fed Torak one half. He gobbled it up and eyed the other piece hopefully.

"Forget it," I said, and sheathed my knife.

"It's not like we have a lot to go around. We need to share. You had your piece already, this one's mine."

But as I watched him, tired and sweaty after all that running, I realized he deserved an entire apple tree. I gave him the other piece. "You're welcome."

I laughed, glad of his silent company. Without the distractions of wicked priests and handsome men, I could figure out a plan to get me back into this race. I tied the reins around a branch from a pine tree, broke off a piece of bread, lifted a flap from the bag and pulled out the map. I didn't like going into unknown territory. I needed to study the map.

Maybe I could find a shortcut to Goth. With that idea in mind, I felt a new sense of hope and moved to a soft spot under a large pine tree. I sat down and unfolded the map on the soft pine needles. It was good quality parchment, and I was surprised to see how much care had been taken in the details. Only the temple could afford maps like this.

Although I might have been poor, my mother had taught me to read, and it saddened me to think that most of the people in the Pit were illiterate. The priests preferred to keep their cattle in ignorance, the better to rule them.

The map showed the boundaries of Anglia that bordered the West Sea. I stared at a small strip of land that connected Anglia to the small island of Goth to the west. *Death's Arm* was written in bold black letters. It was the only way in or out of Goth.

"Inviting," I said. "It's no wonder nobody wants to go there."

I moved my finger along the narrow passage into Goth and studied the many paths that led into Hollowmere. Even shortcuts and secret passageways were marked on this map. Had the priests been to the Hollowmere? It was obvious that whoever had conjured up this map had taken great care with the details.

If my map was more detailed than the maps of the other racers, then it was clear that the high priest really did expect me to win. If he really had given me a special map and a strong horse, maybe I could win.

I wondered about the golden cage. Was there a connection between the Anglian crown I had stolen and the golden cage? Why was the stone so important to the high priest? What would he gain from having it? The other competitors wanted to win to bring joy to their communities and experience the glory of victory, but what would the temple gain if I captured the stone? What was their true purpose? I would have to think about that later.

As I studied the map, I remembered the handsome man with sparkling blues eyes who had made the gesture of helping me, even though I was a competitor. The memory of his warm mouth on the skin of my hand sent a jolt rippling through me. A man hadn't had that effect on me for years...

I was still haunted by Mad Jack's apparent look of disappointment and anger at my conversation with Landon Battenberg. Why should he care if I'd enjoyed being treated like a lady by a handsome stranger?

I realized the truth. This was a competition. Sooner or later we'd all face each other. We might have to fight or even kill to get to the stone. What if Landon was playing me? Could he have been charming his way into my heart so I wouldn't see the blade of his sword until it was too late?

I'd been seduced in less than a minute, my new record for stupidity. I'd let my feelings overwhelm me. It was with my brain I needed to race with, not my heart. My face burned with shame and humiliation. I swallowed my nausea. I was weak. But I wouldn't be fooled twice. I wouldn't let some pretty face deter me.

Suddenly, I was all too aware of how dark it had become, as though the trees had purposely hidden the last of the sunlight from me. I could hardly see the map. It was getting late. There was no way I'd ride on in the dark. I needed to make camp.

Torak seemed happy and rested. Perhaps with a good night's sleep, we could ride hard at sunrise and catch up to the others. Yes. That was definitely a good plan.

Feeling more optimistic, I folded up the map and stuffed it back into the bag. I picked out a small pot and, to my surprise, tea. Tea sounded like a dream.

I went in search of kindling for a fire and threw a look back at my horse to make sure he hadn't run off. He was still where I had tied him. Technically he wasn't *my* horse, but he was mine for the duration of the race. I'd never had a pet before. It's not like we could afford to feed a dog or a cat … or even a bird. This was as close to owning a pet as I'd ever come. I smiled.

Tomorrow I'd catch up, maybe even lead, if the Creator were on my side.

I had a small meal of dried meat and tea and settled on my back in the pine leaves. It only took a few seconds before my eyelids were so heavy that I couldn't keep them open. I fell asleep with a smile on my face.

I didn't know how long I'd slept when the snapping of a branch woke me.

I froze. My heart fell to my stomach. I jumped to my feet and went for my daggers. But it was already too late.

A dark cloak swept past my eyes, metal rang, and a blade pierced my throat.

CHAPTER 13

WARM BLOOD WELLED INSIDE my throat. I gasped as the metallic liquid poured from the corners of my lips. I was choking on my own blood.

I reached up, wrapped my fingers around something cold and hard, and pulled. I tossed the knife to the ground and instinctively covered the cut in my throat with my hand. The blade had struck deep. I felt the blood pump between my fingers, and I knew it had hit an artery.

I spotted my assailant through my tears. Even in the dark there was no mistaking that it was a man. He wore a golden mask fashioned with the face of a skull, and he was covered from head to toe in a black cloak. He held two curved daggers, and his soulless dark eyes spied me from the holes in the mask.

I hadn't even arrived in Goth, and yet I stood before a demon, or a man disguised as one.

My attacker watched me gurgle and choke on my own blood. He almost looked carefree. He watched me patiently, like he was waiting for something.

"The priests are liars, and they can *never* possess the stone. You should never have agreed to this race," he said. His heavy accent sounded Fransian.

"I do not rejoice in the killing of a woman, but I will do what I must to protect the stone. We know what you are, and what you can do. You must die tonight before you murder us all."

His eyes showed a fierce resolve as he watched me.

"For our wrestling is not against flesh and blood," chanted the man. "But against principalities and powers, against the rulers of this world of darkness, against the spirits of wickedness in the high places. Demons creep in stealthily through all the avenues of the senses. Demons will lead men to falsehood."

I staggered as the world began spin. I opened my mouth to speak, to tell him I had no idea what he was talking about, but my words died in mouthfuls of blood.

"You might not die from the mere blade," he said, and I saw the sneer on his lips from the bottom of the mask. "But the poison *will* kill you."

Poison. Did he say poison?

I knew as soon as he said it that something was very different from when the high priest ran me through with his sword. Then it had stung, and I had felt the tearing of flesh, but it was a clean cut. This wound in my throat felt as though the skin around the puncture was peeling away and burning piece by piece, like salt on a wound. As my blood pumped, the pain spread all the way down and throughout my body. The blade had been tainted with poison.

Whoever my attacker was, it was clear he knew more about me and what I could do than I did. But who had told him?

"It's for the best. It's for the good of Arcania. With your death...millions will live."

My attacker was waiting to see the effect the poison would have on me. The twisted smile on his face showed me that he was enjoying watching me die.

I wanted to spit in his face, to punch him, but the muscles in my face had stiffened as if I were wearing a solid mask. I felt the poison burning my fingers. My body was becoming numb and my fingers stiff. My breathing came in rapid, wet breaths as my throat began to swell. I didn't feel the healing magic I'd felt when I'd been stabbed before. Ingesting the poison was different. It was in my blood stream and spreading incredibly fast inside me.

A cold shiver spread through my body as the fever settled in. Maybe this was it. Maybe I couldn't heal from poison.

"It's Hemlock," said the masked man as he prowled closer.

"It causes paralysis of the various body systems. Paralysis of the respiratory system is the usual cause of death. You won't be able to move, but you will be aware of what is happening. Your mind will be unaffected, until just before you die."

My legs felt like ice blocks, and I couldn't move. I keeled over onto my back. The hot-white pain spread as the poison made its way through every inch of me. I couldn't even cry out. It stung my face like the scratches of a cat. And then it dug through my ears and pounded in my head.

Then the pain stopped altogether, and I felt cold with fear. I couldn't even feel the blood that gushed out of my throat and mouth. With my hand clutched on my throat, I was frozen like a statue in one of the priest's gardens.

I was dying for real this time...

A twig snapped, and the shadow loomed over me again. I stared into the sadistic, skull-masked face of my attacker.

"Demons are always sent to test our faith, to trick the weak as false prophets."

His rough voice was nothing like the priest's soft, melodic tones.

"Many succumb to earthly pleasures instead of following our duty to the one true God."

He talked of the Creator, and yet he was no priest. I was being murdered by a religious fanatic.

"Bless Arcania. Bless the one and true God. Deliver us from the evil of the world, from the corruption that is in the world through the devils; from the evil of every condition in the world; from the evil of death that is plaguing our world. Deliver us from ourselves, from our own evil hearts. Deliver us from evil men and false prophets, that they may not be a snare to us."

He made a sign over the left side of his chest and then kneeled beside me until I could smell his hot, stale breath. The tip of his curled dagger pointed at my right eye.

I couldn't blink my tears away. My eyelids were frozen, and I stared out into the black sky. Stars peered through gaps in the trees. They were so beautiful. It was almost calming.

I realized that I would never experience childbirth. I would never love a child unconditionally, protect it, and have a family of my very own. I had never really thought about it before. That deep, throbbing pain of that one thought alone was terrifying.

I knew I was dying when the world around me began to melt like ice cream on a hot summer day.

I cried as the trees melted. I cried as the stars melted into blots of white ink in the sky. I cried when I thought of the terrible things he'd do to Torak when I was gone. I cried when the masked man's face started melting.

"I can see by the fear in your eyes that you've started to hallucinate," said the man.

His voice seemed far away.

"Soon you will not be able to tell the difference between reality and the demons in your mind. The poison will melt your brain inside your skull. It will be excruciating. And you won't even be able to scream."

CHAPTER 14

I STARED INTO THE masked face of death. If the poison didn't melt my brain like he'd said, then surely he would finish the job.

The tip of his blade dangled in front of my eyes. It was coming. Death was coming.

And when I'd convinced myself to let go, that I was ready to die, that I was *going* to die, something stirred inside me.

My body shook on its own accord. Was this the poison's doing?

I watched helplessly as the masked man moved his blade away from my eye.

He rolled up his sleeve and sliced his forearm with his dagger.

"I believe in the one true God, the creator of all things. Soul of the one true God, make me holy, be my salvation. Purify me. Wash me clean of my sins, strengthen me, hear my prayer."

Blood trickled to the ground as he cut himself again.

"Defend me from the evil enemy and call me to the fellowship of our brethren at the hour of my death. I say this praise with them for all eternity."

He looked over to me and clicked his teeth together in a wild grin.

"And they said you couldn't be killed."

His unnatural laughter cut through the eerie silence of the forest.

I wanted to shout for help. I wanted to kick out with my legs, but my body wouldn't obey my mind. It was as though I was already dead and my soul was waiting to be taken by the Creator.

The man's cold eyes watched me. "It won't be long now."

My vision blurred then, and I was glad that I wouldn't have to look into that horrid masked face anymore.

A soft neigh reached my ears. I went cold. Torak. Where was my beautiful horse? The thought of this bastard hurting Torak woke something inside me.

A new feeling stirred in my chest. And then sensation.

It started with a tingling like tiny insect bites under my skin. And then tingling turned into a throbbing pain.

Pain. What a wonderful thing.

I knew it before it happened. My body was healing itself. My magic was working.

It attacked the poison. I kept my face straight, did my best not to blink to give myself away. Surprise was my only advantage at that point. The pain changed to a warmth that spread through my entire body. I felt my neck wound begin to repair itself. Delicious air filled my lungs.

The masked man continued to mutter prayer after prayer.

Let him keep talking. Keep praying.

He obviously enjoyed the sound of his own voice. I took comfort in knowing that I would repay his attempt on my life by cutting his throat. He had been foolish. In his confidence, he hadn't removed any of my weapons. I waited calmly for the perfect opportunity. It was as though it came naturally to me, like I'd been born to do this.

"This is taking too long. You should be dead by now."

The man's voice was hard and unfeeling, business like. "I'm done waiting."

I watched and waited.

The man grasped his blade with both hands, raised it high above his head, and brought it down.

But I was already moving.

I rolled away, and the tip of the blade plunged into the earth where I'd lain a second ago.

By the time he realized what had happened, I was on my legs, and my own blades were ready in my hands. Although my legs were still stiff and painful from the effects of the poison, I could feel adrenaline surging through the rest of my body.

My would-be assassin spun around. His eyes widened with a mixture of fear and fury.

"Impossible! No one can survive the hemlock. What kind of demon are you?"

I smiled. "And here I thought I was a witch."

My voice sounded strange, muffled, different from how I had spoken before.

My heart thumped hard as I took in deep, wonderful breaths of air, and my healing magic ate away at the last of the poison.

I watched the assassin's fury spread through him like a wildfire. I could see his poisoned blades shining beneath his long black sleeves. I couldn't risk a scratch from those damn blades again. I had to be extra careful.

I swallowed hard and took a chance.

"Why do you want to kill me? Who sent you?"

Instinctively I looked over my shoulder, expecting more skull-masked men to jump at me from the forest. But they didn't. It was only him, for now.

The skull mask gleamed in the light of the moon.

The man snickered. "I shall kill you once and for all, demon. And this time you will *stay* dead!"

Scowling in determination, I crouched with my knees bent and prepared to engage him at close range. I thanked the Creator that I'd been raised in the Pit. I might have been blessed with the gift of healing, but I'd learned to fight, and to fight dirty, from experience.

"You've got that wrong. I'm *not* dying today," I growled.

I wasn't about to let him hurt me again. I was going to fight with everything I had in me.

He snarled as he came at me like a blur of darkness. He was much faster than I'd first anticipated. But I was ready for him.

He lunged for my heart, but just as the tip of his blade brushed the front of my tunic I parried and spun around. With a twist of my forearm, I sent one of his daggers sailing into the air. But that didn't stop him.

With incredible speed, he sliced through my garments but never reached the soft of my skin. I kicked out hard and made contact with his knees with a satisfying crunch. He yelled out in pain and surprise. I ducked and swung my leg at his ankles and swept him off his feet.

He tumbled backward but regained his balance as skillfully as a cat.

He grimaced in the faint moonlight. "I'm going to enjoy killing you, demon whore."

I flashed him a toothy grin, my confidence building with every breath.

"From where I'm standing, you're the one who looks more like a demon than I do. I'm not the one sneaking up on defenseless women in the dark."

His lips curled into a vicious smile beneath his mask. He slashed me with his dagger, but I blocked with my sleeve and slashed my blade across his chest. He stumbled back, his robes were torn, and a large wet stain began to grow over his breast.

"Better than you thought, aren't I?" I taunted.

My eyes narrowed in the dark. "You lack the necessary skills to kill me. The high priests made a huge mistake sending you."

"Ha! You're even more stupid than I thought if you imagined we'd ally ourselves with those false men and their false God."

I could see the darkening fury in his eyes.

"You know nothing."

"If not the priests, then who? Who sent you?"

He roared with wild rage and came at me again. But I twisted easily away from him.

I crouched low, then jumped and slammed my knees into his back. He went sprawling and his blade fell from his hand. He reached for it, and I stomped on his hand.

He shrieked and kicked out with his legs, sweeping my feet from under me.

I barely had time to blink as he threw himself at me again. I ducked, but as I pulled away he managed to get me in a headlock. I kneed the muscle in his thigh and brought my fist crashing against his kidney and groin. I flipped him over, but he slipped out of my grasp like an oily snake.

"Die, demon bitch," he sneered and charged.

Call it instinct, call it the hand of the Creator, but at that exact moment, I sidestepped and spun. He impaled himself on my blades as I held them protectively in front of me.

He toppled to the ground with a grunt. And then there was nothing.

My stomach contracted, and I vomited. I didn't know why. Maybe it was the last of the poison, or maybe it was just my body telling me how I truly felt.

I stood there for a moment, letting the emotions of killing someone run through me.

I wasn't sure what I felt. It's not like he'd given me a choice. I had to protect myself. He was going to kill me. Even though I'd felt rage and wanted to kill him in the moment, now that I stared at his body, I was pretty numb. Remorse? Guilt? This was self-defense. It was odd. A few seconds ago I had enjoyed taking his life and had felt no remorse.

If he wasn't working for the temple, then who was he? I remembered him saying *we*, so there were more in this group, whoever these masked men were. I wasn't about to stay here and wait for more of these lunatics to try and kill me.

I pulled my blades from his chest. After I wiped them clean on the grass, I reached out and pulled off his mask.

I wasn't sure what I'd expected underneath, but the plain face of an ordinary man wasn't it. Maybe I thought he'd be ugly and disfigured, or maybe even a demon himself. But I looked down into the empty eyes of a regular middle-aged man.

Just a man. Not a demon.

I couldn't sit here and wrestle with my feelings while more of these lunatics prowled the impenetrable night forest and waited for me to turn my back. I could almost see them, waiting in the dark. If they were so keen on killing me, who's to say they hadn't sent backup just to be sure I was dead?

I needed to go.

I was alive. And I planned to stay that way until I finished this race. I ran over to Torak. He nudged me gently with his muzzle and neighed.

I reached out and patted his neck.

"It's okay. I'm all right, boy. It's over now."

Torak rested his head on my shoulder. His gesture was almost like a hug. I wasn't an expert on horse emotions or their body language, but I had the feeling he'd been worried about me and was glad that I was safe. God I loved that horse.

There was no point trying to get some sleep because I knew it wouldn't come. The forest was too good a hiding place for masked men. Torak shifted nervously, the whites of his eyes showing as he glanced at the dead man. The smell of blood unnerved the horse, and he seemed to be as eager as me to get out of these woods.

I ran over to the creek and splashed cool water on my face to wash off the stench of the masked man. Then I grabbed our supplies and pulled myself with surprising ease onto Torak's back. I grasped the reins firmly to keep my hands from shaking.

A faint glow appeared through the tangle of trees in the east. It was nearly morning. I said a silent prayer to the Creator and hoped that the forest was not hiding any more masked men.

Then I kicked my heels into Torak's flanks, and we galloped through the forest, racing for our lives.

CHAPTER 15

TORAK RAN LIKE THE Devil himself was chasing him.

At first I wasn't sure if I should stop him. He seemed to be running on magic. His powerful legs dug up dirt from the road and left a trail of dust behind us. Every time I heard a snap or a break I feared that he had broken a leg, but he never faltered. I feared that I was pushing him too hard, but it was as if he wanted to leave the forest behind as much as I did. And even if I wanted to stop him, I wasn't sure I could. It was all I could do to keep from falling.

I tried hard not to think of the masked assassin. *Who had sent him and why? If not the priests then who? Why was my death so important? What had I done to these people?*

As the darkness of the forest began to lift, so did my spirits. Crisp white light spilled through a break in the trees up ahead. We finally emerged from the woods and galloped into bright midmorning sun and crisp blue sky.

Torak slowed as if he had finished his race with the foreboding darkness of the forest and left behind the memory of the masked man. He seemed as happy as me to be in the golden fields and warm delicious sun.

We rode at a comfortable gallop for a while, just enjoying the sun and each other's company. I'd made a friend for life, and I smiled into the wind. Flocks of starlings swooped overhead, riding the wind like a horse. A small red squirrel chased a much larger gray one, but we were going too fast to see the outcome.

The road was trampled, and even though my tracking skills were limited, I could tell by the fresh tracks that my competitors were just a few hours ahead.

I patted Torak's neck. "See, we're not too far now."

A new sense of confidence and determination welled inside me.

But my smile soon faded.

Up ahead, a white shape was coming at us fast. I drew my short sword instinctively and slowed Torak to a walk. I peered into the brightness of the morning light. A beautiful white mare came into focus less than a hundred feet away, and I took a steadying breath when I recognized the rider.

"Isn't the race that way?" I snapped, and pointed behind him. I remembered the look of hatred he had given me a few hours earlier.

Mad Jack pulled his horse to a stop. There were no traces of anger on his flushed face, but the dark circles under his eyes showed that he hadn't slept. His face was still radiant in the morning light, however, and a sheen of sweat covered his golden skin where he'd left his tunic unbuttoned. I felt a flutter in my chest, and I hated that he had that effect on me.

"I came to find you," he said a little breathlessly.

144

He looked mildly surprised to see me, but real concern shone in his eyes. "I waited for the first light."

"Why? What the hell do you care?" I kept my face blank, but my breath had caught in my throat.

His mouth tightened. "Because I realized you were really *far* behind, and you weren't catching up to us…"

He paused like he wasn't sure if he should continue.

"I was worried," he said finally.

His voice was a little strained as if it was an effort to say such a thing.

"I was worried something had happened to you. And by the looks of it I was right. It looks like you had a rough night." His eyes moved over the dirt, cuts, and dried blood on my cloak and tunic.

I shrugged it off. "Nothing I couldn't handle."

I had almost died. The masked man had nearly poisoned me.

"What happened to you?"

The concern in his voice made me want to trust him and tell him about the assassin, but I couldn't. I didn't know who had sent him or why.

Was Mad Jack really concerned about me? Or was he only checking to see if I'd been killed?

I just couldn't trust anyone, especially the man who had put me here in the first place.

"Fell off my horse a few times," I lied.

I was surprised how real and true it sounded from my lips, and how incredibly weak I was making myself out to be.

"But I'm all right now. Nothing broken as you can see."

Mad Jack was silent. His eyes locked onto mine, and I could see he didn't believe me.

He nodded. "The others are still camped a few miles down the road. We can catch up before they leave. Come on."

He turned his horse around and urged it forward.

I wanted to tell him to get lost, to go to hell, to jump in a lake, and hold his breath. I kicked Torak into a gallop instead, and we raced after Mad Jack.

We rode side by side in silence. From the corner of my eye, I caught him staring at me a few times, but I forced myself to look straight ahead. I wasn't sure I understood him. He was bad, dangerous, and a liar, all wrapped up into a gorgeous package. I couldn't help but feel empowered whenever he glanced my way. I wanted to believe that he cared for me, and that he hadn't planned on handing me over to the priests, that it had been a terrible mistake.

But part of me screamed not to let my guard down, and not to let him creep into my heart. I couldn't let my feelings get in the way if I was planning to win.

Although it appeared that he had betrayed me, a part of my soul hoped somehow that I was wrong.

Finally, we spotted the others. Groups of men and women were dotted along a small river that weaved through the fields and out of sight. I could smell the remnants of a fire. I watched as they gathered up their things, folded their bedrolls, and tended to their horses as they prepared to leave. None of them looked even remotely concerned or disturbed that I was here still alive and still in the race.

And then I noticed that there were a few black eyes, puffy faces, and bloody noses.

"What happened here?"

I couldn't see any bodies or serious injuries, but the marks on their faces and bodies were definitely signs of a brawl.

Mad Jack watched the campsite with indifference. "A fight broke out after a few of the men started drinking."

I spotted a tall dark-skinned woman with a bloody nose and her right eye swollen shut. She smiled at me as I looked on, and I was glad I wasn't the only rough diamond of the opposite sex in here.

"What was the fight about?"

"The usual when you put different clans together with too much ale," he said like it was common knowledge. "Add a race that will shower the winner with gold and glory, and you're asking for trouble. This is nothing."

"Doesn't look like nothing to me."

Even from a distance I could see the fury in their eyes.

His expression hardened. "Soon they'll be cutting each other's throats."

A shudder went down my spine, but his words rang true. It was only a matter of time before even those from the same clans killed each other. There could only be one victor.

I scanned the groups, knowing what I was looking for, even though I didn't want to admit it. And I found him.

Landon was surrounded by a group of men. He stood straight with his arms folded around his chest. His expression was hard. They appeared to be in a heated discussion. He did not look up.

I felt a little deflated.

Serves you right, Elena.

I shouldn't have been thinking about his smiling eyes and his soft, warm lips. I should have been focusing on the fact that he was my opponent.

As we approached the group from the Pit, every single pair of eyes, including Will's and Leo's, shot daggers at me.

I gasped. They were all directing their hatred at me.

The blood drained from my face as I looked away. It hurt. It hurt to be loathed by your own people. I could read their minds. *Traitor.*

Of course I would be perceived to be a traitor to them. I was racing as the champion of the temple. I was representing the very people who forced us to live like animals. How could I explain why I was doing this without putting myself, them, and all our families at risk?

My eyes burned, but I wouldn't let the tears fall. I sat straighter. I wouldn't let them see how painful this was for me. If Mad Jack had seen the reaction from his group, he never gave any indication. I was sure he did. If I saw them, he saw them.

It was as clear as the sky was blue—I was not welcome.

The icy realization that I was alone made me shudder. The other participants all competed as members of teams. My friends from the Pit had rejected me, and I didn't fit in with the highborn and wealthy Anglians. I was an outcast.

Mad Jack seemed to realize how alienated I had become, and the look of sadness in his eyes made it all so much worse.

"We're about a half a day's ride away from the border. The horses are well rested so we'll be heading out soon," he said softly as though he was afraid I'd burst into tears.

I felt guilty that Torak would not be as well rested as the other horses. He was loyal to me. He was the most *deserving* of a good rest and a full belly.

Mad Jack shifted uncomfortably. "I have a few things to take care of before we leave. You know, the tension between the groups is just going to get worse. It might be safer for you to ride with us. Maybe we could—"

"No. I'm not riding with you."

My voice was harsh, and he stared at me with his mouth open.

"This *is* a race, right? There is no *we*. And the last I checked, I was in this bloody race because of *you*. So you'll understand why the last thing I need is to be around you. We're alone in this. All of us. Only *one* of us can get the stone."

I looked away, not wanting him to bewitch me to change my mind.

"My horse needs water."

Mad Jack opened his mouth to argue, but I left him and steered Torak to the riverbank.

I was not alone. I had Torak.

I slipped off his back and let him relax a little. He deserved it. As he began to drink, the thunder of stampeding horses filled the air. I whirled around to see the Girmanians dashing across the road. The other groups saw them leaving and rushed their packing, too. In a few moments most of them were mounted and racing across the fields to catch up to the Girmanians. It all happened much faster than I could have imagined.

I coughed as the last of the riders hurried off, and everything was covered in a blanket of dust and dirt. I blinked through the mist and saw that Landon was watching me. Our eyes met for a moment. He gave me a meaningful smile, like he was pleased to see that I was still in the race, and then he turned his horse and galloped after the fury of rushing horses.

Mad Jack's great white mare shifted nervously, anxious to be let loose and join the others, and he looked at me anxiously, pleading with me to move.

I had told him that I didn't want to race with him or anyone. But *I* would race.

I met his gaze and nodded my head.

He kicked his horse, and they were off.

I pulled myself up on Torak's back and grabbed the reins.

"So sorry for this, my boy," I whispered and caressed his mane. *Creator, forgive me.*

"I promise it's only for a few more hours. Then you'll have a whole night to rest."

But Torak didn't seem tired. He was excited, and his eyes were wide and fixed on the other galloping horses. He *wanted* to run.

"You are a true godsend, my friend."

I didn't need to slam my heels into his flanks to encourage him. We flew into the open fields, and when I stole a look behind me, I spotted riders eating my dust. I couldn't see their colors, and I didn't care. I welled with pride and urged my horse faster.

This time I *wasn't* last.

CHAPTER 16

WE TORE DOWN THE central road, finally passing out of the mountainous wilderness of Anglia and into easier country. And I was still not last.

Mad Jack and his crew rode ahead of me, and I could see him glancing back over his shoulder every few minutes, just to make sure I was still there. I ignored him completely. I didn't want him to think that he was doing me any favors.

Again Torak was the model of strength. He ran with an effortless grace that put all the other horses to shame. I understood why Landon had seemed so sad that he had had to sell this magnificent creature to the priests. He was a prince among horses. Although I knew nothing about riding, and even less about a horse's pedigree, I was sure that Torak had come from a line of kingly horses.

I caught a glimpse of Landon's gold and red banners about a half a mile or so ahead, and I knew he was there somewhere, riding with the rest of the champions from Anglia.

By midday we had reached Gray Havens. It was a small village protected by forest, and I knew from studying my maps that this was a legendary witch village. Stories were still told of the strange and deadly witches who lived here. They were said to be cruel magic bearers that stole children in the night and feasted on their bodies.

Gray Havens was a small part of Witchdom, a giant realm east of Arcania. Regular folks didn't dare enter. There was no invisible wall or anything like that. But the legends said that the witches ate human flesh, so I guessed that was enough to deter anyone from entering.

Personally, I never believed in such nonsense. I didn't think women could *actually* eat people, let alone children. It conflicted with our maternal instinct to protect the young. It sounded more like a manmade myth to keep children at home at night and to prevent them from doing mischief.

Legend said that in the days of the kings, the royal guard had been charged with destroying the village and killing all the witches. But the guard had gone in and never returned. The people of Anglia never set foot in the village again.

As we approached, I could see a road that wound into the forest but then was lost in shadow. And then I heard a strange humming sound, like the buzz of giant bees. I could see that the sound came from tall wooden posts in which grotesque faces had been carved. They were part human and part animal, with horns, holes for mouths, and long protruding tongues.

The posts stood like giant guards at the entrance to the town, to warn off intruders no doubt, and I felt their eyes following me as I galloped by.

A strange energy was thick in the air, like lightning before a storm. I couldn't see anything, but I could feel it—a warning of some kind. But I wasn't sure if it was a warning not to enter, or a warning about something else entirely. Even Torak stiffened beneath me. I was terrified.

"It's witchcraft," shouted Will twenty feet ahead of me. "Demons, disciples of the Devil himself. Do not look into the eyes of their demons, my friends, for they will curse you and take your soul."

He spit on the ground and made the sign of the Creator.

Every rider who passed after that spit on the ground, and each time it made me more and more nervous.

I glowered at them. "Do you think it's wise to insult them like that?" I yelled to anyone who would listen. "If anything, it might make them angry."

A man I recognized from the Pit turned to me. "If you don't want them witches to poison your soul, best spit on the ground and ask the Creator for protection."

He pulled out a trinket in the shape of a sun that hung from a thin leather string. He kissed it. No doubt it was some crude protection charm to ward off evil. I'd seen them before at the traders' market, and they never stayed on display for long.

Why did the people of Arcania fear magic bearers so much? Their hatred for anything magic made me uneasy. I didn't want to think of what they would do to me if they found out my secret.

I caught Mad Jack watching me. He looked nervous and curious, like he knew there was something different about me but just didn't know what. All he knew was that I had managed the impossible when I had survived sorcerer's fire to steal the crown.

I sighed in relief as the village of Gray Havens disappeared behind us. I had the uneasy feeling that the witches had seen the disrespect that the other riders had demonstrated at the doors of their village. I suspected they wouldn't forget.

We rode on in silence for hours after that. When we finally reached the border of Anglia, the sun was a fiery red orb of light sinking beneath the waters of the West Sea. The sky was ablaze with warm oranges and searing reds, and I could see that the outer edges of the blazing sky were cooled with the indigo of the coming night.

Even before I saw it, I smelled the delicious salt scent of the West Sea. We came over a rise, and I could see the waves that beat golden beaches that stretched into the distance.

The long strip of land that was called Death's Arm disappeared into a blanket of rolling mist out at sea. It was wider than I'd first thought, the size of a farmer's field, and although I couldn't see past the fog, I knew that it stretched out all the way to Goth.

At the border between Anglia and Goth, Death's Arm connected the two realms with the miles of dead grasses and rotted trees that were known as the Eternal Bog. Tree skeletons were foreboding shadows that loomed up in a thick gray mist to warn off intruders. Weeds covered most of the dark greasy surfaces of the sullen black waters, and white mist coiled above the stagnant pools of the bog. A faint smell of sulfur tickled my nose, and I could smell something more foul that I didn't want to think about.

The Eternal Bogs looked more impenetrable than I'd first thought.

I felt a sudden pull, like something in the bog was reaching out to me. And then I heard a droning sound. At first I thought it was the sound of the waves hitting the rocks around the cliffs, but I quickly realized that the sound was something else. It was coming from the bogs. It was almost as though the mist itself was alive and breathing.

A chill rolled down my spine, and my pulse raced. There was something evil lurking beyond that gray mist. I couldn't see it, but I felt something in my bones, something inhuman. A dark entity was waiting for us on the other side.

How are we going to cross?

Torak shifted nervously, and I eased him into a full stop. I stared out into a white evil. He could sense it, too, the evil that lurked in the bogs.

I spotted the Girmanians, the Espanians, the Anglians, the Romilians, the Fransians and the Purtulese. They were all camped out on the beaches. While many of them regarded me with animosity, I couldn't help but feel invigorated. I was still in the race. And by the looks of it, everyone was at a standstill. Everyone was equal now.

I took in a long breath of fresh air and relaxed a little.

"Quite a sight, isn't it?"

Startled, I turned to see Landon. He walked over to me with his head high and looked very regal in his red and gold tunic. There was no mistaking his noble birth. It practically oozed off him. He smiled with that too perfect smile, and I cursed self-consciously that the blood always seemed to rush to my face when I saw him.

I looked away quickly.

"It is. It's like a white evil. I've never seen anything like it before. It doesn't even *look* real, more like a dream, you know, like a nightmare."

He didn't say anything, but I could feel his eyes inspecting every inch of me. I felt my ears burn, and my heart raged in my chest.

He came up and stroked Torak's neck, soothing him softly with words I couldn't hear. Torak nickered in greeting, a hello to an old friend, and rested his head on his shoulder. They stayed that way for a while. Finally, he peered up at me, and our eyes locked.

"You're holding your own," he said, impressed. "Glad to see it. For someone who'd never ridden before, I wasn't even sure you'd make it past the gates in Soul City."

When I saw the mischief in his smile, I couldn't help but laugh.

"Well," I said, trying to compose myself, "you haven't gotten rid of me just yet."

He was so close I could smell his musky male sweat. It was intoxicating.

"Who says I want to get rid of you?"

His gaze met mine again, and he didn't try to hide the flirtatious tone in his voice.

I looked away again as my treacherous cheeks began to give me away. I blurted the first thing that came to my head.

"Why has everyone stopped? Shouldn't we continue?"

"Because it'll be dark soon." Landon looked over to the bogs. "And no one, not even the strongest warrior in all of Arcania would venture into Death's Arm at night. It would be suicide."

"Because of the bogs?" I asked and shivered.

I had to admit that just looking at them almost caused me to break out in hives. I peeled my eyes away from his, and with a straight face I asked, "Tell me more about this bog. Something tells me you know more about it than the rest of us."

I wasn't sure he would answer, but I felt it was worth a try. I needed to prepare myself for whatever devils were lurking out in Death's Arm.

Landon spoke lightly, but his eyes were grave.

"Well, from what I've heard, the bog is a perilous swamp that goes on for miles. Some say that it never ends. Some say that it's a doorway to hell, and that you'll be lost when you are sucked into their shallow waters. Only your bones will resurface, years later," he added with a knowing expression as though he'd witnessed this first hand.

"Well, it's really creepy and disturbing that we have to cross it." There was no way in hell I'd go in there at night. "Is there no other way around the bogs?"

I peered at the swamps that bordered Death's Arm. "There might be some dry areas that would be stable enough support us."

Landon shook his head. "No, there's no other way around, unless you fancy a swim. Even then there's no telling what demons lurk in the waters. I've heard stories of folks who've only just dipped in their toes, only to die the next day of a mysterious illness. No, I wouldn't chance it. The waters are treacherous."

"Such nonsense is probably just old wives' tales," I said. "But I believe there's a bit of truth in any tale, so I suspect it's wise to stay away from the water."

When Landon grinned, tiny dimples formed below his cheeks.

"Beauty and brains. A dangerous combination. Is there anything you *can't* do?" His eyes sparkled mischievously.

"I don't know, to be honest."

I laughed softly, shocked at my own forwardness. "I haven't discovered anything yet."

He laughed hard, and then watched me for a moment, drinking me in slowly with his eyes. "You are a remarkable woman, Elena. No doubt with many more *secrets*."

I was complimented that he remembered my name, but it was the way he emphasized the word *secrets* that had me twitching on the inside.

I tried to look composed. "So everyone will camp here for the night, then?"

He watched me for a moment longer. "For the most part, yes."

The camps that were set up already surrounded small fires, and everyone's expression was rather gloomy. No one was smiling. Did they feel the evil that I felt coming from the bogs?

"So, what part of Anglia are you from," I asked and then regretted it, the second the words left my big mouth. This was becoming way too personal.

He didn't answer right away, and I thought he was about to lie. But when he did finally answer there was no lie in his eyes.

"Erast," he said finally. "Just south of Soul City."

He looked at me sharply and said, "From your accent, you're definitely from Anglia. And if I had to guess, I'd say you were from the Pit."

He watched me with eyebrows raised.

"I am." There was no point in lying, but I furrowed my brows in frustration.

"A woman from the Pit riding for the priests," he said perceptively. "Odd. Don't you think? I'd have never believed it if it weren't for Torak here and the temple's emblem. I hate to ask, but are you one of their concubines?"

"The hell I am," I shouted, surprising us both. Did he think I was some sex pet? My anger rose to match my voice.

Landon lifted up his hands in surrender, but he was smiling.

"I don't mean to offend you. It's just..." he paused and his smile vanished, "it's just very unusual for a woman from the Pit to have such vivacity of spirit. You are clearly *not* in a sexual liaison with the priests, and yet you are riding *for* them."

Of course he'd think I was in league with the priests. I was traveling on a warhorse clad in the finest saddle blankets and emblazoned with the emblem of the temple. It made me want to vomit. But it was quite plain from the expectant look on his face that he was anticipating an answer. Why was he so interested in me? What was in it for him? I had the feeling he would keep on asking until I told him.

I couldn't tell him that the high priest had forbidden me from speaking, and that I was being blackmailed. Perhaps it would be better to avoid him after all.

Finally I answered, "I race for the priests, and that's all there is to it."

He hid his disappointment with a casual smile.

"Of course, and I apologize for being so impertinent and forward. I'm just very intrigued by you."

I caught his eyes staring at my chest. So that was what he had wanted. He had thought I was a concubine. Surprisingly, I wasn't upset. I felt rather flattered that someone of his status would even consider bedding someone like me, a skinny woman from the Pit.

I sat straighter in my saddle. I turned my attention back to Landon and dared to look at him, really look at him. He was tall, a few inches taller than Mad Jack, and while Mad Jack was dark and mysterious, Landon was light and airy. His forearm was three times the size of mine, and I could see that he was well muscled under his tunic. Nobleman or not, he'd had to train hard to acquire muscles like that. It appeared as though the nobleman had secrets as well.

Landon gave Torak a last pat and stepped away.

"You're welcome to join me and my friends at our camp. There's a warm fire going already, and we have some nice sweet wine from my family's vineyard."

Wine, the drink of the rich. I'd had it before on a few occasions, but very rarely. I'd preferred it to the bitter taste of ale, but I couldn't afford it. I couldn't even afford a glass, let alone a bottle of the stuff.

I didn't understand why he was being so kind to me. I was poor. He was rich. We were from entirely different worlds, and we were competing against each other in a race...

"We're just over there," he waved his hand towards the beach.

I followed where he pointed. The group from Anglia was sitting around a small fire, although I wasn't sure a fire could warm the chill I felt at the back of my neck. I recognized some faces from Soul City on the day of the race. A beautiful young woman with long blonde hair caught my eye, not because of her delicate features, but because she was shooting daggers at me with her icy blue eyes.

I doubted that anyone from the Pit would've invited me to join their camp so openly. Landon was different from the others. It was as plain as the smile on his face. When he spoke his eyes were honest, and I didn't suspect a lie in anything he'd said so far. There was a quality and a natural grace about him. He was a true gentleman.

I saw that the young woman knew it, too. She wasn't about to let him go, and she was definitely not ready to share.

I smiled. "That's very kind of you, but I think I'll just stay on my own. I'm more of a lone creature anyway. Gives me time to think."

"Ah, ha," he said." So you're a great thinker? I thought I saw that spark in your eyes."

His smile grew. "Well, if you change your mind, you're most welcome to join us."

He walked away, and I didn't stare at him long enough to make my feelings known.

When I looked back at his camp, there she was. The blonde was eyeing me with hatred. But as soon as Landon neared the camp, her face brightened, and she looked even more beautiful. She took his arm in hers, pulled him close, and whispered in his ear. They looked perfect together, a lady with her knight. I couldn't help feeling a little jealous. She looked back at me triumphantly. For half a second I thought she was about to stick out her tongue at me.

I sighed. I didn't have time for games. I was tired, and I didn't have the energy to chase someone else's lover. She couldn't have been more than twenty and really was stunning. The way she stood, by itself, told me she was from a wealthy family, too. She was a lady in riding clothes. Her cloak moved, and I noticed the sword tied to her waist. I thought she looked too delicate to be in this kind of race, but looks could be deceiving.

I dismounted and stretched. I steered Torak in the opposite direction from the Anglians on the beach, passing the other groups on my way. Mad Jack stood up as I wandered past, but I didn't meet his eyes. I didn't feel like chatting at the moment, especially not with him. Just the thought of him made me quiver with anger.

Most of the other horses were tied up in clusters on a nice stretch of grass above the sand dunes. A stream trickled down between the great boulders on the other side of the little field and provided the horses with the fresh water they needed.

I moved carefully around the other horses and led Torak under a tree near the widest part of the small stream at the far edge of the clearing. I looped the reins in a loose knot around a thick branch. After I had unpacked my saddlebag and my bedroll, I emptied most of my provisions from Torak to lessen his load. I settled down next to a patch of shrubbery.

I didn't have the energy to make a fire, so I settled for some stale bread and cheese. The bread could have been moister, but I was used to it. The goat cheese was divine.

The priests would have eaten like kings, no doubt. Wine would have been perfect with my small supper. I took a sip of water from my canteen and finished it. I couldn't leave it empty, so I got up and filled it at a clean and fast moving part of the small stream. When I was done, I sat back down. I was the farthest one away from the bogs, not the best spot from which to restart the race, strategically speaking, but it gave me a good view of everyone else.

They were all friends. They passed their food and drink around without speaking, like family. But it was clear that they were all warriors, too, even the women, even that delicate Anglian blonde.

I watched them and planned.

The boisterous and loud Girmanians were physically the biggest. They would obviously be ones to watch out for, if and when they decided to take a hit at me. They feared nothing, and they wanted everyone else to know.

The Anglians were more subtle. They smiled and laughed, but they were more controlled than the Girmanians. Every now and again, I could see Anglian men spying on the other groups and then huddling with Landon to discuss whatever they had discovered.

My heart raced whenever I saw Landon. His arms were crossed over his chest, and he was staring at a piece of parchment that was obviously a map. Everyone was trying to figure out a way to cross the bogs.

I felt the tension in the air as much as I felt the evil that lingered in the mist. No one appeared to be taking any chances.

I couldn't help but smile when I saw the Fransians. It appeared that they, too, had brought some wine or some hard drink on their journey. They danced around their fire, singing songs in Fransian, and their faces were red with drink. They would probably miss tomorrow's early start.

The Romilians were roasting some animal over their fire. Even from where I was, my mouth watered at the divine smell of spices and roasting meat. They gestured with their hands a lot when they spoke, and they were just as loud as the Girmanians. I knew they must have been skilled hunters because none of the other groups had been successful killing any game. The Romilians' hunting skills would give them an advantage in the race.

The Espanians were restless. They paced back and forth on the other side of the bogs. They thrust their weapons into the swamp to test the depth of the waters, looking for an advantage at tomorrow's start.

But I didn't know where the Purtulese fit. They were the quietest of all the groups and seemed to be watching everyone else, just like I was. It would be strategy over strength with them. I would have to watch out for the Purtulese. There was something unsettling about their behavior. It was almost as though they were planning something.

Mad Jack and his crew from the Pit would probably be prepared to commit murder to get their hands on the stone. A handsome prize wasn't something he'd give up easily. I would definitely have to watch my back around everyone from the Pit. It was clear they hated me and wouldn't think twice about cutting off my head.

The man I had seen before, with the temple trinket around his neck, was making a circular impression in the sand around their camp. It was either to protect them from the witches he'd insulted earlier or from whatever evil lurked in the bogs. I might have done the same if I'd had a pendant like his, anything to repel the evil that lingered so close in the air.

As the evening sun started to set, the voices grew louder, and I smelled ale. I was still uneasy about the hatred that they all seemed to show for witches. I had magic, too. Did that make me a witch? Or was I something entirely different?

The high priest had said that I was more than just a witch. So what then? I wasn't schooled in magic, and magic was a taboo subject anyway, so I really didn't have much to go on. I never really believed in magic until I saw it with my own eyes. I saw the golden light that healed my fatal wound. I didn't know why I could heal and others couldn't. My magic had frightened me when I first felt my skin healing. But I wasn't afraid anymore. It was part of who I was. And it was the only thing I could use to my advantage in this race. While they had strength in numbers, I could heal from a fatal wound. Maybe my magic could do even more, I didn't know.

I relaxed and let my thoughts wander about the rest of the race. I leaned back against the bushes and noticed that the shadows around me seemed longer than usual.

That's weird. It's not even late in the evening yet.

The sky was thick with gray clouds that covered the sun and turned the sky into night prematurely.

And then darkness fell.

CHAPTER 17

TORAK SQUEALED, A HIGH-PITCHED, ear-piercing scream, and I jumped to my feet.

He was stiff and twitching. The whites of his eyes shone in the semi-darkness. He rose up on his hind legs and squealed louder. The other horses shifted nervously, too, and looked like they were about to bolt.

The horses all seemed to be looking at the bogs. Something in there was setting off the animals. I strained, but I could only see swamp and sickly vegetation. Then I smelled rotten eggs and damp earth. It filled my nose until it burned. Grimacing, I searched for the source of the smell in the bogs. And then I saw it.

A giant wave of light gray mist was rolling silently onto the beaches. It moved faster than any normal mist, but when I looked to the top of the trees next to me, they weren't moving. There was no wind. The air was eerily still.

My breathing came in rapid bursts. I watched as giant fingers of gray mist searched the beach as though they were alive and had minds of their own. The smell of sulfur choked me. My eyes burned, and I had to blink the tears to see clearly. Something was wrong.

My pulse raced as I grabbed my daggers.

"The mist!" I bellowed. "There's something in the mist!"

Heads turned my way, but they ignored me. Some of them pointed at me and laughed. They must have thought that I was mad or drunk.

"Bloody idiots," I hissed.

I ran a few paces forward all the while jumping in the air flailing my arms like an idiot.

"Listen to me, you fools!"

I pointed towards the evil white mist and bellowed as loudly as I could.

"The threat is real. The mist is coming. There's something unnatural in the mist. You need to move!"

They stirred then. Some of them looked frightened as the gray devil approached, but it was too late.

I watched helplessly as a giant wave of mist rushed silently onto the beach and engulfed the unsuspecting men and women. The great, mist-like hands of the bogs had decided to come and get us.

Earsplitting screams echoed from inside the eerie fog. And then I heard the sound of metal hitting flesh. Horses trumpeted, but the mist muffled the sounds and made them seem far away.

The mist kept coming. It spread out and rolled along the beaches to where the others camped. My fear and dread increased. I couldn't see farther than a few hundred feet now, not even the fires that burned along the beach. Everything was covered in a blanket of fog. Horns blew, and the long and desperate screams increased.

And then I heard wet guttural snarls and growls that were unlike any living animal I'd ever heard before. It was the sound of nightmares, the sound of creatures from another world. And it was all coming from inside the mist.

In a mad panic, the horses pulled free of their tethers. I caught a glimpse of Torak's black tail as he galloped away from the mist. Two bronze colored horses and a white mare followed him. Seconds later the spot where they had been grazing was completely submerged in the mist.

I wanted to call out to my friend, Torak, to call him back, but I knew he wouldn't come. The horses had sensed the evil before we humans did. They weren't stupid. They ran with wild speed, and the mist would never reach them.

"Goodbye, my friend," I whispered. I felt a little bit of comfort that he was safe, but I knew I would need all my courage to face this new evil.

I turned towards the rancid, burning fog. Glowing red eyes peered at me greedily from inside the mist. They were so close that I would make contact if I slashed out with my weapons. The hatred and hunger in the eyes were unmistakable. It wanted to taste *my* flesh. We hadn't even made it into the bogs, and yet something evil was attacking us.

There was no time to think. I lunged forward, blades flailing. But in an instant, the eyes were gone, and I was alone again. Although I'd often wished for solitude, this time I didn't. I longed to have someone, anyone, next to me. How could I fight an enemy that I couldn't see?

"Mad Jack?" I cried and took a careful step forward.

"Mad Jack!" I bellowed as loudly as I could.

I listened and prayed that he'd appear before me. But the only sound was my beating heart. The air had gone silent. The mist had silenced every living thing. Were they even still alive?

The mist billowed like great storm clouds. I turned to the path behind me, thinking about bolting like the horses. But how far would I go before the fog monster reached me? I could never outrun it. I would have to stand and fight whatever monsters emerged from the fog or die trying.

The mist swelled towards me. It swirled as if it had a mind of its own, soaring and twisting, surrounding me. I choked out a sob as the smell of sulfur burned my nose. I desperately fought my nausea and tried to keep my breathing shallow. But the mist burned my lungs like the smoke from a fire.

I pulled my shirt up over my mouth and nose in a makeshift mask so I could breath. I maintained my fighting stance, but my eyes burned so much that I couldn't see through my tears.

How could I fight if I could not see? It was as if the mist had blinded us on purpose, to make us easy targets for whatever demons hid within it. I could almost feel it laughing at me.

I was trapped in a gray hell. Even if I could run now, I would be running blindly. I was too terrified to move, too terrified of what was in the mist. I could barely keep it together.

"Hello!" I cried.

"Is there anyone here? Hello?" But there was no reply.

I wiped my tears with the back of my hand.

And then I heard a cry for help. It was so faint at first that I thought I might have imaged it. But as I tilted my head I heard it again. Faint, but it was definitely human, and female.

"Hello?" I cried. "Where are you?" I waited a moment.

"Tell me where you are. I need to hear your voice so I can find you. Hello?"

Could I even help her?

I tried not to think about those glowing red eyes as I moved carefully forward. I was sure the voice had come from somewhere ahead of me and a little off my left. I took another step forward.

"Please, just say something … anything so I know where you are."

I was probably going to get myself killed. Every instinct in me screamed to run the other way, but I ignored it. Maybe, just maybe, I could help.

Just as I was about to give up, a bone-chilling scream filled the air. All the hairs on the back of my neck stood up and I heard a thump.

I caught my breath. The scream had sounded just like my mother's, right before Brother Edgar had cut off her head. It was a scream that would haunt me forever.

I dashed blindly towards the sound. The fact that I could hear my feet padding the ground brought me some comfort. This was not a nightmare. It was truly happening.

I raced towards the woman's cry, and my own mother's screams rang in my ears again. Tears ran down my face freely now, and I sobbed as I ran. My foot caught on a root, and I stumbled, but I quickly steadied myself and kept moving.

Another scream. This time it sounded as if it were right in front of me. I gripped my daggers and screamed, "I'm coming!"

Images of my dying mother flashed in my mind's eye, urging me forward.

"Stay where you are."

Something caught my foot, and I went pitching forward. I landed hard on the ground and knocked my breath out. I had landed with my daggers pointing up and had nearly impaled myself. My legs were wet. I must have landed in a puddle.

I pushed myself up and gasped.

A shriveled heap lay at my feet. The blood I was covered in was not my own. The body was so mangled and twisted that at first I hadn't even recognized it as a person at all. There was no sign of clothes. The skin had been sliced into strips, and each strip had been peeled away from the body like you would pare an apple. The bloody muscles, flesh, and entrails were strewn about in puddles of deep maroon blood. The body's limbs were scattered around, and the tendons were still attached at the sockets, as though they'd been ripped from the body. Blood. So much blood. The face was a woman's, but the deep mangled gashes looked as though something with large teeth had taken a bite out of her. Her eyes were two empty black holes.

My body convulsed, and I vomited. I retched again and again until the bile burned my throat. I was crying so much that the world was a blurry haze.

What kind of monster could do this?

"Elena!"

Mad Jack's voice sounded behind me, and I nearly collapsed in relief.

"Mad Jack! I'm here! I'm here!"

I forgot about the dead woman and rushed to the spot where I'd last heard his voice. But he wasn't there.

A pair of glowing red eyes peered at me through the mist. And just as my scream caught in my throat, the creature lunged.

CHAPTER 18

THE CREATURE CAME AT me so fast that I barely had the time to lift my arms and block the attack. But still, I wasn't fast enough.

My right arm burned with pain as I spun around with my blades out in front of me and slashed at the beast. I jumped back, and it let out a shriek that chilled me to the bones.

I didn't wait to see how badly I had injured it. I veered away and dashed in the opposite direction.

It caught me by the edge of my cloak. I heard a rip and fell head first into the ground. The creature roared, and it lunged for me again. I could see black blood oozing from the wound across its abdomen, but I hadn't cut deeply enough.

We were both injured now. I leapt to my feet. My arm burned where three sharp claws had sliced through the sleeve of my tunic. My skin was already swelling with infection and discharged a yellow liquid that mixed with my blood and smelled of rotten flesh. The thing had venom in its talons.

My breath came fast and hard, but I felt the warmth of my healing powers fighting the infection, and I prayed to the Creator that I'd heal fast enough to survive the next attack from this monster.

The mist cleared, and the creature hesitated for a moment so that I had time to examine it more closely. It stood over six feet tall, upright like a man, but hunched over. It had long gnarled arms that nearly grazed the ground with a thicket of coarse gray fur that covered its crooked, misshapen body. Its gleaming skull was bare except for sparse clumpy tufts of fur. Its rough body was crisscrossed with scars that looked as though they had been ripped open over and over again and had never healed. Its broad brutal face with a flat nose, large twisted maw, and glaring red eyes shone with intelligence and hunger. There was nothing remotely human or even warm blooded about it. This thing was dead and rotting. Strips of pink flesh hung from its talons, and I thought I was about to be sick again.

I was in such a panic that I couldn't breathe. I could hardly move.

Could I kill it? The fighting skills I'd acquired in the Pit would not be enough to defeat this nightmare.

Where were the others? Had the others escaped? I was sure that Mad Jack had called out to me from somewhere nearby.

The monster and I faced each other alone in the small clearing.

A gurgling escaped from the creature's throat, and when it opened its jaw, I could see rows of brown fish-like teeth. Then four fanged tentacles writhed out of its mouth and lashed towards me.

I flailed with my weapons in the attempt to cut them, but the tentacles grabbed me, and sank their sharp fangs into my arms and legs. They wrapped around my waist and lifted me in the air. I screamed as the poison from the tiny fangs entered my blood stream and burned like liquid fire. The tentacles squeezed my body and crushed my lungs. I opened my mouth to cry out, but vomited from the smell of rotten flesh instead. I could feel the suction of the tentacles pulling at my skin. I felt weak and nauseated again, and I could see that the creature was drinking my blood.

I was horrified. I could heal from cuts and deep gashes, even from some poisons, but I knew my healing abilities couldn't replace buckets of my blood.

I was going to die.

My head fell forward as my loss of blood sapped my energy. I couldn't hang on to my thoughts.

Miraculously my blades were still in my hands. Whether the Creator had decided to help me, or the thing didn't bother to disarm me, I didn't care. I gripped my blades with all the strength I had left and hacked at the tentacles in one powerful upward slash. I heard a shriek as my blades tore into its flesh.

It retaliated, and I hit the ground hard with a horrible snap. A shock wave of pain shot up my left arm. I could see that my arm lay in an awkward position, and I could no longer feel my hand.

But I didn't have time to dwell on it. Just as soon as I hit the ground, I was up again. I could see a tangle of severed tentacles at my feet as I fought the nausea that washed through me.

The thing came at me. It was crazed and slammed into me, pitching me hard to the ground again. But I could feel that the poison was leaving my body, and I felt rejuvenated. I rolled back onto my feet just in time to block a clawed hand that had come within inches of my eyes. It was so close that I felt the icy numbness of death.

I knew I couldn't risk the creature taking any more of my blood. That would finish me.

I kicked out hard and caught the creature in the knee. I heard a satisfying snap and the thing staggered back.

The beast lunged again, but this time I was faster.

My left arm was a useless weight at my side, but I still had one good arm and my wits.

I drove my blade into the creature's open maw and ignoring the razor sharp teeth that cut into my hand, I pushed my blade all the way into its brain. The creature went limp and crumbled to the ground.

I kicked it once, nudged it, but it didn't move again. *Was it dead? Did the dead stay dead?* I reached down and pulled out my dagger.

I took a minute to examine my left arm. I had never suffered any broken bones before, so I didn't know what to expect. I pressed and squeezed around my forearm where I believed the break to be, but felt nothing out of the ordinary. And as I stood there examining my arm, I felt my feeling return.

It was still pretty stiff. I'd have to be careful with it until it completely healed.

An anguished cry echoed through the mist, followed by a series of blood-curdling howls. The air was filled with the clang of metal hitting flesh and bone. I heard another muffled cry, and then the sound of flesh tearing, but the ominous silence that had made my insides cringe was gone. What was happening?

I rushed blindly through the impenetrable mist, following the sounds. A thin, damp layer of film coated my face and clothes. I stumbled clumsily over rocks and leapt over fallen trees and chunks of stone, straining to see through the fog. I barely kept my footing as I slipped on mist-covered rocks and grass.

I was going to break my own neck if I continued this way. I skidded to a halt and listened.

"Hello? Mad Jack?" I called out into the fog.

I turned on the spot. "Is anyone out there? Can you hear me?"

I heard a noise a few yards in front of me. It sounded like the shuffling of feet.

My heart raced, but I waited. *Was this another trick of the mist?*

I knew that if the shuffling feet had been a person, that person *would* have answered me. The hairs on the back of my neck stood up. I could see a collection of fiery red eyes watching me from the depths of the mist. Only a few trees and shrubs stood between us.

I had been lucky with the first monster, but I didn't believe I'd get lucky a second time.

I cursed and held my breath as I crouched in a fighting stance.

"Creator, help me," I breathed.

The creatures barreled over the rocks and through the trees as if they were no more than gossamer curtains. Even the most skilled warrior couldn't fight these things. They were blessed with supernatural strength, and we were mere mortals. I couldn't run. I couldn't hide. They were coming. I swallowed and braced myself. This was going to hurt.

But someone tugged at my arm suddenly

Mad Jack stared at me with wide eyes. "This way! Quickly!" he urged.

I let him pull me away, and I sighed with relief as we ran. How he could see through the mist, how he knew where to go, was a mystery. All I could do was try and keep up with his giant strides. I fell a few times, but his strong arms lifted me as we tore through the haze. He urged me on, faster, and faster, although my thighs burned with every step. I heard the guttural grunts and gurglings of the creatures behind us and ran even faster. My lungs were raw, but I struggled to keep up.

I couldn't believe our luck when we finally burst out of the mist and into a clearing. Mad Jack stopped running and bent over to catch his breath. I drew my blade in a panic and whirled around to confront the monsters again. But there were only trees and grasses at the edge of the clearing. The wall of mist was yards behind us, and the monsters didn't come.

The mist rolled and coiled back on itself as quickly as it had appeared. I could see it clearly now, thinning out and retreating into the bogs from whence it came.

In less than a minute the mist had completely disappeared.

I did a quick head count. More than half the groups were missing. Many of those who had survived were wounded, some more seriously than others. One man, a Fransian was missing an arm. They had managed to bandage it up quite well and stop the bleeding, but I suspected he wouldn't compete in the race anymore.

But when I searched the grounds, the beaches and the small meadows, there were no bodies. It was as if the creatures had taken them without leaving a trace of blood behind. They were lost.

And that chilled me to the bone.

CHAPTER 19

Nobody slept after that.

Those of us who were left unanimously decided that it would be safer to spend the rest of the night away from the sand dunes. We moved to a large meadow that wasn't so close to the bogs.

The mood in the camp had changed drastically. The losses had been great, and I suspected that many of the dead had been brothers and sisters of the survivors, family rather than just friends and allies. I watched as they wept for the loss of their loved ones.

The loss of the horses hit hard on everyone as well. We would have to make the rest of the journey on foot. Although I hadn't been accustomed to riding, I felt the loss of the horses, too. I missed Torak already. That great warhorse had given me a sense of protection. I felt naked and vulnerable now.

I had thanked Mad Jack for saving me. If it hadn't been for him, I would most likely have been killed or pulled into an unknown fate in the mist. I knew he was trying to make up for betraying me. I could see the guilt plainly on his face now. And he ought to feel guilty about sending me on this hellish journey. I didn't want to owe anyone any favors, but he had saved me, and I was grateful for that. I knew that he really was sorry now.

I wouldn't wish our experience in the mist on anyone—except maybe the priests.

I was glad to hear that Landon was amongst the survivors. I wasn't entirely sure what I was going to say when I spoke with him, but I felt I needed to tell him that Torak might be safe.

I found him in a glen in the forest just as the sun began to rise. The parties hadn't left yet, and most of them were in a group with Landon. I didn't know why.

They stood together in the early morning sunlight, atop a grassy knoll that overlooked a glade of pine trees. It appeared the pretty blonde had survived, and she eyed me warily as I approached. But I ignored her and kept my focus on Landon.

He stood with his hands clasped together. His expression was grim, and he looked like he was praying. A woman with long black hair knelt beside him on the stones. I could see that her shoulders were shaking as she rocked back and forth.

Everyone was silent, and they all stared at a small clearing in front of them that was carpeted with stones. Each of the stones was marked with a name.

"What is this?" My words were half-mumbled.

Landon turned around, a look of surprise.

"A graveyard of sorts," he answered solemnly.

He looked at me sadly. "We have no bodies to bury, so this is purely symbolic. But we need something to remember them by. We must never forget what happened here."

The little glen was a beautiful place for a graveyard. After last night, it was exactly what it needed to be.

The blonde continued to glare at me, and I was glad that looks couldn't kill.

"I came here to tell you that Torak's fine," I said. "He and the other horses ran off before the mist could reach them. I thought you might want to know, seeing as he was yours once."

Landon's face brightened. "Thank you. I'm glad to hear it."

He pressed his hand on my arm gently, and my face felt warm. "And I'm happy to see that you're well and still in the race."

I didn't know what to say. I was only too aware that we were having a three-way conversation. I smiled and nodded.

His hand remained on my arm.

The blonde cocked her head and rounded on me. "Shouldn't you be with the rest of your kind, *peasant?*"

Blood rushed to my face, but I kept my expression blank. After the night we'd all spent together, I couldn't believe that she would still dismiss me with this type of class snobbery. It was a low blow, even for a highborn woman. It meant that she felt I was a threat, a real threat. It was clear to me that she wanted a fight. It was also clear to me that she wanted me to start it so Landon would see that I truly was a peasant.

I calmed my breathing. An argument was the last thing I needed or wanted.

"Thea," growled Landon, and he let go of my arm. "There's no need to be rude. We're all equals in this race."

"She'll never be *our* equal," Thea spat.

She smiled and drew herself up to her full height, which was several inches taller than me.

"She looks and smells like the peasant she is. She's nothing but a priest's whore. Anyone can see that."

Her icy stare met mine, and she laughed. "You must have bedded an entire legion of priests to have been given permission to participate in this race."

"That's enough, Thea."

Thea's winning smile disappeared, and she shrank back into the shadows.

But Landon persevered with her. "Apologize to Elena."

Her brows narrowed. "I will do no such thing!"

She crossed her arms defiantly.

Landon exhaled an embarrassed breath. "I must apologize for my friend's behavior. There's no excuse for her rudeness. I'm sure she meant no offense."

My jaw clenched. "Yes, I'm sure."

I turned towards the scowling woman. "But for the record, my *lady*—I would rather be a peasant and a priest's whore than socialize with the likes of you."

I did an exaggerated curtsy and left.

"Elena, wait!"

But I was already walking back towards the spot where I'd left my bag. If Landon socialized with the likes of her, I didn't want to be near him either. More importantly, I didn't want to give her the satisfaction of seeing that her words truly did hurt. I was a peasant. Although I had been born with nothing and would probably die with nothing, I had a head on my shoulders and more than a whisper of magic in me.

I swung the large bag over my shoulders and set off studying my map.

I made it to the edge of Death's Arm. There was already a line of people waiting at the edge, but no one had made a move to cross it. It was like they were all waiting for the first fool to venture into the stinking bogs.

Well, let me *be the first fool.*

I sucked in a breath and moved. The ground was soft and stinky, and I had to pull my boots from inches of gray-green muck with each step. But once I started it was surprisingly easy to keep a steady pace.

I didn't have to turn around to see that the others had followed in line behind me. I heard their curses and the suction of their footsteps.

We traveled through Death's Arm for the next six days. The nights became colder, and the days shorter. But nothing attacked us. No monsters came in the middle of the night or during the day. It actually became repetitive and quite boring after a while. From time to time I'd chat with Mad Jack, and his friends from the Pit, Leo and Will. They were the only ones who cared to speak to me. But mostly I kept to myself and kept my senses sharp.

Icy rain dogged us for three days. With each gust of frigid, cutting wind, I wondered when my skin would peel from my face. I was miserable and cold, and I missed the warmth of my small cottage. I missed Rose. More than once I wondered what I was doing here, and many times I contemplated turning back. I tried to convince myself that the high priest would never hurt Rose or my friends in the Pit, that maybe he was bluffing. But I knew I was being foolish.

I kept moving with everybody else, but the heavy weight of responsibility that I felt for everyone back home was wearing me down.

I was soaked through, and my stiff wet toes were frozen. My boots were wet. Everything I owned was wet. I couldn't change into my spare clothes because they were soaked as well. Each night, I'd wrap myself in whatever dry spot I could find in my tunic and try to rub the feeling back into my toes.

I never imagined that I'd ever find a worse place to sleep than in my cubbyhole under the floor, but this bitter cold and icy rain was much worse.

We were drawing nearer to Goth, and I began to ponder seriously what my plan of action would be once we had arrived there. There were a lot fewer of us now, and we were all solemn and wet, but I was not about to underestimate the capacity for greed of this lot. They were warriors, and if they were anything like Landon, the stone meant a great deal to them. They would do anything to get their hands on it.

I knew there was eventually going to be a great battle between us all, and that the victor would come out with the stone. Battles weren't my forte. I wasn't as strong as the Girmanian women, or even as clever or a swift as the Espanians. My best chance would be to steal the stone. I would lie low, hide in the shadows and wait. When my chance came, I would sneak up and pinch it from whoever had it. No one would see me.

It was a horrible plan. But it was the only one I could come up with.

That night I lay staring up at a starless sky. I tried not to think about Thea, but her slights never left me. I had always longed to be something more than just a peasant woman from the Pit. I had always wanted to make something of myself, to own property and make my own living. Her words resonated, and they hurt. I wasn't sure if they hurt more because Landon had been there, or simply because my pride had been hurt as well. I wanted Landon to think I was more than just a peasant woman. I could be so much more if I were given the chance.

And when finally sleep came, it was a sleep of bitter disappointment.

CHAPTER 20

WE ARRIVED AT GOTH on the eighth day of the race. I wasn't even sure I'd call this a race anymore. No one was rushing to the finish line or towards the stone. Well, not yet. I was sure that things would begin to change the closer we got to the Hollowmere. And although I had thought to keep the location of the stone a secret, I had overheard Hollowmere mentioned by name on more than one occasion, first by the Espanians, and then by the Fransians. The whereabouts of the stone was not a great secret now. Everyone knew.

I had half expected the clouds to clear up as we left Death's Arm behind us, but I was sadly mistaken.

A perpetual gloom hung over the realm of Goth like a dark shadow. While the land was gray and lightless, the trees were so tall that I had to lean back just to see the tops of some of them. I had no idea that trees could reach such a height. It was like they were trying to reach God. Aside from the woodlands and patches of desert, there were a few areas of sparse dry shrubbery with long, black, thorns. Goth was a mountainous realm of gray sand, rock, thorny bushes, and giant, creepy trees. It couldn't be more unwelcoming.

The rain had stopped, and I took comfort in that.

We were all too tired and too wet to start the long journey north into Hollowmere. I found a comfortable spot next to one of those colossal trees and unloaded my pack and bedroll. I was blessed to find dry kindling and some moss that I peeled off the rocks. I had a fire within a minute.

I nearly sobbed in relief as the warmth of my little fire brushed my face. I heard the sparkling of a nearby fire and saw that most of the other groups had settled happily to warm themselves by their fires, too. I made a rack with sticks and laid my spare clothes over the fire to dry. Without a sun it would take a while, but the stale air was better than rain. And yet I still couldn't shake off the coldness I felt inside. I realized it was this place. Its coolness clung to my very bones.

A distant screech cut through the silent night air. The long grating *cak-cak-cak* call was one I recognized as belonging to a bird of prey. I found it odd that any such birds would find themselves here in Goth. I hadn't seen any signs of food like squirrels or field mice. Come to think of it, I hadn't even seen a bird for days.

I was half-asleep on my bedroll when Landon came strolling towards me carrying a silver flask. His golden locks bounced, and his red cape rose and fell in a crimson wave as he walked. His crisp white shirt was snug across his broad, muscular chest. With his tall leather boots, he did look quite regal, and too handsome.

I pulled myself up from my bedroll and rested my back against the tree trunk. He eyed my undergarments that hung on crooked sticks over my fire and smiled. Although I was slightly embarrassed, I kept my gaze as steady as possible. I was thankful that the redness of my cheeks was masked with the darkness of night.

He settled himself down next to me and added a few more sticks to the red embers of my little fire. We sat there staring at the fire without speaking for a little while. My heart beat so loudly, I was certain he could hear it.

Finally, he handed me the flask. "My family's wine. I was saving the last of it for a special occasion."

I took the flask hesitantly. "And you figured *this* was that special occasion."

Fire danced in his eyes. "Well, we're both still alive, aren't we? And we've got maybe another few days until we reach Hollowmere. I'd say this does call for a celebration."

He tilted his head. "Try it. I think you'll like it."

I was tempted to ask where Thea was, but then changed my mind.

"Why are you here, Landon? This is a competition. We should be at each other's throats, not sharing drink."

He shrugged. "I'm not really sure."

I stared at the flask.

"It's because you don't think I can win, isn't it? I'm not a threat to you, so why not toast to my failure? I'm in this to win, too, you know."

"I never said that you weren't," he said, shaking his head. "I just wanted to come over and chat."

His eyes met mine, and I felt my heartbeat increase again.

"If you want me to leave, say the word, and I'm gone."

It pissed me off a little that he thought I wasn't good enough to be a real threat. But I also didn't want him to leave.

"It's fine," I shrugged.

I sipped some of the wine, and my throat burned a little as the liquid trickled down. I swished the liquid around in my mouth and tasted the sweetness of honey and grapes.

"I've never tasted anything like it before," I said and handed him back the flask. "It's better than anything I've ever had."

He smiled proudly at the compliment and took another mouthful himself. I knew that poor quality wines like the ones I'd had in the past tasted of alcohol. This one didn't. I could already feel the effects of the drink on me, however, and its warmth spread through my body. The wine relaxed me, and I started to feel a little giddy. I started to smile, and I caught Landon's complicit smile as he handed me back his flask. I took it gladly and sipped some more.

"If by chance *you* get the stone," I said as I handed him back the flask. "Do you know what you're going to do with it? I mean, you're already rich. You have your own wine and all. Why would someone like you want more? Isn't what you have enough?"

His smile faded a little, and I knew I'd gone too far. This was a little too personal.

"I'm sorry," I blurted. "None of my business."

But I was surprised when he answered.

"It's not about the riches for me. And yes, I do have enough, more than enough. But it's more than just riches."

He opened his mouth as though he was going to add something more, but then closed it, like he thought he better not reveal too much.

There was something more to Landon than he was letting on. I could tell that his secret, whatever it was, was weighing on him, just like mine. Was it his family? Had they pressured him to retrieve the stone for some family heirloom?

As I wondered about his secret, I stared at his lips, unable to look away. The wine was making me bold. I had to be careful. But Landon caught me staring at his lips again, and his eyes gleamed in the half-dark.

I smiled at him. I couldn't believe I did that.

The next thing I knew he'd pulled me onto his lap. He leaned forward and kissed me lightly. His soft lips pressed tenderly on mine, slow at first, but then harder. And when his tongue entered my mouth, I gave a little moan. The taste of the wine was still sharp in my mouth, and I lost all sense of propriety. My head spun a little, but I didn't want to stop. I didn't want him to stop. His tongue was restless against mine, and he kissed me long and deep.

He pulled away and slid his hands up my body to cradle my face with his hands.

"You're so beautiful," he whispered and kissed me again.

He pulled his lips from my mouth and trailed his kisses down my neck. Every kiss sent a jolt of desire pulsing through my veins. I pulled him closer, my arms around his tousled mane and broad shoulders. The intensity increased. He growled in anticipation, and I trembled with desire. He kissed me, and I was overwhelmed with my need for him.

"Elena," he breathed as he kissed my neck. His tongue lingered on a delicate spot, and one of his hands slipped under my tunic and began to explore the soft skin of my chest and the slope of my breast.

I pulled his mouth to mine again and slipped my fingers into the soft hair on his chest. Then I moved my hands over his back. In the cold night, his hot body was intoxicating. I hadn't realized how much I had missed the feeling of a man's strong arms around me and the crushing weight of a body on top of mine. I needed to feel his touch and I luxuriated in his warm hands as they continued to explore my body.

Suddenly, Landon grabbed my hands and pulled me away.

"What?"

His face was serious. He looked behind my shoulder.

I turned around in his lap.

Mad Jack was standing behind me. He held a small cup and a plate with assorted cheeses and dried meats. But he wasn't glaring at me; he was glaring at Landon and at the empty flask on the ground next to us.

"Thought you'd get her drunk and take advantage of her," he growled.

His knuckles had turned white on his fists.

"Don't you have your own women to do that to? Or do you think you own our women, too, Your *Highness*?"

It took a few seconds for me to compose myself and register what was happening.

I giggled. Clearly he had lost his mind.

"Go away, *Jack*," I slurred. Trying to focus on one Mad Jack was proving a difficult task. I laughed again.

"Is that the kind of man you are?" accused Mad Jack.

Landon was quiet for a while. I tried to focus on his beautiful face, but it kept slipping away in a foggy haze. The desire was gone from his eyes, and he looked serious. He grabbed me, lifted me up, and gently settled me on my bedroll.

"I'm sorry, Elena. But your friend is right. This was a mistake. I'm sorry."

He stood up, and the two men exchanged a silent look. And then he walked away.

My face burned as I watched him go, and I tried to control my anger and embarrassment at being disturbed.

I glowered at Mad Jack.

"What is your problem? Can't you just leave me alone? Why do you have to ruin everything? You've already ruined my life. Why? Why are you doing this?"

He looked at me, and I didn't understand the look that flashed into his eyes. He shook his head.

"What are *you* doing, Elena?"

I cringed at the blame in his voice.

"What am *I* doing?" I barked, angry at his accusing tone. "None of your damn business! Who the hell do you think you are?

My father? Mind your own damn business. What I do with my life is of no concern to you."

Mad Jack shook his head and looked stunned. "You're drunk."

He said it accusingly, his expression hard. "You don't know what you're doing."

"I'm *not* drunk." But I knew I was. "Why don't you stay the hell out of my life?"

He looked a little surprised at my tone, but at this point I didn't care what he thought of me.

He scratched the back of his neck. "You don't understand—"

"I do understand," I hissed, the blood was hot in my cheeks, and I could feel my ears burning.

"I understand that you're doing this on purpose!" I yelled. "Like in some sick twisted way you're enjoying ruining my life."

I felt all my bitterness at his complicity with the priests rushing out of me. His betrayal had made me abandon Rose and had ruined my life.

"That's not true," he said. I could see that his face had darkened.

"I would never want that."

"Really, well you could have fooled me."

I looked at him in frustration. "Then why? Why are you even here? What do you want?"

His eyes fell on the plate in his hands.

"I came to see if you were hungry," he said, his voice soft.

"Well, I wasn't." I brought my knees up and rested my head on my arms, fighting the angry tears that I knew would come.

"Yes, I can see that now." He sighed emptily. He stood there like he wanted to say something, but he couldn't bring himself to say it.

My brows knitted together. "I don't get it. I just don't get it."

Mad Jack shook his head. "No, you don't."

He walked away, and I felt even worse than before.

I couldn't think straight.

What had he meant by that? What didn't I get? Why did he look like a lost puppy?

I put a hand down on the ground to steady myself. Resolved to put the conversation behind me, I lay back down on my bedroll and stretched my arms out to keep me from vomiting.

I wondered why Landon had been so quick to leave me, and why he had looked ashamed. I thought of the command in Mad Jack's voice when he had spoken to the noble man. What had Mad Jack said that had affected Landon so much that he had to excuse himself and leave?

If Mad Jack hadn't appeared when he did, I knew I would have slept with Landon. I had not abandoned all reason, and although I could blame my behavior on the wine that Landon had brought, I didn't care that he might have planned to seduce me.

I closed my eyes and focused on the feeling I had felt in Landon's arms. I had craved it for so long. For a short moment, in Landon's arms, I had felt safe.

CHAPTER 21

Every muscle was sore when I woke the next morning, but I felt worse about what had almost transpired between Landon and me the night before. It wasn't like me to bed a stranger just because I was longing for some intimacy. I knew I would have never let it go as far as it did if it hadn't been for that damn wine and his smug gentility.

I shuffled around in a funk, folding my bedroll and getting ready to set out again. According to my map, Hollowmere was about a two-day journey on foot. The sooner I got there the sooner the race would be over, and the sooner my life could get back to normal. That is, *if* I brought back the stone. Although my innards felt like churned butter, and I felt as though I had been slammed by a galloping wagon, I could feel the comfort and warmth of my healing power surge through me. It was becoming familiar now, and I could feel my muscles easing and my cramped neck beginning to loosen. Unfortunately it didn't appear to cure hangovers.

That wine had been treacherous. Its sweet taste disguised its strength. I was drunk with only a few sips. Well, I had more than a few sips. In fact, I couldn't remember how much of the wine I had.

Just thinking about Landon's hands all over me made me flush with embarrassment. I didn't think I could face him this morning.

Perhaps what was done was done. I couldn't go back and erase things. I just had to accept what had happened. When I found him he was lost in conversation with his team, and he did not once look up to meet my gaze. My face burned with shame again.

I couldn't let what happened between us deter me from my goal.

Get over it, Elena.

It had happened, and I had to accept my own actions. I needed to get my hands on the stone. That's the only thing that mattered.

With my bag over my shoulders, I set out towards the North. I was just behind a few Espanians and Romilians, and I let them set my pace.

The mood of the groups had changed. Everyone moved with more haste and more energy now, and I knew it was going to get worse. The nearness of the prize weighed heavily on everyone. I had to watch my back.

I kept to myself as I wandered along the hard desert floor. The air was hot and stale. The endless gray terrain seemed to spread its gloom into me as well, and I walked in silence.

I was deep into my thoughts when I was surprised to find Mad Jack walking along beside me. He forced a smile.

"How are you feeling?"

"Like I'm about to cough out my liver, and like I've been hit with a blunt object. Other than that, I feel great."

He laughed and handed me a canteen. "Here, drink that. It's beef broth. It'll help settle your stomach."

The last thing I wanted to do was drink, but I did as I was told and gulped it down. I raised my brows.

"This is good. Surprisingly good." I handed him back his canteen. "Is it from a stew you made yourself?"

"It is," he answered proudly. "I like cooking. It relaxes me."

I raised an eyebrow at that. I'd never thought he'd be the type to cook. I was even more surprised at how relaxed I felt with him, even though he had seen me in a scandalous entanglement last night. His easy demeanor comforted me somehow. I didn't quite understand it.

We walked side by side in an awkward silence for a while until he broke it by asking plainly, "So, what's going on between you and his highness?"

I nearly tripped.

"Nothing. Not that it's any of your business," I added sharply. "Have you stooped to name calling now? Can't you use the usual...I don't know...*bastard*...*son of a bitch*...or something of that sort?"

Mad Jack shrugged. "Because he's not a bastard. Landon Battenberg is the real royal prince of Anglia. Well, at least he would be if the monarchy still existed."

I nearly spit up the broth. I knew I had heard the name Battenberg before. Of course, I had read it in one of Rose's history books. The Battenbergs were a long line of kings from Anglia. They went back for generations, long before the priests established their empire.

I had nearly slept with royalty, and I wasn't exactly sure how that made me feel. *Good? Bad? Really good?* And what were the prince's motives? *Was I a prize? A tool? A cheap thrill to distract him?*

Mad Jack frowned. "I thought you knew."

"Well, obviously I didn't," I exclaimed. My knees were wobbling.

He had treated me with true kindness since the beginning of this journey. Royalty or not, he was the only one who had bothered to come to my aid. Maybe he was just lonely. Maybe all he wanted was some company, just like me.

I searched the long line of heads and found his tousled dark blond hair and broad shoulders easily. There was something regal about the way he carried himself, and the way others always looked to him to lead. I knew he was highborn, but I would never have guessed he was of the highest sort. I steadied my heart.

"Well, it's not like he's parading his position anyway." I had noticed, however, that most of the wealthy and noble Anglians addressed him by his title.

I thought of Thea's murderous glare and her use of the word *peasant*. It all made sense. She didn't want me to taint her beloved prince. And I couldn't blame her.

"I thought the priests had stripped away all their titles and their lands," I said after a moment, my heart still pounding in my ears.

Mad Jack watched me through narrowed eyes for a moment.

"They did. Officially, the priests took away the nobility's power, their crowns, and their castles. They don't have any real authority anymore. But if you travelled through the other parts of Anglia, especially in the south, you'd find that most folks still speak of the monarchy like it still exists. They still believe in the monarchy."

"Really?" I wasn't surprised. "The Anglians were lucky to have kept their way of life after the rebellion. They still live in the exact same way with all their gold and their grand houses. Nothing really changed for them. They weren't forced into the Pit to rot like us."

"No, they weren't, that's true," he answered. "Those with gold used it to their advantage when the greedy priests came to collect. The wealthy kingdoms signed a treaty with the priests and paid to keep their lands and way of life."

"Sounds pretty hypocritical to me."

I pictured Landon and Thea laughing and drinking his fine wine from golden goblets as they looked out over his vast vineyards and crystal castle.

"Not really," he shook his head. "It's more about biding their time. Would it surprise you to know that most of the noble families want the monarchy *back* in power?"

I stopped walking and turned to him.

"It would, yes. But…Where are you getting this information? I mean, since when did you become an expert in everything royal?"

Had I been blind all these years not to have noticed? Had I been too preoccupied with my own agenda to have seen this coming? Could it even be true?

A sad smile spread across his face.

"There's a lot you don't know about me, Elena."

His comment stung a little, but I kept a straight face. He started walking again, and I followed.

"I'm sure there is," I said.

I thought about my own secret and wondered if one day I'd be able to trust him enough to tell him the truth.

"I conduct transactions… I do business with a lot of wealthy families from time to time," he informed after a moment of silence.

This came as a surprise to me. I furrowed my brows. "What kind of business?"

He chose not to answer my question. What kind of *business* did he mean?

"I meet with them on a regular basis," he said and raked his fingers through his dark locks.

"I know you look at me and see a nothing but a street thug," he said quietly. "I've seen the way you look at Landon, and it's not the same way you look at me."

I felt an edge of jealousy in his tone, and I felt my ears burn.

I didn't know what to say. It was true. That's how I'd always thought about him. And now that I knew that Landon was a prince, it did make things more … *complicated.*

"But there's more to what I do in the Pit, and why. There's a reason why I keep a close relationship with the priests, you know, and it's not because I admire their wardrobe."

"Such as?" I didn't care to hide my skepticism.

"Such as I need to keep them close to know what they're up to."

He paused and then added, "And there are other reasons, too. But I can't tell you, not yet at least."

"What the hell is that supposed to mean?" I said firmly.

"It means that there are things that I can't tell you *yet*," he said abruptly. "Things that are not entirely up to me to tell you, to discuss with you."

I snapped my head back to him. "I doubt that. You've never needed anyone to tell you what to do."

"This is different."

"How so?" I pressed.

"I can't talk about it."

I shook my head. "You're so infuriating. What can you say then?"

A sly smile spread across his face. "Did you know that Prince Landon isn't the only royal in this race?"

My mouth dropped open in shock. "What? You mean in the Anglian group? Prince Landon has siblings?"

Mad Jack laughed, and I found myself smiling.

"No, in the other groups. There's Philippe Touraine, Duke of Fransia." He pointed to a short, stout man with too much lace around his high collar.

"And over there is Enrico Caserta, Duke of Romila." He pointed to a tall and handsome young man around my age.

"The big one over there," he pointed to a giant of a man with light hair and fair skin, "that is Otto Sassen. He's the would-be-king of Girmania."

"And over there," he pointed behind us cautiously. "The older gentleman with the hat is Bartolomeu Dias, a nobleman from the royal household of Purtula."

"The only female royal here is Isabella Velasques, Princess of Espan." He motioned towards a tall, dark-skinned woman who carried more weapons than Mad Jack and I together. Her eyes were fierce, and she resembled a warrior more than a princess. I remembered her from the first day of the race. Her eyes had sparkled with curiosity when she looked at me then.

If he hadn't pointed them out to me, I would never have known.

It was obvious Mad Jack knew much more than he let on, and much more about the royal families, too.

"Why would any of these royal families risk their lives in this race? Why are they even here if they want to restore the monarchy?"

"Same reason as everyone else, for the stone. I think that getting the stone is part of bringing the monarchy back. Well, in essence at least."

"How so?"

"Well," said Mad Jack. "The stone is called the Heart of Arcania because it is a talisman that represents power. To possess it would bring great honor to the winning kingdom. It would bring back hope to the kingdoms who had lost it when the priests turned everything to hell. No one has ever been able to claim it before. It would show strength to claim a prize that even the priests had failed to grasp. And if someone actually does manage to retrieve it, then I think it'll signal a new beginning."

We walked in silence. The high priest had told me that the stone was a symbol of power, too. But what if it was more than that? Would the royal families risk their lives for a stone that was merely symbolic? Or was there more to this mysterious stone?

CHAPTER 22

WE PASSED THE REST of the day in agreeable conversation, reminiscing about our childhood in the Pit. I was surprised at how much Mad Jack and I had in common. We both grew up poor. We both got into loads of trouble as kids. We both stole fresh bread from Mr. Aird's bakery, and both our parents were dead. (I didn't tell him that my father was a priest. To me he was just as good as dead.) His mother had died of the fever eight years ago, and his father had died a year later in a fishing accident.

After a while I noticed that Will and Leo were walking alongside us. They had been listening in on our conversations, and now they began adding their own thoughts every now and then. I wondered if they knew of Mad Jack's involvement with some kind of revolution. The three of them were as thick as thieves, and as we talked some more, it became very clear that they did.

They never spoke to me directly. It was always more along the lines of *ask her,* and *tell her,* and the occasional *would she...* It became clear that they distrusted me and even feared me because they had seen me bring the crown to Mad Jack. They were suspicious because they couldn't explain just exactly how I had acquired it. Those touched by sorcerer's fire died, and here I was—still alive.

Their apparent hatred for witches or anything remotely magical made me nervous. I had hoped to keep my secret hidden at least until the end of the race when I put this damn stone into the high priest's hands. The priests had been drilling the idea that magic was evil into our young heads since I can remember, so Will and Leo's fear of me was understandable. Magic bearers were demons. Anyone involved with magic had always been executed—until me.

At nightfall, we made camp in a miraculously green glade. As usual I set out my bedroll away from everyone else. I was able to make a fire easily because it had been so dry. But the nights were surprisingly cold, and I was grateful for the warmth of my little fire.

I had caught Landon throwing glances my way a few times during our excursion today, but his face had been unreadable. I suspected that he felt what had happened between us had truly been a mistake.

It didn't help that I felt ashamed, too. Nonetheless, I couldn't help the heat that flushed my face whenever our eyes met. I'd been a fool to think there could ever be more between us. He was a prince while I was a peasant and probably a witch.

My stomach growled, and I attempted to ease my hunger with tea. Tea, I had plenty of. Food on the other hand was scarce, and I was too proud to beg for it. It's not like I wasn't used to starving, I could always manage to find food if I had to.

I was conscious that Mad Jack seemed to have taken it upon himself to watch out for me, not that I was going to need it. I wasn't planning on another fling with the prince. But I was surprised that I wasn't annoyed by his supervision. In fact, I was rather pleased that he was keeping an eye on me. I didn't feel so utterly alone.

We reached Hollowmere City near noon of the second day, earlier than I'd first thought. Although the sun was hidden in dark clouds, the city itself was alight with blazing yellow fires. We marched through the iron gates in silence. It was a wretched city surrounded by iron walls, and the fires we had seen as we arrived turned out to be burning above the countless tombs that dominated the landscape.

I couldn't see any bodies, but I could smell the dead flesh. Bone dust blew in the unforgiving winds. And when I inspected the ground more closely, I could see that the cause of the dust in the air was bones that had been shattered. It was as though someone had taken a great hammer and crushed them. The air smelled of sulfur and rotten flesh. There must have been the bones of thousands of bodies littering the city. Where had they come from? And who lit the fires?

"This place smells like death. Is it what you expected?"

Mad Jack's expression was just as alarmed as mine. I regretted sharing my doubts and fears with him, but it was too late now…

"I'm not sure what I expected," I answered truthfully.

A cold shiver rolled down my spine, and I tried not to panic. "There's no life here, only death. I feel like I'm staring at a glimpse of hell."

"I think you're right." Mad Jack stiffened. "This place gives me the creeps. It feels like all the happiness would drain out of me if I stayed here, you know. Like this place feeds on it."

There was no use pretending that I didn't feel it too.

"Yes," I nodded absentmindedly. "I know exactly what you mean. I can feel it too. It's like a perpetual doom is waiting for us, waiting to devour our souls."

"Makes you wonder what the hell we're doing here, don't it?" I turned to see Will and Leo walking towards us.

"This place is unnatural. I'm sure that witches live here. See all those bones? That's their doing. They eat us and spit out our souls. I can feel their wickedness all around. It's everywhere. We shouldn't be here."

Leo's pale eyes met Mad Jack's. "Hope you're sure about this."

The two men watched one another in what I believed to be a silent argument. The stiffness in Leo's shoulders revealed that he wasn't here of his own accord. Perhaps they came at Mad Jack's orders.

"Smells vile," said Leo. He wiped his nose rudely with the back of his hand.

"Best be moving if you don't want to fall behind."

"Why don't we wait here and let them fools get the stone for us," said Will. "Then we can steal it from them. Makes more sense to me that way. Why should we risk our necks for a bloody stone, anyway?"

It was the same train of thought that I had had earlier. I was surprised at how openly they discussed their plans in front of me.

"Forget it," growled Mad Jack with such authority that the other two men were silenced. "Stick to the plan."

Pinching the stone wasn't a bad plan, and I was pretty sure we weren't the only ones who had thought of it.

"Are you ready?" he startled me. "This is where the *real* race begins."

I'd been staring out into the city, lost in my own thoughts.

"Not really," I said, which was the truth, and I tore my gaze away from his. "But what choice do I have?"

Not for the first time, I wished I were back in the Pit with Rose, conversing about our simple and uneventful lives.

"Everyone will be out for blood. It won't matter if they're a prince or a princess or a street peddler from the market—don't let your guard down for anyone."

"Even you?" I said dryly.

Mad Jack clenched his jaw. "Don't worry about me. Focus on what you need to do and get out."

My jaw dropped, and I didn't try to hide my surprise. "Don't you want the stone?"

Mad Jack drew his sword.

"We'd best be moving. Watch your back, Elena. Don't trust anyone."

He moved away with his trusted bodyguards at his side. Their job was to keep him safe, but their faces were pale and their weapons twitched nervously in their hands.

I followed behind them, staying alert. I gasped when we reached the gates. I could see mountains of human bones inside the iron walls.

Statues of dark gods and demons, temples, and tombs were scattered throughout the city. I had felt a darkness emanating from the witches' carved poles when we had come across them earlier, but this was by far more terrifying. It was a nightmare. Human bones lay everywhere. Some were so old they looked like fossils, while others oozed with fresh flesh still clinging to them. And yet, there were no worshipers, no demons, nothing. I don't know why, but this horrid place reminded me of the priests and the Temple of the Sun.

A cold and heavy rain started to fall, and the bones of the people who had been sacrificed here lay in a filthy mixture of shadow and putrid water. I retched. My throat was burning with bile, and my eyes welled with water.

We all gathered around the gates.

The large man, Otto Sassen, pushed his way to the front with large battle-axes in both hands. The Duke of Fransia looked as if he were snickering as he let Otto and his people move towards the gates. Princess Isabella glared at me briefly as she whispered to the other Espanians.

It was starting.

I braced myself and followed the others through the iron gates.

Hollowmere wasn't a large city. It was more a village. A few stone structures had doors and windows, so people did live here, but it was hard to imagine anyone thriving here. There were still no signs of life. Hollowmere was more like a shrine where you went to sacrifice animals. The silence was unnerving.

An array of fantastic gods and grotesque sculptures were etched into the walls. Their faces had been carved to ward off intruders and to make sure we knew we were being watched. *But by whom?*

Fires blazed in iron braziers that were spaced randomly around the city. Someone had lit those fires. *So where were they?*

I recognized the tallest building as the temple-like structure on my map. It was the complete opposite to the lavish golden temple in Soul City. This structure was made of high stone walls covered in stucco. It was a square building with a flat top and with a wide, double-stone staircase that led to a large archway. The architecture was simple, elegant, and unique.

The stone was in there.

It was obvious that everyone knew where the stone was being held. Nothing in this great race was secret. It seemed strange that a stone called the Heart of Arcania would be in such an obvious place. It didn't make any sense.

We were afraid that any sudden noise would jinx us, so we moved as quietly as we could. While I could see that everyone was uneasy about entering the building, they also watched their opponents with suspicion. The tension in the air and the gloom of this place gave me goose bumps.

The Espanians and the Girmanians moved with purpose towards the temple. They moved faster and faster, until Otto sprinted ahead.

I dropped my bag, drew my short sword, and started to jog. But something held me back. I felt eyes on me. I stopped and looked behind me. Nothing. But I felt it. There was something lurking in the shadows behind the stone buildings. Something waited.

My senses screamed for me to run, but I stood there. I turned around. Mad Jack had stopped, too. He was watching me, and his scowl showed that he felt the same fear as I did.

"I think..." I frowned at him and fought the chill that ran down my arms. "I think this is a trap."

And just as the Girmanians and the Espanians arrived at the large stone steps of the temple, an army of men wearing billowing black cloaks and golden-skull masks jumped out at us from the shadows.

CHAPTER 23

THEY DROPPED FROM THE top of the temple like a rain of slashing silver swords. The sound of metal against flesh chilled me to the bone. The air filled with guttural shouts as many of our number died at the foot of the stairs. They were foaming at the mouths, convulsing, and screaming as the poison from the swords entered their blood streams. They never stood a chance.

I was shoved and pushed. I cried out as someone elbowed me in the face. And in the confusion and screams, I stood frozen in panic for a moment. I knew what violence just one of these masked men was capable of.

Blood trickled from my nose as I blinked away my tears and found my courage again.

"Their blades are poisoned!" I shouted.

Mad Jack looked confused for a second, then he ducked and parried the sword of a masked man. With surprising skill, he spun and ran his sword through the masked man's back.

"How do you know?" he shouted back.

He blocked another attack from two masked men and drove them back. I watched as the masked men spread out like a shaken silk sheet. They spilled out of the building like an army of ants.

"Because I've fought one of them before."

The blood pounded in my ears. I heard Mad Jack shout something to Leo and Will, but I couldn't make it out over the screams and shouts that surrounded us.

My attention shifted to the three masked men that came at me.

I didn't have time to think. I could only react. I raised my sword and parried the first fierce blow instinctively. My attacker's cape entangled him for a second, but it was all I needed. I rammed my sword into his gut, and he spit out blood into my face. As he hit the ground next to me, I was already moving towards the other two.

The other two assassins came at me from two directions. I parried them, one after another. Then they both slashed sideways, trying to behead me. I ducked and pulled out a dagger. I spun and came up behind one of the men. He slumped to the ground as I embedded my dagger into his throat.

I stumbled forward as something hit the back of my head. The adrenaline of panic gave me the strength to steady myself and turn around. Blinking the spots from my eyes, I felt for blood or any signs of a cut, but there were none.

The second masked man roared as he flew at me again. His sword cut the air in a side-to-side movement and when our swords met, he pushed me to my knees in a show of strength. I strained to keep my sword against his and looked up into dark eyes behind the mask.

"You will never get the stone," he hissed.

He pushed his sword dangerously close to my neck.

My arms burned as I strained to keep his blade from slicing my throat. But I was no match for him, and I knew I couldn't defend myself like this for much longer. He smiled wickedly at me, knowing all too well that he was winning. My arms slipped a little, and his blade inched down closer to my throat. But just as victory gleamed in his eyes, I kicked out my leg and made contact with his ankle. I heard a snap. He yelled and as he dropped his guard, I drove my sword into his heart. His eyes widened in shock, and then their gleam was gone.

I pulled out my bloody sword and stood up. I jumped over his body and made my way towards the battle. Bodies lay scattered in puddles of their own blood, but I'd say there were more bodies of the masked men than there were of us. Combatants circled and feinted towards each other in a dance of death.

I spotted Princess Isabella. She proved to be the warrior princess I thought she would be and moved with deadly skill and grace. She spun and parried as if she were dancing while masked men fell at her feet. If I hadn't been in mortal danger myself, I could have watched her cut a path through our attackers all afternoon.

A glimpse of red and gold caught my attention. Prince Landon lifted his sword to parry a blow at his shoulder. His sword met with a masked assassin's, and in a swirl of flashing silver the masked man lay on the ground at his feet. The prince moved with the deadly grace of a tiger. He skewered the assassins so fast and precisely that they were dead before they realized it.

While about a dozen men and women from different groups lay dead with white foam in their mouths and blood that had thickened like pudding, I was in awe at the warriors around me. Although we had suffered a considerable number of causalities and had been outnumbered, we had managed to kill every single one of the masked men.

Something caught Landon's attention, and he bolted towards the temple's stairs just as Otto disappeared through the arched entrance.

That's when the race truly began.

The surviving crowd rushed to the temple as Prince Landon galloped through the archway. In the melee a man came tumbling down the stairs, and another brawl erupted. Only this time we were fighting amongst ourselves.

Not wanting to get caught up in this madness, I hung back and waited for an opening. Once again the air was filled with the sounds of metal clashing against metal and grunts.

I felt something on my lower back, and in a flash I whirled my sword around and parried Mad Jack's blade with a ringing clash.

He made to lower his blade, but I wouldn't lower mine.

"Easy. It's just me," he said.

I clenched my teeth. He could have easily rammed me through, but he hadn't. My gut told me to trust him, so I lowered my sword but kept it in my hand.

Will and Leo both looked wild eyed, but they were alive and had been unscathed by the poisoned blades.

Mad Jack crouched. He looked at me.

"On my mark, you run like hell up those stairs and get that god damn stone! You hear me? We'll be right behind you."

Even though I was still unsure why he was here, or whether I should trust him, I nodded anyway. I didn't have time to second-guess myself.

I waited. Mad Jack's shoulders tensed, and he whispered, "Go, go, go!"

I ran up the stairs two at a time, careful not to trip, and all the while watching to protect myself from any attackers. But I reached the top of the stairs without incident and kept running.

I heard footsteps rushing behind me. I could only hope that they were Mad Jack's. I didn't stop running.

The temple was larger than I'd first thought, and the first hundred paces of passageway were carved from stone. Soft light from torches that were held in sconces on the walls lighted my path. I felt the same strange sense of power that I had felt at the poles and at the entrance to the city. Only this time it was stronger. Energy pulsed through the walls of this place.

"Don't stop," Mad Jack encouraged me from behind. I hadn't realized that I had stopped.

He whispered, "Unless you want twenty more people crushing us in this small tunnel, we need to keep moving."

There was an anxiety in his voice that I had not heard before, maybe even fear, and it made me move more quickly…

I held my breath and ran as fast as I could. The strange, humming tunnel continued for what felt like miles, and then it opened into a cavern.

Prince Landon stood in the clearing along with King Otto and several others of their entourage. They were examining a section of the wall at the opposite side of the chamber. They looked up at our arrival, but then quickly returned their attention to the wall. Even in the dim light I could see that both men were sweating in concentration. And when I moved closer I could understand why.

A single oval-shaped stone that looked like a giant egg sat in a niche carved in the stone. It was the size of a hand, but it didn't sparkle, nor was it made of red diamond. It looked like a smooth river rock. But as I got even closer, I could see six red lines marked on the front of the stone. They were the only indication that this wasn't just a regular rock.

"What the hell are they waiting for?" Mad Jack's hot breath tickled the skin on my neck.

I looked around at the wall of stones and shrugged. "I don't know. Maybe they feel it's just way too easy. That's what I think. It can't be as simple as this. There's something else."

He leaned so close I felt his cheek brush up against mine.

"You think it's a trick?"

I shook my head and shrugged. "I don't know…maybe…it just feels off, you know. If this stone is so precious, then why isn't it better protected? Why aren't any of those masked men in here guarding it?"

"You have a point."

"Something's not right."

Even as the words escaped me, I felt dark and light emanating from the stone. I smelled the stench of death, but I also smelled the blossoms of summer and the flow of life.

There was a rush of voices behind us, and the rest of the surviving clans stumbled into the room. King Otto's eyes narrowed, and he roared something in Girmanian. Then he thrust out his great big arm and reached towards the stone—

"Don't touch it!" I warned in a hasty whisper.

King Otto stopped. His hand was still outstretched.

"Why not?" he said with a heavy accent.

Even though he looked at me with eyes that showed his mistrust, he had paid attention to me and had hesitated.

"I don't know," I said. It was the truth. "It's too easy. Think about it. It doesn't feel right."

I didn't know why I was helping him. We were competing, and yet a part of me felt it was wrong not to help.

King Otto stared at me and then glanced at his men. He said something that immediately resulted in laughter at my expense. Prince Landon did not laugh, however, and I could see that he agreed with me.

The room went still and all eyes turned to the king.

He smiled at me, and with eyes gleaming with greed he grabbed the stone.

"No, wait!" I shouted and then held my breath.

King Otto's face paled. But then the color returned to his cheeks when nothing happened.

He raised his hand in triumph, and the Girmanians exploded in cheers and threw their swords in the air. They had won the race.

But then the king's flesh started to glow a bright yellow. His eyes opened wide with fear as the yellow light broke through his skin, and then he exploded into thousands of bloody chunks of burned flesh.

CHAPTER 24

Bits of King Otto got me in the face, and I nearly vomited right there. I could see that the only solid parts that were left of the king were his shattered bones. That explained why we had seen all the bones outside in the city. They were the remains of the thousands of unlucky souls who'd already tried to retrieve the stone. Blood of Arcania.

The room erupted in a cacophony of screams and blood-curdling wails. People ran for cover, slipping and falling into the mess of what used to be the king of Girmania. They didn't know if they were about to explode as well. The blast had been so sudden that most of us just stood transfixed and stared at the spot where King Otto had stood moments before.

"La pierre est maudite! C'est une pierre des démons!" Spit flew from the mouth of a Fransian man whose face was covered in blood that was not his own.

The man said something about the stone being cursed. And I believed him. A consensus of murmurs reverberated around the chamber. The blanched faces spoke for themselves. I just stood there shivering and sweating.

The stone rested in a pool of blood in the middle of the chamber. The Heart of Arcania was such a small thing, and yet it possessed remarkable power. I had sensed it. And I was no fool. I had warned Otto, but he hadn't listened. And now all that was left of him was a sticky, slippery, red mess.

I looked around the room, trying to piece together a plan. My gaze fell upon the nobleman, Bartolomeu Dias, not because he was about to share his thoughts, but because he was watching Prince Landon. In fact, as I surveyed the room, I could see that all eyes fell on the prince. It was as though he had become their leader now, and it would be up to him to decide their fate. Besides, he and Otto had been first to enter the chamber, so Prince Landon was next in line.

I watched the prince. He hadn't moved either. He'd been closer to Otto than me, and by the sloppy mess of flesh and blood that covered him, he'd gotten it worse than I had. As though he'd read my mind, he pulled out a handkerchief and wiped his face. But his eyes didn't leave the stone.

The tension in the room continued to grow. The hair on my arms stood up, and I instinctively grasped my sword. Something was about to happen and it wasn't the stone.

A brute of a man from the Pit turned on Mad Jack.

"This whole damn race was a waste of time," he growled, and took a menacing step forward. "We lost valuable men and for what? All for nothing! We can't even touch this damn stone."

Mad Jack didn't flinch, but I saw his knuckles turn white around the hilt of his sword.

"Get back, Mason. We all knew the risks when we *volunteered* to come."

Mason stood his ground, but he shook his head.

"Well, it's not a fair race. It's a trick. This whole damn thing is a hoax. The priests tricked us. They knew we couldn't win. They sent us all on a fool's mission, another way to toy with us. I'm sick of their games!"

"He's right, they knew this would happen." Everyone turned and stared at me.

I was shocked that I'd actually spoken my mind out loud, but it was too late to take it back now. I thought Mad Jack would be the first to talk, and I was surprised when the prince spoke first.

"What do you mean, Elena?" His voice, although a little gaunt, still retained the royal quality I had heard before. But there was something else in his look that I didn't understand.

I swallowed hard. "They knew. They knew all along."

Mad Jack leaned towards me and narrowed his eyes. "Did *you* know this would happen?"

I understood his silent accusation and denied it angrily. "Of course not! But they knew…they knew this was going to happen."

As I spoke, everything began to make sense. Why I was here. Why the high priest had looked so triumphant when I had healed myself. It was all for this very moment. Right now.

I knew that the high priest had sent *me* because he knew I was the only one who could touch the stone and live.

Before I knew what I was doing, I walked over to the stone and picked it up.

"Elena! No!" I heard Mad Jack's voice behind me.

The stone was warm, like it'd been sitting in the sun all day. It was smooth and surprisingly heavy for its size. It felt as though it should have been twice as large. I felt its power reverberate in me. It pulsed like the beating of a heart. I heard it in my ears and felt it pounding in my own chest.

All at once I felt a monstrous pain, and my legs buckled. I lost my breath and couldn't focus. I heard voices call my name, but they were far away. A buzzing sensation shivered through me from the top of my head to my feet. Hot. Cold. Hot. Cold. I felt like I was being pulled in every direction. My body burned from the inside, and then I felt as cold as death. And when I thought I was going to explode like Otto, I felt a shift in the power of the stone, and it released me, as though I had passed some sort of test.

"She touched it, and she's still alive!"

"How is that possible?"

I blinked as the chamber around me shifted back into focus. My heart beat madly in my chest like I had just run a mile.

Mad Jack stood next to me. He was breathing heavily and sweat trickled down his face. His dark eyes were wide with fear, and he shook his head in disbelief. His left hand was slightly raised as if he half expected me to give him the stone but was too frightened to take it.

I glanced at Landon, and he tensed. He was watching the stone in my hands closely. No doubt he was wondering if he would have

226

survived, if he had picked it up instead of me. Although he was expressionless, I felt the same unexplainable shudder spiraling down my spine that I had felt when I had looked at him before.

"Maybe the stone chooses who it wants, who it thinks is worthy to wield it," he said.

He looked at the stone and then back at me.

"It seems to have chosen you, Elena," he said quietly.

I could tell that he felt *he* should have the stone, not some peasant woman like me.

The others in the chamber shifted nervously and cast the same envious glances in my direction. But there was something else—like a pull. It was like everyone had gone mad for the stone. They seemed compelled to possess it. They needed it. It was like they were all under some sort of spell. The stone was doing something to them, but somehow I wasn't affected.

I caught a glance exchanged between Prince Landon and his battle-proven wingman, and I shifted uneasily. Was it frustration, arrogance, or greed? Whatever it was, it was catching and spreading to the rest of the company fast. I knew with certainty that they were going to *try* and take the stone from me.

I swallowed hard and subconsciously rubbed the tiny lines on the stone with my thumb. I couldn't help but feel a sense of pride. *I* had gotten the stone.

But the race wasn't finished yet. I had to find my way back to Soul City with the stone. Landon's watchful stare made me anxious now. The flirty man was gone, and in his stead was a mighty prince.

Mad Jack cleared his throat. "Elena has the stone now. She's won."

He motioned across the chamber to the exit. "You should all leave and be thankful you're all still alive."

"The race isn't over yet," said Philippe Touraine, the Duke of Fransia.

He pushed past his companions but stayed away from me. His expression was just as irritated as Landon's.

"She needs to cross into Soul City *with* the stone to win the race."

Mad Jack turned towards the duke. I could see the tension across his shoulders.

"Is that a threat?"

The duke sneered. "What are you? Her bodyguard?"

He smiled lazily. "I'm just saying, do not be too hasty."

The duke looked at me and there was something cold and foreign in his eyes. I had to force myself not to look away.

"Elena, right? Well, there is still a continent to cross and many days of travel. I'm sure we'll all face more *challenges* along the way. There could be new developments. To win the race, you must have the stone in your possession when you enter Soul City. And to quote the high priest, *there are no rules.* Anything can happen between now and then."

He was right of course. I knew that he had just spoken aloud what everyone else in the chamber was thinking. At some point on the way back, someone would take it from me, or at least they would *try*. They'd all seen what had happened to the late King Otto. Who would be reckless enough to try again?

I glanced around the room and met a few determined faces who certainly looked as if they might. Someone would try.

I sheathed my sword. I had to put the stone inside its golden cage. I pulled out the cage and slipped the stone inside. It fit perfectly, as though the cage had been designed around the stone. I clamped it shut and dropped it safely back inside my pouch. I supposed someone could just cut it off with a blade, but it was close enough to my body that it was not easy to get at, and I could defend myself. I adjusted the thick leather belt slung low across my hips.

I wiped my sweaty palms on my thighs, hoping no one had seen my trembling fingers, clenched my jaw so much it hurt, and stood up straight.

They all wanted the stone. I could feel it.

A little over twenty of them were left from the original racing company. I was alone. The odds weren't in my favor. I felt like a cornered rabbit inside the wolf's den. I only realized I was trembling when I prepared to step back and flee as fast as I could. The stone pulsed at my waist, sensing my fear, and urging me to run. My mouth was dry. I took a step back.

"Miss Elena will leave the chamber *unharmed*," Prince Landon announced suddenly.

His regal voice resonated around the chamber walls as a challenge to any who might try to interfere with me. Though his features remained neutral, he raised his chin, and I could see that his threat was not to be taken lightly…

"I can promise that my company will not harm you, nor will the others." He stared at everyone else, challenging anyone to disagree. Nobody moved.

Then he looked at me and lowered his voice. "But I can't promise anything outside these walls."

"Fair enough," I said.

I felt a little mesmerized by him. I struggled to keep my feelings at bay. I could still remember his salty scent, and how he had gotten me so hot and bothered. I swear I could see a tiny smile tugging at the corners of his lips.

I turned away. I couldn't let myself be intimidated by this handsome man, prince or not.

I pulled out my sword and surveyed the room one last time. Mad Jack was watching me closely, but I didn't look at him. I tried to memorize the faces in front of me. I knew that any one of them could jump me at any moment.

Once I was satisfied I could identify any of them if I saw them again, I spun around and made for the exit.

Mad Jack fell in line behind me, and I felt my chest tighten. Could I really trust him? Was this just a ruse? Was he waiting for me to let my guard down?

I walked faster, and then a little faster, until I was practically jogging. Mad Jack was right behind me. I felt his hand press on my lower back, urging me to go faster.

I flinched. I didn't want him or anyone so close to me. The faster we went, the faster my heart thumped against my ribcage until I thought it might explode. The weird thing was the stone seemed to feel my panic. As my heartbeat increased, I felt the stone's pulse increase, too. We seemed to be joined in some way. Our pulses beat together as one.

I could see light at the end of the tunnel. I was almost outside. I hurried faster. Once I was out there would be lots of places to hide, and then I could make my way home to Rose and freedom.

Mad Jack was still behind me, so close that I could feel his breath on the back on my neck. Would he try to take the stone from me? I was almost sure he would. Why not? He wasn't called *Mad Jack* because he was insane. He got his name because he stopped at nothing to get what he wanted. He never passed up an opportunity to make some gold. He was going to take it.

Almost there, don't panic and don't trip down the stairs.

My heart leapt when I reached the threshold, and cool fresh air brushed my hot cheeks.

I felt a wind at my back, and I heard a shout. Then I heard what sounded like bodies hitting the ground. But I couldn't stop.

Just as I reached the top of the stairs something hit me hard on the back, and I pitched forward. With a startled cry, I threw out my arms to break my fall and immediately regretted it. My palms and elbows scraped on the hard stone stairs, and my head hit a corner of sharp stone. Black spots exploded behind my eyes, and the wind was knocked out of me. I couldn't believe that I hadn't broken my neck in my fall down the stairs. I rolled over on my hands and knees and looked up.

My breath caught in my throat. It was not Mad Jack standing above me with a sword pointed at my neck. It was Princess Isabella Velasques.

CHAPTER 25

THE PRINCESS WAS TALLER than many of the men she kept in her company and much taller than me. I could see her thick muscled forearms through her sleeves. She held her long sword steadily at my throat, as though it weighed nothing more than a stick. While her face was plain, there was no mistaking the nobility of her posture. She had probably trained as a warrior since she could walk, and I had seen her take down those masked men without breaking a sweat. Her dark eyes widened suddenly with madness, and she lunged forward.

I moved, but not fast enough. Her blade nicked the side of my neck, and warm blood trickled down my shoulder.

I jumped to my feet just as she came at me again. Her eyes were wild, and she was striking and slashing with the strength of a man. I blocked a right, then crouched and spun, knocking her blade out her hand. She was surprised at my skill.

"If you want to live, you better give me the stone," said the princess.

The others had made a ring around us, and I felt like I was in one of the fighting rings back in the Pit. But there was no cheering in this fight, only silence. The Espanian guard stood with their swords drawn. Up close, their faces were squashed and brutal. I couldn't see Landon or Mad Jack anywhere, and my heart thundered with fear and anger.

The evil looks in my opponents' eyes said it all. They were all waiting for the outcome of this encounter before making their move. Somebody would challenge whoever came out with the stone.

"Give me the stone. It's *mine*."

I turned on the warrior princess. "Back off, bitch. I won the stone fair and square."

Her cocky smile infuriated me.

"Or is it bastard? Quite frankly, I'm not so sure myself. I mean, look at you? Are you a woman or a man?"

Princess Isabella's expression hardened. She was livid and appeared even more threatening than her brutish company. I needed her to be a little unbalanced if I wanted to beat her and save myself.

But before I could rejoice in my cleverness at having surprised her with my lack of deference to her, her black eyes filled with delight, and she crouched in a defensive stance. She would not be distracted with anger. She was smarter than I thought.

"You must have a death wish, peasant wench. You dare to challenge me! I can kill you with my eyes closed."

I raised an eyebrow. "Probably. But you're not getting the stone."

"Then you will die."

The princess' voice was steady in her confidence that she was going to kill me.

She waved her sword. The tip was still dripping with my blood.

"I am a princess! You are nothing but a peasant. The stone belongs to me!"

My blood ran cold, but I kept my composure. I could feel the nasty welt on the right side of my face beginning to fester. Although my clothes were torn, and I favored my left leg, the look of scorn on the princess' face caused my fury to grow.

The stone pulsed at my waist, growing warmer and steadier, mimicking the beating of my own heart. I don't know why, but I felt as though it was trying to communicate with me.

"You can't wield the stone. You will die," I said. "You saw what happened to dear Otto. If you touch the stone you will suffer the same fate."

She smiled wickedly at me. "You didn't die, and neither will I. Perhaps the stone needs a woman's touch. Perhaps only a woman can yield it."

Many of the men from the different realms muttered their disagreement and glared at the princess.

Princess Isabella pointed her sword at me. "I'll take my chances. The stone will recognize me as its true bearer."

My logic screamed at me to run and take my chances in the wild land of Goth. But something else possessed me and commanded me to stay and fight.

"Kill her! And take the stone!" said one of the brutish men from the princess' company.

"Why should Espan have the stone?" growled an even bigger red-bearded man who wore the orange and yellow colors of Romila. "The stone belongs to Romila!"

"It belongs to Espan!"

"To Girmania!"

"You fools. The stone is meant for Fransia!"

I didn't see who charged first, but the clans' greed for the stone escalated into a full-fledged war, and for a moment we were forgotten.

"My patience has run out, priest whore," growled the princess.

My attention snapped back to her. Her voice rose as the muscles in her neck throbbed.

"The stone is mine!"

She charged like a wild beast and hurled her sword at me like a spear. I barely had time to duck as the massive weapon nicked my left side and buried itself in the earth near my feet. I threw myself on the ground and rolled back onto my feet. Something else slammed into me, and I pitched headlong to the ground.

I cried out in pain as cold metal sank into my shoulder. I grabbed the sword and managed to pull myself free and slither out of the princess' way. Blood poured freely from my deep wound, but I struggled to my feet.

236

I covered the wound with my hand to prevent anyone from seeing the streams of yellow light. But my cloak and tunic hid my secret for now. Although the pain flamed in my shoulder, I felt the warmth of my healing power as it stitched up my sliced flesh, eased my pain, and gave me new strength.

I shifted my weight and balanced on the balls of my feet.

"Give up?" taunted the princess.

"Never," I growled. I held my sword in a fighting stance and waited.

The princess gave me a bloodthirsty grin. "We are going to play a game, you and I."

"Is that so?" I mocked. "And here I thought you wanted to kill me."

She smiled. "And you've already lost."

The princess charged.

I spun and dove to avoid the impact of her attack. As I rolled back onto my feet, her fist connected with my cheek. I fought a sharp wave of nausea, and without giving the princess time to react, I kicked my foot into her jaw. Then I twirled and kicked my other foot into her lower back.

The princess staggered, but hardly looked injured. She spit some blood from her mouth, and smiled. Her teeth were smeared with blood.

"I'm going to rip out your heart and—"

The last of her words died in her throat as a sharp silver sword from the back of her head emerged through her mouth. Her eyes rolled back in her head, and she toppled like a great dead tree.

The great red-bearded Romilian brute behind her withdrew his sword from the princess' head and growled at me like a bear.

"The stone is mine! Mine! Mine!"

His small eyes narrowed as a dark grin grew on his face.

I stood on the tips of my toes, balancing my sword in my hand.

"Give it to me!" He lunged faster than I would have thought a man his size could move.

I raised my arm to parry the thrust, but the brute's violent strength nearly shattered my wrist. Miraculously I managed to hold on to my sword.

My attacker howled and sprang again. I dodged backwards and then ducked as his sword brushed the top of my hair. A few more inches and I would have been decapitated.

I could hear the sound of battle all around me, but I couldn't take my eyes off my attacker for one second.

I could never beat him with strength. I needed to outwit him.

As he came at me again, I rolled to the side and countered with two short jabs into his stomach. I raised my sword up and was about to swing it in an arc at his head, but in that split second before I swung, I could feel the life flowing from him. His guts suddenly spilled out onto the ground at his feet. He babbled unintelligently and then collapsed in a heap.

The violence disturbed me, but it also unleashed a fearless and unyielding ferocity from inside me.

I felt another presence behind me, but it was already too late.

I whirled around just as a sword rammed straight through my chest.

I staggered back as my assailant pulled out the sword in one rapid motion. Blood poured down my front, and I looked up into my assailant's face.

Philippe Touraine, the Duke of Fransia, looked jubilant.

"La pierre est à moi! Donne-moi la pierre!"

Madness cast a dark shadow over his face as he reached for the stone in my pouch. But then a light shone on him, and he faltered. The blood left his face.

He stared at my shredded tunic. My chest was exposed, and golden light spilled out of me like the rays of morning sunshine.

CHAPTER 26

EVERYONE AROUND ME GASPED at the spectacle of golden light shining out from the wound in my chest. My secret was out.

The Fransian duke pointed a finger at me, all the while taking careful steps back. Spit flew from his mouth as he cried, "Witch! She's a witch!"

"I saw it," a woman from Romila affirmed. "The sword went right through her. She should be dead, and yet she lives like nothing happened."

"Demon!"

"Accursed!"

"Burn the witch!"

Damn. Things were not looking good. It was clear that most of them wanted me dead. And yet no one came at me. While they made menacing noises and gestures, it was fear I saw on their faces. Some individuals spat on the floor, and I saw a few men make the sign of the Creator and mumble prayers under their breaths.

I searched for Mad Jack, but he wasn't there. I felt my stomach contract. Maybe he'd been killed. And when I finally saw Prince Landon, I saw confusion, terror, fear, and then revulsion on his face. I felt something crush my throat, and I couldn't seem to get enough air. I tried hard not to think about the disgust I saw on Landon's face. How he must regret ever touching or kissing me.

I still wasn't sure if I was either a monster or a witch. I felt the magic healing my wounds, and I fought the tears that filled my eyes. It didn't matter anymore. My sword felt heavy in my hand, and my tears fell. I was whimpering.

I felt my strength return. I met their disgusted gazes and straightened up. No one tried to approach me. They were all too frightened.

So I did the only thing I could. I spun around and bolted towards the iron gates.

I dashed past the strange tombs and sculpted gods. When I made it to the gates, I heard feet rushing behind me. I didn't turn around. I kept going. I knew I had a few seconds lead, and I wouldn't waste it.

The thought of Rose and of a new life somewhere away from all of this gave me the strength to push on. I wouldn't let them crush my spirit.

To hell with them all. I had the stone.

It was only when I had left Hollowmere and was running across the barren land that I sneaked a peek behind me. The Duke of Romila and his company were close behind me. They were followed by Bartolomeu Dias, with Prince Landon and his group who weren't far behind. The Girmanians had fallen back, and I still couldn't see Mad Jack or his two bodyguards.

I had escaped death twice. I couldn't help but feel empowered. Yes, I was different, but it was a *good* different. I still didn't understand what it all meant, but I'd have time to figure it out. I had a feeling that Rose knew a lot more than she let on. She was the first person I'd interrogate when I got home.

I realized that I'd been running with my sword in my hand, so I sheathed it in my weapons belt. I could run much faster with my hands free. I kicked up sand as I went and didn't slow down.

After what felt like hours of running, I felt a giant cramp in my side, and I had to stop. I wheezed as I caught my breath but continued walking. I had lost my bag in all the confusion. All I had were my weapons and the stone. I could feel it at my waist, pulsing in time with my heart. I had no food or water. My body was used to poor nourishment, but it could not survive without water.

I smelled terrible, and I was sweating like a real peasant. I recognized a weedy field up ahead. It was one of the places we'd made camp on the way, and I headed for it. It had been one of the only areas in Goth with a reasonably sized woodland. I quickened my pace and hiked through the waist-high grass and piles of dry leaves that crunched under my boots. There were woods to my right.

I can lose them there.

My thighs burned with every stride as I plunged into the stand of pine and birch trees. Branches nicked my face and sliced through my skin like the thinnest of knives, but I never broke my stride.

Eventually I began to falter over the fallen trees and underbrush. I was getting tired. Every step became more difficult, and I felt like my legs were made of iron blocks. I was drenched in my own sweat. Finally my cloak got caught between two birch trees, and I was flung backwards. I didn't have the energy or the patience to untangle my cloak, so I ripped it free.

I moved carefully now to avoid slipping on the moss-covered stones. The little light I had was fading into the semi-darkness. The air was surprisingly wet and cool. I shivered uncontrollably as my wet clothes clung to me but gave me no warmth.

But the stone did. It pulsed warmly at my waist. Even through its cage, I could feel its energy, and I was tempted to pick it up to warm my hands. I decided against it at the last minute. Although I was curious, I was still terrified of the stone.

I leapt a rotten log and then climbed up a gentle slope and jogged down the other side. I slowed and sped up again as I made my way in a zigzag motion. I hoped to throw my pursuers off with my crisscrossing. But I had to be careful, if I got too deep into these woods I'd get lost for sure.

At the top of the hill I stopped and glanced back. The Fransians had pushed ahead of the Romilians, but both were catching up to me. The Anglians and their prince had fallen farther back and seemed to be flagging.

I tore down the slope, heading south, and scurried into another cover of woodland. Branches slapped my face, roots tripped me, and thorns scratched my arms and tore holes in my clothes as I ran through the forest

The undergrowth was thicker here, and I had to slow down, but I kept up as good a pace as I could. Another hill rose steeply in front of me and I went up and down again. I ran and ran.

I seemed to get nowhere. It was as if the woods went on forever. The dead trees sprouted around me and the ground beneath my feet grew wetter and swampier. I slapped away mosquitoes that were the size of horseflies, but they bit my neck and forehead anyway. I cursed. I hated bugs. I ran faster but the earth turned soft and muddy beneath my boots, and I stumbled and fell. When I rose again my pants were soaked through and covered in dark green muck that smelled like sewer water.

I stopped to catch my breath and realized it was getting even colder. Night was falling, and soon the forest would be too dark for me to run anymore. A damp chill closed over my skin, and I strained to find my footing. I needed to get out of this swamp.

Then I heard them. My pursuers' voices carried easily though the woodland. I could even hear their footsteps tromping through the brush. They were still behind me, but they were getting too close.

"She went this way…"

"Here…look…footprints turning left…"

"Stay on the path. We'll get her, and then we'll kill the witch and take the stone."

I didn't recognize the voices, and I didn't care. The voices were getting louder, the footsteps closer. I struggled through the wet ground, and when I found harder soil I was able to run faster.

I ran until I was finally too exhausted to take another step. I stumbled through a thick patch of weeds and into a rushing stream.

"Thank the Creator!"

The icy-cold water stung my face and neck as I splashed the glorious water over me. I was waist deep. I washed some of the grime off me, and I drank long and deep. I trudged up and out of the stream on the other side, but my strides were slow and heavy because my wet clothes added unnecessary weight. It hadn't been such a good idea to plunge into the stream, but it was too late now to second-guess myself.

As I stood twisting the water from my cloak, something stung the back of my neck. I reached back and felt a lump.

"That hurt, you little shits—"

I held my breath and went cold with fear. I felt a presence. I went for my sword, but it was already too late.

Something hard hit me in the back on the head, and I pitched headfirst into a tangle of sharp branches. I spit the dirt from my mouth and whirled around.

I recognized what he was even in the darkness. A red monk, an assassin from the temple, stepped out of the shadows of the forest.

CHAPTER 27

HIS BRIGHT RED ROBE stood out like a light in the gloom. I had never seen a red monk before, but I had seen the mutilated bodies they left behind. I'd always wondered why professional assassins would choose to wear such a bright color. His wool gown was tied around the waist with a simple rope, and soft light reflected off the shaven bald spot on the top of his head. Monks called the shaven spot *the blessing* because it symbolized a direct connection with the Creator. If I didn't know better I would have assumed that he was an ordinary monk.

But these monks were such skilled killers that it didn't really matter what color they wore, since no one ever lived to tell. He wore a glove fashioned with the talons of some beast on his right hand. Red monks were the notorious assassins. I'd never heard of anyone surviving after a monk had been unleashed to kill them.

I struggled to my feet and stumbled at the pain that throbbed in my neck. Those bloody horseflies left a nasty large welt.

I looked into the fury of the monk's eyes.

"Why did the high priest send you? I've got the stone. *I* got it. I was on my way to bring it back."

My anger boiled up to the surface. "I haven't told anyone of our arrangement, if that's what you're worried about. Everything is exactly like we agreed."

"It doesn't matter."

I frowned.

"Stop speaking in riddles, monk. Tell me why you're here, and stop dicking around!"

He looked amused. "I can't let you live, being what you are."

"What the hell does that mean?" My voice rose, and I motioned towards the bag tied at my waist.

"I did what he asked. I got him the bloody stone!"

Deep down I had known all along that the high priest wouldn't let me live. I'd been kidding myself. What else had he lied about? My blood froze, and I felt sick. Rose...

The monk looked at the bag around my waist, and I saw a flicker of stifled admiration that disappeared quickly. "Yes. Impressive for a *woman*. You must have been lucky."

"Lucky?" I spat furiously. "It wasn't luck, you prick."

He laughed, and I could feel waves of contempt coming off of him like heat.

"Always so dramatic and emotional, you women are all the same. You are pathetic, weak creatures that need to be tamed and conquered."

I narrowed my eyes. I wanted to kill this bastard.

"It's obvious you know nothing about women. We are certainly *not* weak."

I moved my right hand carefully towards my sword.

The monk's face was blank and emotionless. I saw only contempt in his eyes.

"All women are the property of the temple," he continued like this was a well-known fact. "No matter what their station."

I thought that if Princess Isabella were still alive, she would beg to differ.

"The noble women are not the property of the temple, or have you forgotten the treaty that you signed with the kingdoms. I'm sure the noble women from Espan would have your head if they heard you talk like that."

"Things are changing. Soon, it won't matter if you're wealthy, highborn, or simply from the Pit like you. All women will belong to the temple priests. You'll see."

"See what? You spineless dick."

"Women have always been inferior to men in every way. A woman is nothing more than a handicapped version of a man. You have smaller brains, weaker muscles, and you are submissive and unable to think rationally or logically. You are too emotional and lack the intelligence to rule and govern. You only have two purposes in life: to breed and to bring pleasure to men."

I wanted to cut out his tongue and feed it to him.

"You know nothing about women. And what would *you* know about pleasure? Everyone knows that you monks have been castrated. You are nothing more than ball-less tools of the temple."

I looked at the spot between his legs, and I smiled.

"You're not even a *real* man. And you probably have to force yourself on a woman because let's face it, what woman would have you *naturally*?"

I laughed. "You're a freak. You monks are nothing but the temple's bastards."

His face darkened, and his lips grew taut. He drew a long silver sword. "You'll die for that."

I glowered and pulled out my sword. "We'll see."

The monk charged faster than I had anticipated. I blocked his sword with the broad side of my blade and managed to avoid the sharp edges. I could smell his rancid breath as I leapt back. I parried his next blows and looked for an opening while I tried to stay alive. But I never saw an opening. Every time I struck, he had already moved his sword to counter my attack. It was like he had anticipated my every move before I had even thought of it.

I dodged as the great silver sword came swinging at my head. He struck unnaturally quick, and I barely had time to block and recover. I was tired from the running and from the lack of food, and I felt my strength failing me. My neck burned where I had been bitten, and I could feel the welt growing down to my shoulders and onto my collarbone.

I rotated my blade and parried, then feinted to the left, coming to his right side and striking out hard—but I only hit air. He caught me on my thigh, and I cried out. I spun around and blocked a killing blow that would have decapitated me. I managed to jump clear, and did my best to ignore the throbbing in my thigh.

He hesitated for a moment when he saw the golden light that spilled out through the gash on my thigh.

"Damn you, witch!" he hissed at me. "I'm going to enjoy watching you die."

He dropped his blade and attacked my injured leg. I spun, but he rammed his sword into my gut. I opened my mouth in a silent scream as he pulled away. Blood poured out of my wound for an instant, but then it slowed. Another inch to the left and I'd probably be dead. Although my leg wound had already healed, the wound in my gut needed a little time to seal itself, and I knew I couldn't keep getting wounded like this. I needed to find a way to end it now. My sword was getting heavier and heavier, and I knew I wouldn't be able to wield it at all soon. Witch or not, I wasn't immortal. I was tired.

"I want to see your face as you die, witch," hissed the monk. "I want to be the last thing you see before you meet the Creator."

A dizzy spell came over me, and his face blurred. I shook the white spots from my eyes and thrust my blade into his side.

But my sword faltered and didn't pierce the monk's skin.

"Did you think your miserable weapon could harm me?"

The monk laughed. "You might have some skill with the blade, but you're no match for a red monk, woman. And now you're out of time."

He snarled, and I could see and smell his sharp brown-stained teeth.

In a flash of red, and before I could react, the monk surged towards me again, thrashing wildly. I could only bound back and deflect his blow with my sword. He was a blur. How could a natural man move so fast? It was impossible. There was no way a normal man could move that way. It was almost as though he was magic.

The world around me became foggy. I threw out my arms to steady myself, but the ground wavered at my feet.

"Told you I would kill you," laughed the monk.

Pain from my neck and collarbone seared through me.

"What—what is this?" I felt the numbness from the bite on my neck spill down my arms and legs. I had to strain to keep my sword in my hands.

"You will die eventually," said the monk, and he curled the talons of his gloved hand.

"The poison is already working through you."

I realized with horror that I hadn't been bitten by a giant horsefly but rather stung by his clawed glove. I reached up and touched the back of my neck.

"Poison doesn't kill me."

He smiled wickedly. "This is no ordinary poison."

I couldn't keep this up. He would kill me eventually.

"I'll make you a deal," I said, trying not to sound desperate.

The monk laughed. "I don't make deals."

I shook my head, trying to clear the blurry vision.

My voice trembled, "I'll disappear. The high priest will never know you didn't kill me."

"But I will kill you," the monk smiled darkly. "Like I said, I don't make deals."

He made to move towards me, and I stepped back.

"I'll give you the stone," I blurted.

He stopped and studied me for a second.

"That's right," I said, and I dropped my sword to my feet.

"I'll give you the stone, all right. I'll give it to you."

I unfastened the bag at my belt and pulled out the golden cage. I popped open the lid and slipped the stone into my hand. It was hot.

"Here, take it. That's what you came for, isn't? Take it, and I'll go. The high priest will think you've killed me. I'll disappear, and you'll never see or hear from me again."

He hesitated. The temptation to possess the stone consumed him. I could feel the stone's pull reaching out to the monk.

"Yes," he said, nodding strangely. "The stone is mine. It has always been mine. I can feel its power."

Suddenly, his smile disappeared.

"Give it to me," he ordered.

"Catch." I tossed him the stone and took several steps back.

The monk caught the stone easily. He dropped his sword and held the stone in the air, staring at it lovingly, adoringly.

"It's mine. The stone is mine! It's—"

But he didn't finish his sentence. He glowed bright yellow and then shattered like glass.

This time I'd been far enough away not to get hit with bits of him. I reached into the liquid mess that had once been a monk and picked up the stone.

After I'd rubbed it clean with my cloak, I slipped it back into its cage and secured it in my pouch. I was relieved to feel its warm pulse against my skin.

The others would still be coming for me, and I had wasted precious time battling the monk, but I staggered and nearly fell as I tried to start running again. I knew the effects of whatever poison he'd used would eventually wear off, but it was hard to concentrate.

When the masked man had poisoned me I had recovered, but somehow I knew this poison was *different*.

My vision blurred, and I saw images of men and women dying, creatures eating children, oceans of blood, maggots, darkness, and the dead rising. I was cold and hot all at once. I fell to my knees and vomited a black liquid that wasn't blood. *What was happening to me?*

Cold seeped through my skin, and my mouth tasted as bitter as raw onion. My tears felt like hot iron on my face, and my pulse roared in my ears. I watched in horror as some kind of black ink spread under my skin and filled my veins. My arms and hands were covered in thick black threads. *What kind of poison could do this?*

The nausea hit me again and I vomited. I tried to stand, but the ground shifted. The trees zoomed past me, and I felt like I was running around, but I wasn't. I closed my eyes in an attempt to keep the dizziness at bay, and I fought off another wave of nausea.

I heard the sound of leaves and branches crunching under the weight of feet. I heard the rustling of the brush and then muffled voices. They seemed to be coming from all around me. I kept my eyes closed and focused on the noises. They were getting louder and louder. My heart pounded in my ears. Was another red monk coming to finish the job? Or was one of my competitors out to kill me?

"Elena?"

I opened my eyes and nearly cried out in relief.

Prince Landon stood over me, watching me as if he hadn't expected to find me. I could barely make out the faces of the five men standing behind him. He stared at the mess of blood and the chunks of flesh on the ground beside me.

When his gaze returned to me, I couldn't understand the look in his eyes.

"L-Landon ..." I breathed.

I retched again and a thick liquid dribbled down the sides of my mouth.

"I'm sick. Help me. I think I'm dying." I was crying now.

I wanted to fall into his arms and let him make everything all right again. I opened my mouth to speak, but I was hit with another violent fit of nausea. I fell forward on my hands and puked.

"We thought we'd lost you."

I was so happy to hear Landon's voice so close.

"We've been tracking you for hours. We thought we'd lost you for good, until we saw the light."

I wanted to ask what light, but another sick feeling rushed through me so powerfully that my muscles slackened like I was made of water. I had no strength. I swayed to the side, my arms shook, and I knew I couldn't hold myself up for much longer.

I raised my head, and with some effort I reached out to him with my right hand.

"Landon."

He moved towards me with his hands outstretched.

I wanted to feel his warmth again. I was so cold. I wanted him to hold me, to take me to his healers and mend me. I closed my eyes and willed myself to feel better.

But I never felt his hands wrap around me. I never felt the warmth of his body against mine. He didn't take my hand.

I gave a little gasp as the prince untied the pouch at my waist and took it away with the stone inside it. He dropped the small pouch into a larger leather one and clasped it securely around his baldric.

I was too horrified and too hurt to speak. I struggled with words that wouldn't come.

Finally, I said, "Landon … what are you doing … please … help me…"

He looked at me. *Was it pity in his eyes?*

"I'm sorry, Elena," he said without emotion. "But this is more important than you can ever understand. The high priests promised to give me back my title and my lands if I brought them the stone. Think about all the good I can do. I can rebuild the Pit and remove the caste system. I'll even put a stop to the concubines. Think of that. Our people, yes Elena, *our* people will heal. I have to do what's best for my kingdom. I hope you can understand that. You would have done the same thing."

I opened and closed my mouth. I couldn't speak.

Trembling with heartache, I finally managed to mumble through my tears and spit, "Landon, I don't care about the stone. Just find me a healer."

But there was no kindness in his eyes anymore. I wasn't sure there ever had been. He looked as cold and bitter as a harsh wind.

"I wish things could have been different between us. I'm sorry."

He turned on his heel and left.

The world went spiraling out of control. My heart had been shattered by a man whom I'd come to care about. The last of my strength gave way, and I fell face down into my own vomit.

I sobbed. "Landon?"

I cried, reaching out to him, heaving my body across the ground with my hands. But he didn't come back. He had chosen the stone, and he had chosen to let me die. I thought we'd shared a connection, but I was wrong.

I watched through my tears as he disappeared into the tangled woods. My hand fell lifeless to the ground, and I felt my heartbeat slowing down until I couldn't hear it anymore. Maybe I should die. Maybe I deserved it.

When the darkness finally came, I let it take me.

CHAPTER 28

THE VOICES CAME ALL at once, muffled, like they were far away, like in a dream. They shifted and changed, growing louder. They were shouting. I tried to tell the voices in my dream to go away, to let me go with the darkness, but my voice wouldn't come. The darkness lifted, and the voices neared.

"Don't touch her! She's a witch. She'll hex you," said a man's voice.

"You heard what the others said. She's a magic bearer. That can only mean she's a witch."

"If you touch her you'll be cursed forever," said another man, and I heard someone spit.

"I'm telling you, you'll be under her spell like a slave. You'll be the slave of hell. Everyone knows witches are the Devil's whores. She'll probably curse our families too. Is that what you want? Is it?"

"Damn it, Jon," said the other voice again. "Just leave her. She's probably dead anyway. Look at her."

"She's not dead," roared a different voice with authority.

I felt something brush my neck and then press on my skin.

"There's a pulse," the man called Jon sighed in relief. "She's alive."

I don't know why, but I wanted to tell him to let me die. If I couldn't heal myself from the red monk's poison, he wouldn't be able to help me anyway.

"Even if you take her, she'll never make it back in time. She's too far gone."

"Yeah, she looks like a corpse. Leave her."

"Shut up! The both of you," growled the dominant voice. "Or so help me God, I'll kill the both of you!"

Something hard and strong wrapped around me, and the next thing I knew I was floating. I remembered having dreams where I could fly, and my feet didn't touch the ground. This was similar. The musky smell of a man's perspiration filled my nose. I didn't remember ever being able to smell in any dream. Maybe I wasn't dreaming. I was warm and so sleepy. The man's fingers were hard with calluses and fearsomely strong. A wave of nausea hit me, and once again I went tumbling down into the darkness.

I woke to the sounds of angry voices again. I was still floating. When I felt the searing pain of my skin rubbing against the man's shirt, I knew I wasn't dreaming. I trembled violently as a wave of cold fever rushed through my limbs, and I burned with cold.

I felt the man's arms squeeze me in response to my trembling. As my head lolled back, my eyes snapped open. Blurred shapes passed me by, tall shadowed figures, as giant as the mountains. Trees, I figured. But as my eyes adjusted, the trees appeared to have faces, gruesome faces with large, bulbous eyes and fangs. *How can trees have faces?* I felt like I'd seen these trees with faces before, but where? I felt a jerk, and my head fell forward.

The shapes were moving faster now. My lids were like iron, and I couldn't keep them open. It didn't matter. Nothing I saw made any sense. I was confusing my dream with reality, or I was going insane? Maybe a little bit of both.

"That's as far as we'll go," I heard a voice say. "I hope you know what you're doing."

There was a rush of wind on my face, and I was moving faster now. I was moving in a constant up and down motion, and for a second I thought that I was riding Torak again. I thought I heard a loud neighing, but that was impossible. All the horses had left.

I felt a sudden rush of sick, and I vomited all over myself. I didn't have the strength to lift up my head, so I let it loll to the side. Just the smell of the putrid, black liquid almost made me sick all over again. I was thankful when I drifted back into unconsciousness.

I knew I wasn't dead when I woke with a giant pulsing migraine that throbbed through my bones. I couldn't remember any dreams, only a cold, dark, and endless sleep that pulled me down so deep that I felt as though I would never wake.

Something warm washed over me and soothed my headache. I pried my eyes open through my thickly crusted eyelids and blinked in the bright light. I was in a bedroom. I lay in a soft, comfortable bed with white linen sheets and a thick quilt. The walls were paneled with pine and gave off a glorious smell of woodland. I could also smell a faint scent of lavender. When I realized that I was the source of the smell I stiffened.

Someone had bathed me. Where was I, and how did I get here?

I heard something sniff, and without turning my head or moving I rolled my eyes towards the sound.

Mad Jack sat in a wooden chair. His cheeks were wet with tears, and his eyes were rimmed with redness. He was alive. I hadn't realized how relieved I would be to see him and how much he meant to me until that very moment. I almost started crying myself at the sight of his pain. I felt flushed and rolled away. I felt I was intruding on a private movement. I knew he wouldn't want me to see him cry.

But why was he crying? And what was he doing here? What was I doing here? Where the hell was I?

I waited for a moment, and when I figured I'd given him enough time I made a sudden moan and moved a little.

Mad Jack jumped to his feet, and I heard the crash of a chair hitting the floor. I felt a sudden weight on the mattress as he sat next to me.

"Elena?"

I opened my eyes again, more easily this time, and stared up at him.

His dark eyes were rimmed with red, but his tears had disappeared. He moved to take my hand but withdrew at the last second, as though he thought better of it.

"What happened?" My voice was dry. "How did I get here? Where are we?"

I realized that I was naked except for a thin white shift. I flushed at the thought of someone scrubbing the grime from my body.

He let out a shaky breath, and his smile sent a thrill through me. His clothes looked freshly washed, and he had shaved. His golden skin seemed to glow in the light, and standing there he looked even more beautiful than I'd remembered.

"We're in Gray Havens."

I pulled myself to a sitting position.

"What? The witches' village? Are you mad?"

I looked around the room expecting to see human skulls, sacrificial objects, toads, and a large boiling cauldron with children inside. But the room was spotless with a single white painted dresser and a vase full of fresh blue and yellow irises, daffodils, and purple coneflowers. It looked more like a noble's cottage than a witch's hut. But then again, I'd never seen where the witches lived or been inside one of their homes.

"But why would you bring me *here*? Whatever gave you that idea?"

Mad Jack's smile sent my heart racing again. I could see he was still struggling with whether or not to take my hand. He didn't.

"Because," he said, his voice low, "you have magic. So, I figured that you must be a witch, too. And who better to help cure a witch than witches."

I was surprised. "But you *hate* witches?"

His cheeks flushed a deep red, and I didn't understand why. He shifted uncomfortably, and he wouldn't look me in the eyes.

"I saw how you looked at me when I had taken the stone. I saw something dark in your eyes. I saw it. And still you brought me here?"

"Jon did the right thing by bringing you here," said a woman's voice.

I peered over Mad Jack's shoulder. A stout woman with a serious face and kind eyes stood at the bedroom doorway. She wore a shapeless dress of simple green linen. Her face was lined with age, and yet it was still beautiful. Her skin was like porcelain, fair, but not fragile, and her dark eyes stood out against her fair skin. Her white hair was piled neatly in a bun on the top of her head. She leaned carefully on a wooden staff that was carved with faces of different animals. A long chain hung from her neck with a pendant in the shape of a star within a circle.

I was staring at a witch, a real witch, and she looked like a normal elderly woman. She was not green and covered with warts and leathery skin, and her teeth were not filed down into pointy needles. She looked like a regular person.

Surprisingly I wasn't afraid, or even embarrassed that they had bathed me. Instead I felt a calmness, and for the first time in my life I felt safe.

"I'm Ada," said the old witch. Her deep green eyes looked as if they were filled with wisdom.

"I'm the high witch in Gray Havens, and you are most welcome here, Elena."

"Thank you, Ada. And I'm guessing I should thank you, too, for saving my life."

Ada shook her head.

"Jon saved your life. You would have died if he hadn't brought you here when he did."

I stared at the strange woman. There was that name again. I didn't know anyone named Jon, and yet I remembered someone named Jon in my dream.

"I thought Mad Jack brought me here? Who's Jon?"

"I am," said Mad Jack.

There was a hint of sadness in his voice that nearly brought me to tears. My cheeks flushed, and I released a tense breath. I looked at him, really looked at him, and it was as though I saw his face for the very first time. How selfish I'd been never to have asked this man's name. This beautiful creature had saved my life when everyone else had left me to die.

When even the regal Prince Landon chose to let me die, the street lord chose to save me.

"Jon," I said, feeling his real name on my lips for the first time, testing it.

"Thank you for saving my life, Jon. I'm…I'm sorry I never bothered to ask your name, your real name. I was so horrible to you," I whispered.

My voice shook, "I can't believe the things I said."

At the mention of his real name, he flashed me the most dazzling smile I'd ever seen, more beautiful than all the precious stones in the high priests' vault.

Jon looked at the high witch at the foot of my bed and then back to me. I saw that he struggled with something internally, almost as if he'd have preferred to have kept this conversation private.

He brushed away my tears, and I stayed as still as I could. His fingers were warm and gentle. And then he took my hand, squeezed it gently as he brought it to his lips, and kissed my fingers.

My heart pumped in my ears, and I felt my face burn. Mad Jack, or rather Jon, had never ever kissed me, not even on the cheek, and all kinds of emotions welled inside me at the same time. This wasn't a flirty kiss or a sensual one, it was a kiss that signified unconditional love, kindness, and forgiveness.

I'd been such a fool.

I wanted to reach out and grab his face and kiss him until I ran out of breath. But we were not alone, and although I was only too aware of the woman's watchful stare, I sensed that she wanted us to share this moment together.

"Don't worry about it," he said, finally, "it's not like I told you my real name either. I couldn't ... well not at first. I was born Jonathan Worchester. Mad Jack is just a cover I use in the Pit. I was known as Mad Jack, and I just went along with it for so long that I *became* him and sort of lost myself in the process."

"Cover for what exactly?" I felt the old woman's eyes on me as I waited for his answer.

Jon straightened. "The rebellion."

I didn't care to hide my surprise. "There's a rebellion?"

"Yes. And it's been in planning for years."

"I'm head of the Pit division. We needed to infiltrate the empire and where better than from the Pit. It was the perfect location to get the information we needed. We were close enough to Soul City to study them and to make plans to overthrow their empire. Where our forefathers failed, we believe we can win."

"The stone complicates things," he continued. "But I'm still hopeful we can overthrow them."

The strength in his face was achingly beautiful.

"So that's how you knew Prince Landon and the other nobles," I said, putting the pieces together. "This is part of what you couldn't tell me before."

"That's right. We've been secretly meeting for years, carefully planning our coup."

Jon sighed, and I was tempted to reach up and touch his face but didn't.

The thought of being part of a rebellion sent a jolt of excitement through me.

"I want to join." I straightened up. "I want to join the rebellion. I could be useful. My skills and abilities could be a real asset for you. I want to join." I repeated with more conviction.

Jon flashed his perfect teeth. "Usually there's a trial period and a thorough investigation of anyone who wants to join. You know, we can't be too careful. But I'd say you've proven yourself worthy. In your own way, you've always been part of the rebellion."

I was grinning from ear to ear. "Thank—"

Suddenly there was a bustle outside the bedroom door, and three teenaged girls rushed into the room. They all wore the same shapeless white linen dresses as the older woman, but theirs were plain and without embellishment. The tallest one had skin the color of coffee and sparkling hazelnut eyes. The other two had fairer skin — one had dark hair piled high her head, while the other had a long light blonde braid that brushed the middle of her back. They stood together like they had been joined at the waist.

Their eyes widened at the sight of me, but they blushed deeply when they looked at Jon. I didn't blame them; he was very handsome. The blonde caught my eye and I winked at her. She giggled nervously.

Ada looked slightly annoyed at the girls. Her grip tightened on her staff.

"What is it, girls?"

The three girls straightened, and the tall girl took a step forward.

"We've finished washing and mending her clothes, high witch," she said. Her voice was soft, but I could tell she was the bravest of the bunch.

The high witch hit her staff on the dressing table, and I flinched.

"Put them here, Sasha," she ordered. Her voice was stern, and even though she was small I knew she was someone you *never* crossed.

The three girls stared at Jon self-consciously, like they'd never seen a man before, particularly a beautiful one. But when I moved my gaze over to him, I could see that he was oblivious to the girls' gawking stares because he was staring at me.

The high witch hit her staff on the floor.

"Get back to your duties, girls. Off you go, and no mooning around in the corridors."

As Sasha put my clothes on the dresser, our eyes met and a smile played on her face. But it quickly disappeared when she whirled around, grabbed the two other girls by the hands, and rushed out the room, giggling furiously.

I peered out the window in my room. Judging by the position of the sun, it was about midday. My smile faltered a little.

"How long have I been out?"

"Eight days."

"What? That long? But I thought it was only yesterday that I …"

I remembered coming in and out of a heavy darkness, but it felt only like yesterday when I fought off the monk. What had happened?

"We only just arrived here in Gray Havens last night," said Jon. "I thought…I thought I'd lost you. You were cold and gray, really sickly looking."

He paused, and his eyes were full of pain. "Elena, you looked dead. The high witch saved you."

"No, Jon," said Ada kindly, "It was *you* who saved her. Your quick thinking brought Elena to us. She would never have made it if it weren't for you."

My eyes stung, and I felt ill. I recalled the horrid, putrid smell of my black vomit, and I swallowed the bile in my throat.

"You were very, very sick, but also very lucky," continued the old woman. She raised her brows high on her forehead, and she immediately reminded me of Rose.

My gaze shifted to Jon.

"I thought you were dead too, you know. I thought I'd lost you outside the temple. What happened to you?"

Jon scratched the back of his head. "Princess Isabelle happened, that's what. She and her guard attacked us from behind, and I blacked out. The next thing I remember was that I woke up at the bottom of the stone stairs with a giant bump on the back of my head. Will and Leo were both alive beside me, and everyone else was gone. All we saw were bodies."

"Where are Will and Leo now?"

Jon laughed. "Camped outside the woodland barrier. They wouldn't take one step into Gray Havens."

He shook his head, smiling. "Stupid bastards."

I rolled my eyes. "Stupid indeed. But why I am not surprised."

Will had spit on the witches' lands, and I wasn't so sure it would have been a good idea for him to come anyway. Looking at Ada's stern face, I wasn't entirely sure she'd have allowed it.

Jon smiled. "Well, they won't come in. But they have been drinking our hostesses' fine wine and eating their food, and a lot of it."

I raised my eyebrows at this. "Typical, of course they would."

I thought it very generous of the witches to feed such superstitious idiots. As I shook my head, I felt a tug at the base of my neck. I reached up with my other hand and felt a few stitches in the back of my neck.

"I was stitched?" I looked at Ada, but saw nothing on her face.

"We removed most of the poison," said the witch, "but I'm afraid we couldn't get all of it. You will carry some of it in you for the rest of your life. If you had come to us earlier, we would have gotten it all. But we did get most of it."

"I have healed wounds far more damaging than this. Why didn't my healing abilities mend me? Why couldn't I heal? What kind of poison was it?"

"Not the typical kind, I'm afraid." A shadow passed over her face, and she seemed to age.

"You couldn't heal yourself, and your wound will *never* truly heal. You were poisoned with *black magic.*"

Jon flashed a nervous look my way, but I kept my eyes on Ada. "And whoever did this to you knew exactly what they were doing. They knew what to use to kill someone *like* you."

"It was a red monk," I blurted. "One of the high priests sent him to kill me. He wore a glove with talons for fingers. He must have poisoned me with it. But how could a monk use black magic? It doesn't make sense. It goes against everything they believe."

A glimmer of indignation flashed across Ada's face, but she didn't answer.

"Am I a witch?" I asked.

I couldn't help myself. I'd been dying to ask her the question since the moment I'd laid eyes on her. "Like you and the other girls?"

Ada leaned forward and rested both hands on her staff. "Yes and no."

"What does that mean?" asked Jon.

I sensed a little unease in his voice. "You told me she *has* magic."

"She does have magic," answered the old woman.

She turned her gaze back to me. "Just a *different* kind of magic. Magic comes in many forms and has many variations. It's as ancient as the world and is contained in everything around us. Magic is mysterious. And while there is white magic and black magic, magic itself is neither good nor bad. Magic is magic. The only difference between the good and the bad is in how the bearer uses their power."

I felt my confidence slip away from me a little bit.

"So what am I, if I'm not a witch?"

Ada's eyes gleamed with an intensity that almost made me look away, but I didn't.

"You're a steel maiden."

CHAPTER 29

My FIRST THOUGHT WAS to look at Jon, but from the puzzled look on his face it was clear he'd never heard of a steel maiden either.

"What's a steel maiden?" I asked for the both of us.

The old witch looked at me with a smile. "Are you exceptionally good with weapons? Are you particularly adept with swords, or daggers, or anything with a blade?"

"Yes."

"Have you ever wondered where this extraordinary ability comes from?"

"It might have crossed my mind a few times."

Ada smiled. She seemed anxious to reveal more to me.

"Steel maidens are magic bearers. And if you define persons with magic as witches, then yes, steel maidens are also witches. You are descended from the Steel Maiden clan from northern Witchdom. There are six different witch clans in Arcania and Witchdom, and we administer all of them from here. They are the

White and Dark Witch clans, the Augurs, the Elementals, the Shifters, and finally the Steel Maiden clan. I'm from the White Witches clan. Each clan serves a specific purpose, but we are all blood witches."

"What are blood witches?" I was curious and hungry for more information.

"A blood witch is someone who is born with magic. The steel maidens cannot do magic like the dark witches, for example. They cannot conjure objects out of thin air, cannot hex, or curse, and they cannot wield magic like the other witches. Steel maidens are unique. They were the only clan of witches that did not produce any male heirs. Only a *female* witch could be a steel maiden." I had no idea witches could be male, but I decided not to interrupt her. "They are strong," Ada went on, "and have an innate ability to fight and to wield any kind of weapon. Their extraordinary healing abilities mean that nothing can beat them. They are a force to be reckoned with.

"Witches have been at war with the world of men for thousands of years. Men fight with us because they fear what they don't understand. More importantly, we have been fighting because men always wanted more: more land, more power, more of everything. Unfortunately magic cannot defeat steel, not always. And when magic couldn't save the witches, the steel maidens evolved. They began as a fierce group of blood witches that could fight better than any man, could manipulate any type of weapon, and had the unique ability to heal. They became the guardians of all the clans. For centuries the steel maidens kept the race of man at bay.

"But magic comes at a cost, as you have already learned. You cannot use magic indefinitely. If you take something from the Goddess, you must give something back. The magic of the witches was finally exhausted by war with men, and most of us were driven out of Arcania. Some of us, like me, chose to stay to provide refuge to those who were still born with magic in a land that hated it. Soon Witchdom was divided between what is now Arcania, where a few of us remain, and what's left of Witchdom on the other side of the Mystic Mountains where most of the witches reside today. The clan of the steel maidens thinned over time, and they simply disappeared."

"Until Elena," said Jon.

Ada shook her head. "Until Elena's *mother* came to us."

I nearly fell off my bed. "What? My mother?" My heart sped in my chest. "You knew my mother?"

The light in the high witch's face faded.

"I did, yes, many years ago. Your mother, Katherine, lived here with us before you were born. She was a valuable member of this clan, even though she was a steel maiden."

"You are the spitting image of your mother," said she with an added smile. "I knew who you were the minute Jon carried you through the front doors."

"So why did she leave?" I was dying to hear anything that had to do with my mother. I only still had vague memories of her, and it pained me to admit that sometimes I forgot what her face looked like.

A small frown appeared on Ada's forehead, and I noticed the slight hesitation before she opened her mouth. "For love. Your mother's stay with us was very short-lived. She stayed only a few weeks, until she fell in love with a young man and left with him. She never came back, but we kept in touch."

She looked at me again. A shadow on her face made her lines appear deeper.

"I was very sorry to hear of her death," she said and blinked away a tear. "She was a beloved member here." Ada closed her eyes, and I could see the pain in them when she opened them again.

Then her face darkened. "She didn't deserve to die in the hands of that man, that *priest.*"

"You mean at the hands of that bastard," I spat.

My cheeks burned with anger, my lips trembled, and I couldn't continue. I felt Jon's reassurance as he squeezed my hand, and I squeezed it back.

"There's a lot you still don't know about your heritage, Elena," continued Ada. "About your blood magic and what you can do."

The old woman sighed. "You are the last of the steel maidens. I wish you could stay here and learn more, but there's no time."

She had clearly left many words unsaid.

"Where's the stone, Elena?" asked Jon. I suspected Ada had wanted to ask me the same thing. I also had the impression that she knew more than we did about the stone.

Jon leaned closer to me, his face was pale, his eyes haunted. "It wasn't on you when I found you."

I clenched my teeth down hard. "Prince Landon has it," I hissed. "The bastard took it from me while I lay there dying like an animal. He said it was for the good of the realm and some horseshit like that."

I kept my face as blank and as pain free as I could, even though Landon's betrayal still hurt. Just the thought of him threatened to release my tears. It hurt to have cared so much for someone who cared nothing in return.

"He said that the priests offered to return his land and his title as king of Anglia if he brought them the stone."

"Stupid prick!" Jon let go of my hand and raked his fingers through his hair. "How stupid can a prince be? They'll never give him back his throne and title. They'll never give it back."

"Of course not," I answered. "But he seems to believe they will. Those monsters have been lying to us for years, abusing us, raping us, and still he chose to believe them. All he cares about is getting his title back. He doesn't care about the rest of us."

"Damn it. We underestimated the priests. Somehow they got to the prince. If he's been in league with them this whole time, then none of us are safe. The entire rebellion is in danger."

"None of it will matter if the high priests get the stone," Ada breathed.

She gripped her staff until her knuckles were white. "There will be no more lands, no more wealth, no more rebellion, no more of anything. If the priests get the stone, there will be only darkness."

Her eyes rested on mine, her expression hard. "Elena, what did the high priest give you to contain the stone?"

I shrugged. "Some sort of gold cage. Why?"

The old woman just clamped her mouth shut and stared into space. I searched her face. It was unreadable again, but her eyes were focused and full of energy.

"What is it? What are you not telling us?"

"The high priests are not what they seem," said Ada. "There is something unnatural and evil about them."

"Like what?"

Her eyes bore into mine. "Elena, did you ever wonder *why* the high priest sent you on the Great Race? Why would they send an untrained woman on such a deadly mission?"

I nodded, my eyes narrowing. "Because he knew what I was."

I remembered the sick triumph I had seen in his eyes when I had been captured with the crown I had stolen. It made my stomach churn just to think about it.

"He knew the moment his guards brought me to him. He knew I would be able to touch the stone."

"Exactly." Ada shuffled towards the small window and peered outside.

"Steel maidens were famously immune to different types of magic, especially to druid spells and magic stones."

She turned around and our eyes met. "It was no wonder that they made you their champion. You were the only one who could bring it back."

I had always known that I was just a pawn in the high priest's game. But I had never done it for them or for myself.

"He threatened to kill Rose and all of the inhabitants in the Pit if I didn't get him the stone. She's been a mother to me, but she's a powerless old woman. It wouldn't take much to kill her…"

"I told you Rose would be looked after," said Jon. "My people are guarding her."

My blood raced, and I took a deep breath to try to calm myself.

"I know, but I have a bad feeling. If anything were to happen to her, I would never forgive myself. I left her. I left her all alone."

"She'll be fine. I promise," Jon said.

I felt a sudden urgency to go after Rose. Maybe I could bring her back here, to Gray Havens. She would be safe here with the witches, away from the clutches of the priests.

I met Jon's eyes.

"He also said that he would kill all the children in the Pit, the entire village if I didn't get him the stone."

Jon swore, and even Ada looked like she was about to curse something.

"It was the only reason why I joined this stupid race in the first place. I was forced to do it. And it was all for nothing. He's going to kill them, I know he will."

"I won't let that happen. I promise."

"The Empire of the Temple of the Sun will never give back the prince's title or any other titles for that matter," informed the old witch. "The high priests desire power above all else. They want the power the stone can give them."

Although I had felt the power of the stone when I had first held it, I had known, even then, that I had only glimpsed its true power.

Jon stood up and paced around the room. He turned and looked at Ada. "But I thought only Elena could touch the stone. How can the priests manipulate it?"

I nodded. Jon had taken the words from my mouth.

"They cannot touch the stone," said Ada. "Otherwise they would have taken it centuries ago. No, it's something else, but I'm afraid I don't know what. All I can assume is that they have discovered a way to use it. They wouldn't have bothered trying to find a steel maiden unless they knew they could control it."

"Yes," she nodded. "They must have discovered a way. We have our suspicions that the high priests are not what they appear to be. I felt it in the earth and in the waters of the world when the high priests first appeared. Something dark came along with them."

I sat up straighter. I felt a sting where my stitches pulled, but I wasn't sure it was from the stitches themselves so much as the poison that still lingered there.

"What do you mean? What came along with them?"

Ada let out a breath. "The world changed with the arrival of those priests and their Temple of the Sun nonsense. From the moment they arrived three hundred years ago, I felt a shift in the balance of light and dark, of good and evil. Someone or something is trying to call forth demons from the underworld. Something wants to destroy the world as we know it. Not even the most powerful of witches or the most powerful dark sorcerers can conjure creatures from hell and control them unless they can wield the terrible magic that resides in the stone."

I tried to sit up straighter, but I kept sliding off my pillows.

"Why is this stone so special and dangerous? What *is* the Heart of Arcania?"

"In truth, we don't know for sure," answered Ada. "A weapon, maybe? The stone is a magical relic. We know that its power is derived from the world's own magic, and that the stone stores that magic until it can be released. The stone is connected to our world. We don't know who created the stones, only that they existed before the time of witches and men."

"The *stones?*" Jon furrowed his brows. "There's more than one?"

Ada looked tired.

"Three. But the other two were nowhere near as powerful as this one, and they were destroyed long ago. But we couldn't destroy the Heart of Arcania. The witch clans decided to keep it secret and safe. It was meant to be safe on Goth, where it was protected by a secret society of men called the Order of the Stones. They swore to protect the stone with their lives."

Jon and I shared a look. "The masked men in Hollowmere."

Shame burned on my cheeks.

"They were protecting the stone...and *we* killed them."

Ada looked at us gravely.

"The stones were meant to be secret. Magic is magic. It can be used for good or evil. I don't believe that the stones were ever meant to be wielded by anyone alive today. Their power comes from a world long forgotten in this land. It is a power that we should never have discovered all those years ago."

Her eyes looked wild.

"You must stop it. Forget your friends, your lovers, forget everything. There is nothing more important in this world than to get the stone away from the priests before it is too late. Before they damn us all."

"If I hadn't stolen the Anglian crown, none of this would be happening," I said softly.

I could feel Ada's eyes on me, but I stared at the sheets instead. The long silence was enough of an answer. I couldn't just sit here pitying myself. I had to make things right again.

Jon cleared his throat. "There's no point in blaming yourself, Elena. You didn't know. None of us did."

"What's done is done." Ada moved to the foot of the bed.

"Never mind that now," she said and pointed her staff at me. "First we need to get you well enough to travel. Preferably tomorrow, if you can."

I leaned back against the headboard, nodding. "I will. I'll get it back."

She moved closer to me and spoke with a fierceness that made me cower a little.

"Elena, you *must* stop the stone from getting into the hands of the high priest. Do you understand?"

She slammed her staff on the floor, and her voice rose. "The world as you know it will burn if you fail."

CHAPTER 30

I LAY IN BED for about an hour after Ada and Jon had left me to recover and rest. But I couldn't rest. I was haunted by the idea that *I* had damned the world with my own stupidity. I'd always known that the high priests were evil, but hearing it from the witch's mouth just made everything clearer. The high priests were planning to destroy the world, and I had helped them.

They wanted to use the stone to summon some great army of demons to destroy us all. I had only once run across demons, those that had sprung from the mist at the edge of Death's Arm, and I never wanted to face them again. I didn't know how Jon had made it unscathed all the way to Gray Havens with me in his arms. I would have to ask him about that later.

Ada had mentioned that the high priests were unnatural. *What did that mean? Were they men or not? Were they men with corrupted souls?*

I already knew the answer to that, but what if they weren't men at all, but something more sinister and evil? I had a feeling the old witch was keeping information from me, and I was going to find out what.

In the meantime, I was haunted with images of death. Death. Death, and more death. Ada's words haunted me — a burning world, dying children, Rose...

I had to get the stone back before Landon reached Soul City. I needed to leave now.

If my calculations were correct, I'd been here about half a day. That meant he was one day ahead of us. If we left while there was still light today, we might even catch up to him tomorrow or the day after. My memories of Landon made my stomach muscles tighten until they hurt. I had been such a fool to fall for his bright eyes and winning smile.

I swung my legs off the bed and moved to the dresser. I was dressed in a matter of two minutes. The young witches had done a remarkable job on my tunic and cloak. Only an expert eye could see where they had stitched it back together nearly seamlessly. Apart from the pain of the red monk's poison on the back of my neck, I felt fine. More than fine. I was ready.

I smelled food and found a platter with bread, cheese, grapes, apples, cold meats, and a pitcher of water. I didn't realize how ravenous I had been until the only evidence of the food was crumbs on the silver platter. I washed everything down with a cold glass of water.

I pulled open the bedroom door and peered down a hallway that resembled the bedroom with pine wood paneling, wood floors, and wood trim. It smelled curiously like a forest, and it was like stepping into a woodland tunnel. I made my way down the corridor and had passed a number of closed doors when I came to a landing.

My breath caught in my throat.

I stood on the second floor of a grand mezzanine. A massive fireplace centerpiece rose at least fifty feet from the bottom floor to a roof of soaring log rafters. Wooden moldings and wildlife were carved into the red cedar logs. I leaned over a wooden railing that had been carved with leaves, bears, wolves, and birds, and I peered out at another four wings that fanned out from the rotunda. I saw a dining room and another large room that might have been used for ceremonies. The whole place felt like a castle with its massive size and grandiose ornaments, but it was built with logs instead of stone. I had never seen anything like it before, and I beamed at its beauty.

I could see through the windows that this enormous structure sat in a forested wildlife sanctuary and on the shore of a sparkling lake. It was a secluded paradise. It's no wonder the witches wanted to live here. It was a spectacular setting. Rose would love it here.

Energy rippled through the building, the wood beams, the floor, and even in the air. The light in the room pulsed with it, and my skin tingled. I couldn't see it, but I felt it course through me, too. It was magic. And for the first time in my life I felt like I had come home.

Women of every shape, size, and ethnicity moved about the building, busying themselves with chores, carrying books and potted plants, even a few cats, but mostly just walking and chatting amongst themselves. They all wore the same shapeless linen gowns that Ada and the other girls wore, but their colors were different.

Some were dark green, and others were brown or red. The girls all wore white. Maybe you had to graduate to earn a colored robe.

I moved closer to a window where a group of girls were staring at something outside. The girls stiffened at the sight of me, bowed their heads, and hurried off. I was a little put off. I would have liked to have spoken with them, to see how they liked living here.

But when I moved to the window, I forgot all about that. Down by the lake, Jon was sprawled on the lawn with his head resting on his arms. Even from here, I could see his tanned skin and his open shirt ruffling in the wind. It was obvious that the women and the girls here didn't get a lot of male visitors.

I couldn't help but smile as I made my way down the stairs. I received a few nods and bobs from the witches I passed, with lots of *good afternoons,* and *Miss Elenas.* Their good humor was contagious, and I was smiling so much my cheeks hurt by the time I made it downstairs. I wondered about what magic they could do. Was it learned? Could they do magic just by wishing it?

I'd never been this relaxed before, and I didn't know what to do with myself. I felt better when I pushed open the two grand doors and crossed the plush lawn to find Jon.

He turned at the sound of my approach, and his face beamed. He jumped up gracefully, and it was hard not to stare at his chest. His face was even more beautiful in the sunlight. And when he came closer and smiled, my legs were like water.

"Up already?" he said.

I looked over to the lake.

"Yeah. I feel much better. I felt useless just lying there in that bed. And after what Ada had said, well, I couldn't sleep, could I? If we want to catch Landon before he makes it to Soul City we should leave now."

Jon eyed me suspiciously. "He won't make it before we do. Trust me, we still have time."

I frowned. "But we don't. He's at least one full day ahead, maybe more. If we don't leave now, we'll never catch up to him."

"We can't leave yet, not until tomorrow. Ada's orders."

"Since when do you listen to anyone's orders?" I asked skeptically.

"Since they involve your well-being, that's when. Ada said that this place heals, too, that it's healing you, and that we need to stay until tomorrow."

I sighed, but I knew that Ada was right. I had felt the healing power the moment I had opened my eyes and realized that my migraine had gone.

"Fine."

Jon took my hand. "Come with me. I want to show you something."

It was really easy being led by him. His warm hand was rough and callused, and I felt secure with him.

"Where are we going?"

Jon's smile widened, but he didn't look at me.

"You'll see," he said.

I tried to fight down the warmth on my cheeks.

Mountains soared up and away from the edge of the lake. We crossed the grounds and moved towards a meadow of tall swaying grasses, orange lilies, and buttercups. Showers of blossoms fell over us from the Crabapple trees and covered the grass in a carpet of reds and pinks. The air smelled like expensive perfume. It was very different from the hot piss and sewer smells that I had grown up with in the Pit.

It was a shame that people didn't know about this place, but maybe it was better that they didn't know. I'm sure the high priests didn't know because if they did they would have taken it like they'd taken everything else.

Jon stopped at the edge of an open field. A breeze set his hair rustling. His eyes met mine, and he gave me a lazy smile.

"What are we waiting for?" I asked.

"Just wait."

I heard the rustling of thunder and felt it rumble below my feet, but when I looked up into the bright blue sky, I couldn't find the source of the rumbling. And then from the opposite side of the meadow, I heard a loud bugling call that sounded oddly familiar.

And then they came.

Hundreds of horses galloped towards us through the open fields. They moved together in a giant wave, like a school of fish. They were reddish brown, chestnut, tan and brown, white and black. There were even some with patches and spots that I'd never seen before, like the coloring of cows. I spotted foals running alongside their mothers. But one stood out among the throng of horses.

A tall stallion, the color of midnight, stood out from the rest, grand and prince like. My heart jumped. I would have recognized him anywhere.

"Torak!" I yelled.

But when I started to move, Jon grabbed me by the arm.

"Do you want to get trampled to death?"

I stared at Jon, then back at Torak.

"But? How? How did he get here?" I was excited and relieved to see that he was fine.

Jon smiled and let go of my arm.

"I asked the witches the same thing. Apparently, all the horses from the race came here after we were ambushed by the mist. The witches told me that all animals have a sixth sense. They sense danger, and they can sense safety. They knew to come here."

"Clever beasts." My smile grew. "Beautiful and gracious. I could stand here all day just to watch them all. They look so happy here."

I laughed at one of the foals that head-butted its twin.

"We can make real progress tomorrow with horses," said Jon. "Prince Landon and his company are on foot. If we leave early enough tomorrow and ride hard, we may be able to snatch the stone right from under his nose."

"That is good news." My shoulders relaxed, and I took a breath. I felt that we had a real chance to get the stone. I couldn't wait to see the shocked look on Landon's face when I punched him. Prince or not, I hated him for leaving me to die.

"I'm assuming Will and Leo are part of the rebellion, too?"

Jon nodded. "They are. We all joined together."

"How many rebels do we have in the Pit?"

Even in the sun, a shadow crossed Jon's face. "Nearly every able man and a few women."

"Seriously? That many?"

Jon looked out over the meadow.

"You'd be surprised how many people were willing to join. The folks in the Pit are starving. They're slaves to the priests, and they don't want to be anymore. They're desperate and angry, and we'll need that anger and passion to take down the Empire."

I thought of a life without the priests. *Take down the Empire of the Sun.* I played the words in my head. "Sounds like a dream."

"And some dreams do come true." Jon's eyes sparkled, and I felt his fingers interlace with mine again. The gleam in his eye made my heart race.

"So we have the rest of the day to relax. Ada's orders. Come."

He pulled me along to a thicket of trees and bushes. I was almost drunk I was so lightheaded. Finally, we sat under a great crab apple tree with leaves the color of wine.

I sat next to him but not too close. I was sweating, and I could feel my fingers trembling. *Why was I so nervous?* I'd been alone with Jon before, well, with Mad Jack, and I'd never been nervous because there was only room for my anger. I looked at him again, really looked at him. His chiseled cheekbones, jaw, the framing of his eyes below his eyebrows, the strong muscles that peeked through the open neckline of his shirt, he was perfection. Even his scar gave him a dangerous edge, and I hardly even noticed it anymore. My skin tingled at his nearness. I realized then that my feelings for Jon had changed. It wasn't simply a crush. It went deeper than that. And it scared the hell out of me.

"So what will you do now?" I tried to appear calm and collected.

Jon pulled out some grass with his fingers. "What do you mean?"

"Does it change your plans now that you understand the power of the stone? I mean, I'm sure you had plans to sell it once you had it, right? I'm sorry you won't make a killing with it now. I'm sorry about all of it."

"I never planned on getting the stone."

I turned to look at him. "So why did you join the race then?"

He turned his face to me. The intensity in his eyes took my breath away.

"For you, Elena."

My heart beat so fast I feared it might explode. "I joined the race the moment I heard what the high priest's intentions were with you. I wanted to protect you, to keep you safe. I couldn't give a shit about the stone."

He traced my fingers with his index finger, slowly.

It hit me then how stupid and foolish I'd been all these years. Jon had been in front of me all this time, and I'd never truly *seen* him. He'd joined the race for me, to keep me safe. Although he'd spoken to me very little during all those years in the Pit, I realized now that he was a man of few words. His actions spoke volumes.

"How long?" I asked.

His eyes narrowed. "How long what?"

"How long have you been in love with me?"

He looked away and was silent for a long moment. His expression was a mixture of a smile and a wince. And for a long time I thought he wouldn't answer.

"Since the first time you came to me. You wanted to trade a gold necklace you had stolen for some books," he said quietly.

He laughed. "You were so proud and fierce. You didn't fear me like the rest of the girls, and you never ever tried to flirt with me. You were good with a blade, and you made sure we all knew so we wouldn't take advantage of you. You didn't care about me. You didn't care who I was, or what I stood for in the Pit. I think that's why I was so drawn towards you."

"Really?" I said. "That was five years ago, I was fourteen then, stubborn as hell and foolish."

A ghost of a smile appeared on his lips. "You haven't changed, not really."

I found myself laughing with him.

"I know I'm a bit of a hardhead. I'm headstrong, and I do what I want, when I want. You can laugh all you want, but I'll have you know there are worse faults, like being vain and prejudiced. Rose always said I was as stubborn as a mule, and that one day I would pay for it."

I sighed. "I should have listened to her, because I *am* paying for it now. I should never have gone after that stupid Anglian crown. But I did. And now look at the mess we're in because of me. I'm such an idiot."

Jon let out a low groan. "Can you ever forgive me?" he said.

The sadness in his eyes went straight to my heart. Jon might have played a role in all this mess, but *I* had delivered the crown. It was my mistake, and I had to own up to it.

I leaned a little closer to him.

"Maybe," I teased. "If you give me what I want, I might forgive you."

He laughed softly and placed a strand of my hair behind my ear. "Really? And what's that?"

"A kiss." My heart raced.

He looked mildly surprised at my boldness, but then gradually his smile broadened.

"That's it? Just a kiss?"

I raised my eyebrows. "Well, it better be a damn good one."

Jon flashed a smile and then leaned in. His lips brushed against mine, soft at first and hesitant, like he thought I might pull away. But I didn't.

I leaned in, and he kissed me harder, crushing his mouth against mine. A wild passion exploded in me as our tongues touched and explored. His touch felt so soothing and vibrant.

I kissed him with more intensity. His scent and kisses lulled me into a trance. I breathed in his smell, and it woke something primal inside me.

I had kissed my share of men, particularly during my younger years in the Pit, and I had even added a prince to my list. But with Jon, it was different. He kissed with a gentleness and caution that made his kiss into a vow. It was a promise of his love, a promise that he was mine and always would be.

"It's always been you, Elena," he whispered against my lips.

He pulled back a fraction, cupped my face with his hands, and looked at me.

I swallowed hard.

He kissed my neck and my cheeks and then went back to my lips again. We kissed without finding breath, and his hand slid down my arm to my waist. My pulse pounded at the heat of his hands. I yanked off his shirt and threw it to the ground. My hands moved over his muscled chest as a ravenous unyielding sort of hunger welled in me.

He grabbed my wrists and pushed me to the ground, straddling me. While he worked to take off my breeches, I raised my shift and tunic over my head and tossed them in the grass beside his shirt. I was completely naked, and although I wished I had some of the feminine curves the concubines had, Jon did not seem in any way disappointed as he inspected me from my breasts to my thighs.

"If you don't stop me now," he breathed, his chest rising and falling rapidly. "I won't be able to stop."

I reached over and yanked his pants down. "I don't want you to stop."

He kicked off his pants and lowered himself over me. The heat of his body against my skin was electric. Our hands explored our bodies, and I could feel nothing but his touch, his lips, the sound of his voice, his scent.

I didn't care that the witches might stroll by and discover us. There was only Jon and me.

My eyes gleamed with tears, and I became a breathless tumble of sensations. We locked together, and the world revolved around us.

CHAPTER 31

WE RETURNED TO THE castle at sunset. Jon told me it was called Kindling Castle, and that it was a sanctuary for all things magic. It was also a school for witchcraft where witchlings, the young witch apprentices, learned all about magic.

I couldn't help but envy the young girls. I would have given anything to have been one of them and to have grown up here instead of in the Pit.

As we walked I wondered why my mother hadn't come back here with me. I wouldn't have been the same person I was today if I had grown up in a sheltered and nurturing place like this, if I had grown up surrounded by magic. I could have had friends and learned about my abilities. Maybe she didn't want to give up on the man she loved? Maybe she didn't realize how much danger she was in? I would never know.

The log castle looked welcoming. Light spilled through the large windows, and the last of the sun glowed behind us, so that everything on the hillside threw a double shadow. A cool breeze rose, and I salivated at the smell of meat roasting.

I followed Jon to the dining hall where rows of long tables with white tablecloths were arranged side by side. The air was filled with conversations and the sweet scent of food. We moved to the large buffet table, and I topped my plate with sweet potatoes, roasted chicken, boiled carrots, rice, bread, and a slice of meat pie.

Jon looked down at my plate and gave me an approving smirk. My face warmed. I wasn't sure if the witches sensed the feelings we shared for each other, but I knew that Jon and I shared an unbreakable bond.

I had grown up not trusting men. My attitude towards relationships was pretty dysfunctional, and I had always kept a wall around my heart. But now my wall had lifted, and Jon and I were joined together with a connection so strong that I felt it in my soul. I never believed in soul mates, but if I did, Jon would be mine.

Ada waved us over to her table, the only table that sat on a slightly raised platform.

We took our seats facing the high witch and two other witches. The first was a middle-aged witch by the name of Sylvia who had been responsible for stitching up the back of my neck. Sylvia was from the White Witches clan and wore an earth-colored gown with blue trim. She had a pleasant face and short hair with tight gray and white curls. The other was named Maya, a dark-skinned witch in a sun-colored gown. She had silver eyes and a stern expression. Maya was from the Augur clan, the seers. She was completely bald, and her strange eyes sent a shiver rippling through me. I tried not to look at her while we discussed our travel plans for early the next morning.

"What do I do when I get the stone back?" I asked through a mouthful of potatoes.

I swallowed and watched as some unspoken communication passed between them.

"Do I take it back to Hollowmere?"

"No," said Ada. "That place is spent now. We must find another safe place to hide it. Away from the priests, somewhere where they can never find it."

She drummed her gnarled fingers on the table. "Bring it here. We'll need to convene with the other witch clans, and then we'll make a decision."

The witches fell silent. I felt Maya's strange piercing stare, but I did my best to ignore it.

Jon took a sip of his wine and placed his goblet on the table.

"Can't we use the stone against the priests? If it's as powerful as you claim, why can't we use it against them? You said it was a weapon, so let's use it. Let's get rid of the priests once and for all."

Ada shook her head. "It's not that simple, Jon. You cannot wield the stone, none of us can."

"Elena can," said Jon.

He tapped his finger on his glass. "Surely *she* can use it. You said it yourself. Elena is the only one who can even touch the damn thing."

"Touching the stone and wielding it are two different things."

Sylvia looked at me. "While you can *touch* it, you will never *wield* it like you would a sword or a knife. You can't control it. Eventually you would lose yourself to it. You would become something else, something not human. The stone was not meant to be handled by a mortal, man or witch. Its power would kill you."

"Are you sure?" I dabbed my mouth with a napkin. "Jon might be right. What if I *can* manipulate it? You said it yourself that I was immune to most magic, maybe even to the magic of the stone. I was able to touch it when no one else could. I felt its power, truly I did, and I didn't lose myself to it. It never took control of me. If I can wield the stone, and if it's as powerful as you claim, then I should try. It would be foolish not to."

Maya reached across the table and grabbed my hands. I was surprised at her strength.

"You would be foolish to try."

Maya watched me, and I couldn't look away from her unsettling silver eyes. "I've seen it. I've seen *you*."

The blood left my face and I swallowed.

"You've seen *me*? Like in a vision? What was the vision? What did you see?"

I felt Jon tense next to me, still uneasy with all things supernatural.

"Not now, Maya," hissed Ada. She had noticed Jon's discomfort.

"Elena's already been through enough. No need to fill her head with nonsense about what might or could come to pass."

I shifted in my seat. My curiosity was much stronger than my fears.

"It's not nonsense," said Maya. Her eyes glinted with anger, and I could hear the annoyance in her voice. "Just truths of what may be and—"

"—and what very well may *not be*." Ada glared at Maya.

When Maya turned back to me, I looked into those silver eyes and squeezed her hands. "Tell me. I want to know."

Maya smiled at me from her end of the table.

"I will tell you this. Steel maidens are dangerous because their blood magic is dark and can easily turn to evil. If you use the stone, your soul will gradually become corrupted until you become a twisted dark imitation of yourself, a specter. If you use the stone you will die."

She let go of my hands. I was stunned.

I could feel all their eyes on me. I didn't know what I'd expected her to say, but I never expected her to tell me I was going to die if I used the stone. While Maya's visions only predicted what *might* happen in the future, I still felt ice crawl up my spine. She had seen me die in a vision. I drew a long, shaky breath.

"Best bring it here," said Ada, turning her attention back to what I should do if I got the stone.

She gave me a gentle smile. "We can keep it safe until we find a better solution."

The three elder witches nodded their heads, but it didn't sound promising to me. I chose to keep my mouth shut on the subject. An ominous silence fell over us and lasted throughout dinner.

* * *

We left Gray Havens with a heavy heart. I had felt at home with the witches. We said our goodbyes to Ada and the others, and I was surprised at the number of them who had risen so earlier to see us off. I had the suspicion that many of the younger witches had come to feast their eyes on Jon one last time. And I couldn't blame them.

Will and Leo got fresh horses while I rode Torak, and Jon was back on his white mare, Starlight. The two men avoided my gaze and kept as far away as they could from me. It was clear they didn't like traveling with me. Perhaps they would have left me to die, just as the prince had done. I tried not to let their unfriendliness bother me, but it did.

We traveled south towards Soul City, and the rising sun in the east painted the sky in hues of pink. It was a glorious morning, but it wouldn't last. We rode our horses hard to catch up to Prince Landon. He had a date with my fist.

After just a day with plenty of food and rest, and I felt stronger than ever. And yet I still felt a sting at the back of my neck with every bounce. The red monk's poison was a constant reminder that I wasn't immortal, and that we were up against black magic.

It seemed preposterous to think that the high priests could be dabbling in black magic. They had banished everything magic. *What would it mean if they had it, and why?* The stone was connected to all of this, and I was going to find out exactly what that connection was.

I learned from Jon that the others from the Pit hadn't survived, so it was going to be the three of us against Landon's company. If my numbers were correct there were nine of them, eight men, and the woman, Thea.

We rode hard all day and most of the night. We stopped to rest for a few hours in a clearing, but as soon as I closed my eyes, Jon was waking me to get moving again. We ate a silent breakfast of cheese and bread, climbed back onto our horses, and set off again. My joints, thighs, and lower back were stiff, and the optimism we felt about reaching the stone before we neared Soul City was fading.

My spirits lifted when we approached a camp by the side of the road, and I recognized the royal colors of the Fransians, the Romilians, the Girmanians, the Purtulese, and the Espanians. I searched for the red and gold colors of the royal seal of Anglia. But the Anglians weren't there. We were outnumbered, and I prayed silently that the other kingdoms wouldn't interfere. After all, we didn't have the stone.

As we got closer, I could see only bleak expressions on the faces of the riders from the other realms. They were surrounded by devastation. There had been a great battle. Bodies that had been shot with arrows were covered in mud and lay in puddles of their own blood. The coppery smell of rot and decay rose in the hot morning sun like a mist. Limbs and bodies were scattered everywhere, and bile rose in my mouth at the sight them. I felt Torak tense beneath me, and we slowed down.

It had been a massacre. Only a handful of men were left and no women. I tensed, one hand on the reins, while the other rested on my weapons belt. Perhaps they had thought I was dead. The last they knew, I had run off with the stone.

I saw the body of a single Anglian, and it became clear that the others must have caught up with the prince and had figured out he had the stone. They had apparently tried to get it from him and had failed.

He still had it, and we needed to get it from him.

Jon must have come to the same conclusion as me. His expression was troubled, and he, Will, and Leo had all drawn their swords.

Suddenly, a wave of angry, desperate, and frightened men charged us.

And before I could urge Torak away, something hit me on the side of the head, and the world went dark.

CHAPTER 32

IT WAS A MIRACLE that I didn't fall off my horse. The Goddess was protecting me. Warm blood gushed from my temple, and I tried to blink the blood from my eyes and ignore the wave of dizziness. Someone grabbed me from behind and tried to pull me off my horse. I held onto Torak's saddle, but my fingers slipped, and I was hauled backwards until I was practically lying on his back. Two bearded men pulled my left arm and nearly pulled my shoulder out of its socket.

"The horse is mine!" said one of the men. "I'm going to kill you, witch!"

I pulled out my dagger and stabbed him in the eye. He let go with a howl and fell from my view.

"Stupid bitch. You'll pay for that."

The other man backhanded me in the face so hard that I was thrown forward in my saddle. Tasting blood, I didn't give myself time to think and acted on impulse. I whirled around and kicked out hard with my leg. My boot hit his head with a horrifying crunch, and he went down.

I spit the blood from my mouth. Jon and the others were fighting hard against the mob, and suddenly they had cleared a path.

"Elena," Jon turned to me, his face flushed with sweat. "This way!"

He pointed through the opening they had created.

I didn't hesitate and kicked Torak's sides. The big stallion flew past the men in a thunder of hooves. With Jon, Will and Leo behind me, we gathered speed and escaped.

We rode hard, and I was thankful for the flatness of the land. We tore through the forest so fast that I could no longer distinguish the pine trees from the birch. Everything was a blur of browns and greens. I kept my focus on Jon and marveled at the speed of his mare. I let out a shaky breath, when I realized that I'd been holding it, and let my grip on my reins relax a little. My fingers were stiff, and my blisters were bleeding.

After a half hour of riding hard, we slowed our pace. I was glad to be free of the hoard of crazed men, but I soon started to feel wary again.

Where was Prince Landon? Did he take some other route? A shortcut? Were there secret paths to Soul City that weren't on the map?

No one spoke for a long time. The tenseness in Jon's shoulders told me he was thinking the same thing. He kept moving his head back and forth as if he were searching. *But searching for what?*

The silence was becoming too heavy to bear.

"We should have caught up with them by now," I yelled to Jon over the beating of hooves and the wind in my ears.

"It's a two days' ride to Soul City. How could they have moved so quickly on foot? Do you think they found another way in? Another path?"

"They'd be fools to travel through the forest," he said. "It would take them twice as long. No. They came this way. I'm sure of it."

But his face betrayed him, and he looked like he was trying hard to convince himself.

"Are we too late?" I pressed anxiously. "Will they get to Soul City before us?"

Jon's dark eyes were troubled. "Can't let that happen. You heard what the witches said. Come on! Ride hard, men!"

He slammed his heels into his horse's flanks and flew, his cloak flapping behind him as he rode.

I spurred my heels and Torak sprinted with a clean, pure speed that we hadn't achieved before. Perhaps he'd gotten a little push from the witches.

Hooves pounded hard behind me, and a quick peek back showed that Will and Leo were still hard on our heels. The forest flew by me. I was amazed at Torak's speed, but more amazed that I was managing to hold on and hadn't fallen.

I thought about the stone and the ancient power I had felt in my bones. It was wild and dangerous, and the vilest men in all the realms wanted it. I thought about the dirty faces of the starving children in the Pit and about the courtesans, the sick, and the elderly. Tears flew out of the corners of my eyes as I thought about how much the children and Rose had suffered and starved. It would get worse, a hell of a lot worse, if the priests got ahold of the stone. Ada had said that the world would burn.

I had seen pure evil, and I had seen it in the eyes of the high priest. He must never get the stone.

We rode in silence, each of us alone in our own thoughts as we raced through the forest. Torak never tired, and I was grateful for it. We flew up and down the hills we encountered, slowing and speeding up again, but never stopping. After perhaps two hours of hard riding, we cleared the woodlands and were galloping through farmland on the edges of Soul City.

Jon slowed his stallion and assessed the ground for tracks.

"Horses," he said out of breath. "And by the looks of it maybe eight or nine horses."

He threw his hands in the air. "Damn it. Damn. Damn. Damn."

I slowed Torak and looked to the ground. "Are you sure? These could be older tracks from before. These could be our tracks."

Jon frowned, shaking his head. "No, these are fresh."

"He's right," said Leo, and he swung down from his horse in one swift move. He skimmed his hand over the dirt. "These are fresh tracks. If I were to guess, I'd say only a few hours old."

The blood drained from my face. "But how can that be? *Who* would know they needed horses, and how would they know where to find them?"

"Merlins, most likely," said Will as he looked to the sky. "I don't remember the prince having a bird with him, but if he's in league with the priests, then they've probably been communicating."

"And communicating this whole time," said Jon.

I had heard that the priests used pigeon hawks to spy and to transport messages. I felt like someone had hit me across the face when I remembered that I had heard a hawk's cry before, and that had coincided with Landon's arrival at my fire. I didn't believe in coincidences, but I had dismissed it at the time. *Damn.*

I swallowed hard. "But that means ... that means ..."

"It means the royal bastard has been planning this the entire time. He knew what he was doing from the start. He knew how to play you, Elena. And he did."

I glowered at him. "No need to bring that up again."

Will and Leo looked up at me, but I wouldn't meet their eyes. I was humiliated enough.

Jon kept on.

"He made sure to keep you in the race. He waited for you to get your hands on the stone and didn't interfere because he was already planning on taking it from you. That's why he let you walk out of the temple with the stone. He knew he was going to get it back eventually. But he needed you alive and well because he knew *you* were the only one who could touch it. It was all part of his plan."

"His and the fucking priests'," hissed Leo. "Now I know who's been leaking information to the temple guards. It explains the raids on Wedgemore. Landon's people were the moles. They've been playing us too."

Will punched into his hand. "I can't wait to get my hands on the royal prick's neck."

I had to agree with him. I had had my suspicions about the handsome prince, and now Jon had just confirmed it. The wine, the sweet smiles, him helping me with the race, they had all been a ruse, and I had been the fool. I had believed he cared for me, and it had hurt like hell when he had left me to die. I was going to make him pay.

"Let's pray that we make it back before they do." Jon spurred his horse's sides and tore down the road.

When we had ridden on for another half hour, it was clear that we should have caught up with the Anglian company, and we hadn't.

We reached the farming lands and homesteads that dotted in fields just outside of Soul City. I could see the great circular walls that surrounded the city in the distance, and yet there were no traces of the prince.

The road became crowded with merchants and carts moving to and from Soul City. We couldn't continue our fast pace without killing passersby and injuring our own horses.

A woman jostled against Torak and raised her fist at me.

I looked down at the wave of humanity. *Was the city always this crowded?* I shifted nervously. The wound at the back on my neck throbbed. The pain was increasing as we neared the city.

"We'll never get through," I yelled and slowed Torak to a walk.

"Keep moving, don't stop." Jon took the lead.

He yelled and waved his arms to get people to move to the side of the road and let us through. I kept as close as I could to Jon and the others. I recognized a few traders from the Pit. Still, they were slowing us down, and I cursed them for it. I was sweating with anxiety, and my fingers trembled. I tightened my grip on the reins to stop my hands from shaking.

"Keep going," Jon yelled from ahead. "If we stop now, we'll never reach him before he breaches the city walls."

"I'm trying," I yelled. "There are too many people. I can't get through!"

And the farther we went, the more densely packed the road became. Eventually we were at a standstill. I looked over the heads of the crowds. We were nearly there, but we were completely surrounded.

A flash of red and gold caught my attention inside the west gate. A man on a horse turned around, and our eyes met.

Prince Landon had breached the gates. We were too late.

CHAPTER 33

EVEN FROM A DISTANCE I could read the surprise on his face. Clearly he thought I'd be dead. I was glad to disappoint him. I smiled at him defiantly, and he turned around and yelled something to his guard. I caught a glimpse of Thea grinning victoriously, and then they galloped away.

"To the gate!" I yelled. "The prince has breached the gate!"

Jon looked to the spot where I pointed, but I didn't have time to wait and see if he'd spotted the prince. I was already moving.

I slid off Torak's back, and I led him over to a tree at the far edge of the road. After I'd looped the reins around a branch, I stroked his neck gently.

"I'll be right back. Promise."

Understanding seemed to flash in his big brown eyes.

I had lost sight of the prince, but it didn't matter. I knew where he was going. And I had to beat him there. I waved my sword around like a madwoman.

"Out of my way, or I'll slit your goddamn throats!"

It worked. A crowd parted, and I kept my eyes on the gate and ran. Jon slid off his horse when I passed him, but I didn't have time to stop.

I dodged another crowd and kept waving my sword in front of me. I didn't want to hurt anyone, but I would if I had to.

Four temple guards stood at the gate when I arrived. Their eyes darted from face to face, searching, searching for someone. Me.

I ducked behind a cart, and then I used a very fat man as a shield. I slipped through the gate unnoticed. I never stopped moving. I only hoped Jon was behind me. As soon as I cleared the gate, I tore down the main city road, dodging the nobles and merchants. I felt a moment's satisfaction at the fear that flashed on the snotty faces of a group of wealthy ladies as I purposely elbowed them out of the way. I wouldn't soil my blade on the likes of them.

The golden temple glinted in the sun like a giant yellow diamond. Eight horses were tied to a hitching post at the base of the temple. Landon's horses. He was already inside. I cursed and dashed towards the temple. Two temple guards stood at the entrance, their swords already drawn. Someone had told them I was coming. I didn't care.

I threw myself at the nearest guard. He grinned as he lifted his blade. He swung, but I sidestepped and rammed my sword into his side. I yanked my sword from his bleeding body and knocked him aside. As he staggered back, I caught a glimpse of Jon slamming into the other guard's chest. My assailant had only been wounded, and he came at me again. He swung at me hard, and I danced back.

"Make no mistake, whore, I am going to kill you. First I'm going to cut that pretty little face of yours and slice your throat, and then I'll have my way with your dead body."

I didn't have time for this.

The guard sneered and swung straight for my heart, but I whirled away and sliced him in the back. He staggered but steadied himself. He grimaced and charged after me again. I swept forward again and landed a few strong blows on his blade. His shirt was stained with blood, and his movements became slow. It was all I needed. I could see the hair in his nose and smell the ale on his breath. I stepped to the side when he attacked and thrust my sword into his back. Blood spattered my face. A puff of air escaped his lips, and he crumpled to the floor and didn't get up.

I turned to see Jon ram his sword into the other guard's chest, and then I was running again.

I gripped my sword tightly in my clammy hands and ran up the steps and into the main hall without pausing to admire the golden walls or the elaborate stone pillars. I hoped that the footfalls behind me belonged to Jon and his crew.

I bolted in the direction of the altar where I had been brought to face the high priest the first time. I saw the blur of cream and black shapes as I rushed past concubines and priests, but I didn't stop. I had to get to the stone before Landon handed it over to the priest.

Shouts reverberated around the hall, and temple guards came running towards me from a side corridor. I strained to go faster as I flew down the slippery polished floors.

Three priests stood with their backs to me, and I slammed into them as hard as I could, never stopping. They pitched forward and sprawled on the ground.

"How dare you touch a priest! Woman!"

"Damn you all to hell, priests!" I yelled back and hoped I had busted some ribs. I skidded to a stop at the edge of the altar room, and my heart leapt in my throat.

The room was packed with temple guards, priests, and the men I recognized from Landon's company. Their attention had been on the platform and the altar, but like a giant wave all the heads turned when I barreled in. I could feel the weight of the hundreds of eyes that were on me. The priests grinned with that same wickedness as their beloved high priest. Six red monks stood at attention against the walls. I was completely surrounded. I had walked into my own trap.

I saw a flash of blonde hair. Thea glared down at me ferociously from next to the altar.

The high priest stood on the altar. The jewels and golden thread on his white silk robe sparkled like a sun in the dimly lit room. He held a jeweled staff like the one I had seen on the first day of the race, and the same crippled, shadowy creature knelt next to him. Its empty eyes were focused on me.

And there standing next to him was Prince Landon. The Heart of Arcania, safely inside its golden cage, rested in his hands.

In spite of the warmth of the room, a nasty shiver went down my back.

The high priest turned his pale eyes to me and sneered.

"Ah, Elena. You're just in time. I must say, it's unfortunate that you failed to bring me what I asked. And yet you still played your part well. None of this would have been possible without you."

He raised his arms and gestured towards the rest of the room.

I didn't want to think about *what* he referred to, but I knew I had been partly responsible for it.

My gaze fell on Landon, but he wouldn't meet my eyes.

Two long ceremonial tables covered with human skulls and candles were positioned on either side of the altar. Coils of green smoke rose from metal containers and filled the air with a stench of sulfur that burned my lungs. The braziers of green fire of the altars reflected an eerie green light off the polished floors.

A large red ring had been painted on the floor, and it circled the altar. Strange symbols and letters were drawn in maroon and covered the floor inside the ring. All of them were different, and they were written in a language I'd never seen before. There was something sinister about them, like they had been drawn in blood and were the key to unlock some great evil.

I looked down at my feet. My boots were inches away from the edge of the circle, and I wondered what would happen if I stepped on it.

The air moved at my back and Jon, Will, and Leo came up behind me. Their eyes widened when they saw the stone in Landon's hands.

"Bastard," hissed Jon.

Although I couldn't agree with him more, I still felt a pang in my chest for Landon. Maybe he didn't know what he was doing.

Maybe he didn't have a choice. Maybe the priests had blackmailed him, too. Maybe I was fooling myself.

Guards and priests crowded between the altar and me. I would never make it in time.

"We're too late. It's over." Jon cursed.

"Landon!" with panic in my voice I called out into the chamber.

"Don't do this. Don't be a fool. You'll never get your title back. Don't you see? He's lying."

Landon's jaw twitched, but he still wouldn't look at me. Even from where I stood, I could see the flush spread on his face.

"Landon. I know a part of you believes me. I can see it plainly on your face. Deep down, you know it's the truth. You know he's a liar. Landon, look at me. Look at me!"

It took all my effort not to rush across the room and slap the stupid look from his face. I needed to make him look at me. But I knew if I made a move, it would all be over.

The prince still wouldn't meet my eyes.

The high priest glared at me.

"You can shout and cry all you want, but the fact remains that you've lost the race. It seems you are a poor loser, Elena. But it doesn't change the fact that the prince won. He has the right to do what he chooses with his prize, and as it turns out, the prince and I have struck a deal. I am a man of my word, and we have made an oath that neither can break."

He turned back to the prince and bowed. He reached out with his left hand.

"Your Highness," he said so pleasantly it almost felt sincere. "As we agreed. The stone, if you please."

Everything seemed to slow down. The prince turned towards the high priest, and I could see the sweat dripping from his forehead and the tightness in his shoulders. There was no time to think. I needed to act now.

Before I even registered that I was moving, I took three strides and threw my sword like a spear straight at the priest's heart. It flew straight and true.

The high priest reached out and caught my sword like it was nothing more than a harmless stick. He clicked his tongue and shook his head slightly.

"I'll deal with you later."

He snapped his fingers, and the temple guards came at us.

"Run!" Jon screamed as he and his men doubled back the way we came.

I bolted, but I wasn't fast enough. Something hit me in the lower back, and I landed hard on the cold stone floor. I lay still for a moment and blinked the black spots from my eyes. I smelled the faint coppery tang of blood. I pushed myself up on my knees and stared down at a puddle of my own blood.

"You're not going anywhere, *daughter*."

Brother Edgar loomed over me. His sword dripped with my blood.

"I'm going to finish what I started nine years ago. There's nowhere to run this time. No one to help you."

I was not going to let him kill me like he did my mother. I staggered to my feet, but before I could move a beefy temple guard pinned my arms together in his powerful hold. The smell of male sweat almost overwhelmed me. I twisted and kicked, but he yanked me off my feet effortlessly and held me dangling in the air.

Brother Edgar lined up his sword against my neck.

"Time to rectify my mistake, witch."

"Go to hell," I spat.

I moved, but I felt the wound in my back tear, and warm blood trickled down to the back of my thighs.

Brother Edgar lifted his sword, his face contorted in fury.

"Move," he said to the guard. "Or I'll cut you along with her."

The guard's grip loosened, and I dropped to my feet. Brother Edgar raised his sword high above his head. He was going to decapitate me—

"Enough!" the high priest shouted angrily.

Brother Edgar froze.

"Now is not the time, Brother Edgar. I need you *here* by the altar, as I need *all* the priests. Lower your sword and come stand next to your brothers so that we may proceed. You can kill her after the ceremony."

Brother Edgar scowled, and for a moment I thought he might defy his master. But slowly, very slowly, he lowered his sword.

"Don't let her out of your sight," he said and moved towards the altar.

I was dizzy from the lack of blood, but I could already feel my wound begin to heal. I feared it wouldn't heal fast enough to give me the strength I needed.

Jon was moving to help me, but two temple guards stepped in front of him and put their swords to his throat. Leo and Will were both on their knees and surrounded. It was too late to flee. Too late for anything.

The high priest cleared his throat. "Now, if we can dispense with this interruption, we may continue."

He turned his attention back to the prince and stretched out his hand again.

"Your Majesty. The stone."

Prince Landon watched the high priest's face with a myriad of emotions. I could see fear, doubt, anger, and confusion. He stood straight, but his shoulders were tense. He gripped the golden cage and extended his arm towards the high priest.

"Landon! No!" I made to move forward, but a sword appeared at my heart, and I staggered back.

The prince turned towards me and his eyes lit up. For a moment I thought I had reached him, that he wouldn't give the stone to the high priest. But then something dark flashed across his face, and he turned his gaze to Jon. He looked at me one last time, and then handed the stone to the high priest.

CHAPTER 34

I WATCHED IN HORROR as the scene unfolded. The high priest held the stone, and a strange, wicked smile appeared on his face. His hand trembled, and it wasn't from fear.

"Goddess, forgive us," I breathed.

If the witches were right, this was the beginning of the end. And I had failed them. I fell to my knees, stifling a sob and biting my tongue against a scream.

Prince Landon cleared his throat and wiped the sweat from his forehead with the back of his wrist.

"I held my end of the bargain," said the prince.

I saw the muscles in his jaw tense. "Now it's your turn, priest. Swear to all here. Swear that you'll give back all our family's lands, our titles, and our guards. Swear that I will be crowned King of Anglia, and that you will restore the monarchy as it was. Swear that the Empire will recognize my family's titles and the titles of those of noble birth. Acknowledge my right to rule by the will of the Creator. It is what we agreed."

For a moment the high priest said nothing. He held the golden cage with that same wicked glimmer in his eyes. My chest tightened.

"I made no such agreement."

Prince Landon frowned and took a step towards the priest.

"But you said," he complained. "You swore! You vowed before the Creator! What kind of priest are you?"

The high priest gripped the cage and raised his free hand. Black energy sparkled around his fingers. With a flick of his wrist he sent out a blast of energy that hit the prince square in the chest. The force threw the prince across the room, and he crashed against the wall with a nauseating crunch. The wall splintered under the force. Prince Landon slid to the ground in a crumple of broken bones. His blue eyes stared into space lifelessly.

With an earsplitting wail that stopped my heart, Thea rushed across the chamber and fell next to her fallen prince. She cradled him and kissed his face. Her mouth was wet with tears, and she kissed him over and over, as though he was merely asleep, and she could wake him with kisses.

"No, no, no, no," she cried as she rocked him gently. "You can't be dead. You can't be dead. Please don't leave me, please."

I fought very hard not to cry. Although I had hated, truly hated, the prince, he didn't deserve to die like this.

I looked at the high priest with a new sense of fear. Only a witch could unleash such supernatural power. The high priest must be a sorcerer.

The room had darkened, and the smell of sulfur had increased tenfold. I could see the fear in the other priests' faces. They were just as shaken as I was.

The eerie silence that followed was broken by the small voice of a mousy-looking priest.

"Your eminence, what have you done?"

His eyes darted to the dead prince and back to the high priest.

"He was of noble birth. And you killed him. Your actions have desecrated your vows to God, desecrated our holy temple and broken our sacred oaths to the Creator. You are *no* priest. Only the devil could possess such skill. You are an abomination. Are you in league with the Devil? Have you sided with the occult? What was this magic? Answer us!"

The high priest grinned, took the cage with the stone in it, and set it on top of his staff. With a twist of his wrist, the golden cage clicked into place. It had been specifically designed to fit the top of the staff.

He raised his staff with a wild look in his eyes. A hum reverberated throughout the chamber, and then a pulsing of power that I recognized from when I had held the stone. The Heart of Arcania was beating. I could feel it resonating inside me.

Suddenly, the stone flashed bright white, and then it dulled to black. I could still feel the pulsing energy in the walls, in the floor, and in the air, but this time it wasn't warm. It was as cold as death.

The high priest threw back his head in a high-pitched laugh that sounded anything but human. A chill rattled in my bones.

"Elena. What's happening?" Jon pulled me to my feet.

"I'm not sure," I said. "But Ada was right. The high priest is no mere man, but something much worse."

"Well, if I had to take a guess, I'd say our high priest is a sorcerer."

While I felt noticeably sturdier than before, and the tear on my back had healed, the wound on my neck burned like hell. It was almost like it was warning me. *But warning me of what?*

If dark magic could wound a steel maiden like me, who was supposedly immune to magic, I could only imagine the effects it would have on a normal person, let alone on an entire village.

Jon shook his head. "This is bad. Really bad."

"And I have a feeling it's about to get worse."

Brother Edgar had managed to make his way to just below the altar, but the familiar loathing frown on his face was not directed at me this time.

He pointed a finger at the high priest. "The Temple of the Sun will not stand for this! How dare you masquerade as a priest when you're nothing but a male *witch*."

He spat. "You put shame on the name of the Creator. You have shamed us! You will hang for this. Imposter! Charlatan!"

Spit flew from his mouth, and soon a handful of priests who felt bold enough to denounce the high priest joined him.

But the high priest ignored them. He stood on the altar with his arms spread out like he was about to take a bow. He was waiting for something.

I noticed that the shadowy creature was still cowering behind the priest's gown. Again, no one seemed troubled at the sight of it.

The red symbols on the floor suddenly glowed green. The stone pulsed, and a wave of black energy blasted into the priest. He staggered, and his face contorted as though he was in pain. The chamber shook, small rocks fell around me like a hailstorm, and the air moved with an invisible wind. Then the room went silent again.

All eyes were on the high priest. It was as though we were all watching a performance on stage and waiting for the grand finale. The high priest paled until he was nearly translucent. I could see black veins pulse through his face, his neck, and his arms. He opened his eyes, and they were completely black, like the bottomless pits of hell.

"We need to leave," said Jon. Both Will and Leo's eyes were wide with alarm, but they didn't move.

"It's too late to get the stone. We'll have to come up with another plan. There's nothing else we can do right now."

I nodded, but I couldn't tear my eyes away just yet. I had to see if my fears would come true.

The priests below the altar had stood frozen in fear momentarily, but then they scattered like a herd of frightened deer, pushing and shoving each other.

"I've waited three hundred years for this moment," the high priest boasted.

He looked at the priests below him.

"You God-fearing, paranoid, delusional fools. Your minds are weak, and your bodies are weaker. You never understood the true purpose of the Temple of the Sun. You want to fear a real God? Then fear me!"

The high priest surveyed the room again. "I'll give you the cleansing you've all been waiting for. I give you the Black Blight."

I watched transfixed as he lifted his staff and spoke an incantation in a language I'd never heard before. The stone pulsed, and a black radiance spun like the wind around the room. It wrapped around me, wrapped around everything and everyone in the room, and tightened until I could barely breathe. And then a surge of black tendrils blasted out from the stone. Like a fork of black lightning, it struck the priests first, coiled around their bodies, and paralyzed them.

"Get back!"

Jon pulled me down against the far side of the wall, next to Will and Leo. The energy shot out again and connected with the temple guards this time. If we hadn't moved when we did, we would have been hit, too.

The guards opened their mouths in silent screams as the black magic wormed its way into their souls. The whites of their eyes dulled to black, and their skin paled and thinned until they looked like corpses. Their emaciated faces reminded me of the demons we had seen in the mist. I could see black pulses through the veins on their necks and faces. Their skin began to rot and blister. It looked like an infection of black magic.

Every priest and guard inside the temple had become an emaciated demon.

Brother Edgar's black eyes flickered with an eerie intelligence, but the man was gone. I wasn't sorry about that. Only the red monks appeared to be untouched by the black magic. I wondered if they weren't already creatures bent to the will of hell.

It had all happened in under a minute. What had once been a throng of pompous and vile priests and guards had become an army of demons possessed by black magic.

The high priest turned to me.

"I have no more use for you, Steel Maiden." His voice sounded as though he was right next to me. His smiled widened. "You're far too dangerous to keep alive. You'll die today. Kill her. Kill them all!"

A hoard of black-eyed priests and guards stormed towards us.

CHAPTER 35

IN THE BLINK OF an eye the high priest's creatures had surrounded us and blocked our only exit. There were at least a hundred of them, and we were only four. They moved like a great swarm. Their teeth were chattering, and black liquid trickled down the sides of their mouths. We were backed into a corner.

"Whatever you do," I said, "don't let them touch you."

I wasn't entirely sure, but I suspected that the black magic that coursed through their veins could be transferred by touch.

The three men nodded, and we held up our swords and stood back to back. I couldn't think of losing Jon in this fight. There was no time for fear. There was only time to act.

The temple guard that had assaulted me before charged. There was no recognition in his black eyes, only an evil fury to kill. Like puppets on a string, they were compelled to obey. I shifted my grip on my sword and braced for a fight.

The creature lunged at me at exactly the same time as the other creatures sprang at Jon. I dodged his mangled fingers and kicked him as hard as I could, sending him flying.

But just as I kicked one creature, four more lunged at me. They were coming at me from every direction. I had lost Jon and the others in the commotion. I hacked and sliced. My sword connected with flesh and bone and sent arterial spurts of black blood spraying my face. I couldn't stop. Stopping meant death.

A priest with blackened teeth leaped at me, but my sword hit his chest, spurts of black blood showered the ground, and the monster squealed and hissed, backing away.

He lunged again, but I blocked his thrust and stabbed straight into his thorax. He crumpled to the ground. But another wave of possessed guards and priests attacked me right away. I swung my sword in a giant arc and managed to slice across their navels. Their entrails and guts spilled to the ground in a mess of black liquid.

I turned and saw Jon holding his own against six of the demon creatures, but I couldn't see Will or Leo. I could only hope they were still alive.

Neither Jon nor I could go on like this for much longer. The priests and guards were too strong, too fast, too many. The savage magic had given the creatures enormous strength. We needed to get out now.

A mass of flailing arms and guttural screams came at me again. I swung my sword around, and the creatures jumped back, afraid. I could see the fear of death on their gaunt faces.

But one wasn't afraid. Brother Edgar faced me. I hated him. Whether he was a creature or man now didn't matter, my father was going to die. I raised my sword.

"Hello, Daddy."

He hissed and ran towards me at a frightening speed, and I charged towards him fearlessly. He went for my throat with his teeth, but I pivoted and the creature only tore into my cloak. I spun and parried a blow from the creature's left hand. I thrust my sword into its side and out its back.

The thing that was once my father howled. I wrenched out my sword from its back, but the creature seemed unaffected by its wound as we faced each other head-on again.

A flicker of recognition flashed in its eyes.

"That's right," I said. "It's me. Remember me? Your daughter? Remember what you did to my mother? It's time to make things right."

I could smell his decaying flesh, and I suppressed the bile that rose in my throat. My mother's terrified face flashed before my eyes. Every muscle in my body tensed, and I gripped my sword so hard it hurt.

Brother Edgar leaped. I ducked, but I wasn't fast enough. The creature's fingernails cut the side of my throat, and it burned like hot wax had been poured over my skin. I whirled around, but something hard hit me from behind with such force that it knocked the air from my lungs.

My skin sizzled where I'd been cut, and I could feel an icy burn in my blood. I jerked backward and nearly dropped my sword. The creature hesitated, waiting to see if I'd been infected so that I'd be weakened and easier to kill. But I wasn't.

My father came at me yet again. I ducked and lunged up with as much force as I could.

I severed his head. Brother Edgar toppled over, and his bloodied head thumped to the ground.

I looked up. Jon plunged his sword into the chest of the guards. He pulled out his sword, and our eyes met. I could see his terror. I loved him in that moment. I knew it wasn't the time to come to terms with my emotions. But I knew I would crumble should anything happen to him.

"Run," he snarled, more a plea than a command. "Get out of here."

"The stone. We need to get it back."

"It's too late for that now," he said breathing hard. "You need to get out, Elena. Now."

"Not without you."

He was about to argue but then his eyes widened suddenly at something behind me.

I gripped my sword, ducked and spun, bringing my blade up into the belly of another demon priest. But just as soon as it keeled over, another one replaced it.

It was fast and strong despite its gangly limbs, and thrashed violently as it launched another attack. I deflected the blow, but it knocked me down. A flash of blinding pain hit me as I tried to stand, but it shook me out of my stupor.

"I've had enough of you, Steel Maiden." I could hear the anger in the high priest's voice as he ranted on.

"I thought you might be useful. But you are as wild and unpredictable as all the others of your kind. I could never trust you. And if I cannot trust you, then I cannot bend you to my will. I have no use for someone like you."

I raised my head. "Lucky for me. But I am going to kill you, priest."

I could barely make out his face, but I saw it contract in fury.

With a flick of his fingers, another shot of black filaments caught me in the chest and sent me sailing backwards. I slammed into a wall hard enough to crack my ribs. My skin burned like ice as the dark magic pulsed through me. I couldn't breathe.

Just as I started to see black spots, heat bloomed inside my chest, and my own magic started to build again. It resonated through me and pushed the dark magic away.

And then I was back on my feet.

The high priest, sorcerer, whatever he was, sneered at me. He was angry that I was partly immune to his dark magic. I was just as surprised as he was. I felt a bloom of confidence well in my chest, but it quickly deflated.

"Kill the witch whore," bellowed the high priest. "Bring me her head!"

I saw red move in the corner of my eye, and I knew we were in real trouble.

The red monks came at me. The priests and the guards that we had killed were nothing compared to the killing machines that were the red monks. I had defeated only one, and I had nearly died.

I planted my feet in a defensive stance, but I knew there was no way I could defeat this new threat.

"Elena!"

Jon eyed the red monks that pushed their way towards us.

"Listen to me. We can't defeat these red devils. There're too many of them."

He stepped in front of me, shielding me. "Go. I'll distract them."

"What are you saying?" I felt the lump in my throat. "You can't defeat them either."

"No I can't."

His eyes flashed with urgency. "But I can keep them off long enough for you to get away."

"What about you?"

He winked. "You know me. I can disappear in the blink of an eye."

He smiled. "Don't worry. Right now, you're more important. I promised the high witch that I'd keep you alive if things went badly."

"That's an understatement."

"You're the only one who can touch that goddamn stone. We need you *alive*. And that's what I'm doing. Now get. Meet me back at the Dirty Habit. Just go. I'll be right behind you."

I gauged the distance between the red monks and the exit.

"Fine," I said. The need to feel him, to feel his lips on mine took control, and I reached out and kissed him fiercely. I couldn't kiss him enough. I didn't realize I was crying until I felt the wetness trickle down my hot face. This might be the last time we kissed.

I pulled away, fighting the sob that threatened to escape from my throat. "For luck."

Jon grinned. "I'm going to need it. Go. Run hard." He nudged me roughly.

I gripped my sword. "Be safe."

I turned on my heel and ran.

CHAPTER 36

I BOLTED DOWN A hallway and out through the front entrance.

I met no one. I wondered if Thea had managed to slip away. I didn't like the woman, but I didn't want her to become one of the high priest's new pets either.

I suspected that the other high priests were sorcerers as well. There were six of them in total and that realization only made me feel worse. While they were probably powerful, too, only *one* of them had the stone. I had to take comfort in that.

The stone clearly amplified the powers of the sorcerer who possessed it. The others weren't so lucky. There had to be a chance to stop the sorcerers and get the stone back.

Men and women jumped out of the way as I barreled past them and headed towards the west gate. Their eyes and skin were still normal, but I wondered how long it would take the black magic to infect them. Would it spread through contact? Or were they already infected?

The Black Blight had already caused the trees and grasses to sicken and wither. And it was spreading. I thought of Torak and ran faster.

I searched for a sign of Jon, but he wasn't behind me.

I caught a glimpse of a red cloak, and a red monk came into view. His eyes locked onto mine, and he smiled.

"Shit."

I spun and ran through the gate. I cried at the sight of Torak still tied at the tree where I'd left him. The Goddess had kept him safe. He looked up as I approached and his nostrils flared in readiness.

"Hello, my sweet, beautiful boy," I gasped, out of breath.

I untied the reins and was up on his back in no time. I kicked my heels, and we flew away. I could see the look of fury on the red monk's face.

We galloped out of Soul City and kept to the only real road that led into the Pit. *What would happen to the people of Anglia when the Black Blight reached them?* I had seen how fast it had infected the people in the temple. It would probably infect thousands within a week.

The Pit came into view, and I had to slow Torak to a trot. The roads were narrower here, and I couldn't take a chance of injuring him. We rode through the dreary streets in silence until we arrived in Bleak Town.

The Dirty Habit loomed into view, and I slid off Torak's back. I immediately felt uneasy about leaving him out here. I'd bet my life he'd get stolen. I'd kill anyone who tried, but I couldn't keep him out in the streets. I had called too much attention to myself already by waltzing in on a horse. I had to wait for Jon inside.

I recognized one of Jon's men.

"Hey," I yelled and got his attention. "This is Mad Jack's horse. He asked me to bring him here, but I need to wait inside. Keep an eye on him, will you?"

The man perked up at the mention of his boss' name and made his way over.

"No problem. I'll watch him for you." I knew I could trust him, and I immediately felt more at ease. I sighed with relief and tied Torak's reins around a post.

"Thank you. He'll be here soon."

I pushed my way through the overcrowded inn and made my way to Jon's office in the back. Only then did I stop to catch my breath.

I paced the room waiting. I wanted to see Jon's face through the door. I wanted to know that he was safe. I'd never wanted anything so badly. I began fantasizing of the life Jon and I could have after all of this dark magic business was settled. I'd get the stone back, kill the sorcerer priest, and then maybe we could all move to Gray Havens together. Rose would love it there. The thought of it almost made me smile.

An hour went by, and then another. I rubbed my clammy palms on my breeches. I hated the feeling of helplessness. I paced around the room pulling at my hair and yelling at the whores who kept asking me about what was happening and where Jon was.

Footfalls sounded outside. My heart hammered out of control, and I turned towards the door.

The door opened, and my face fell.

Will and Leo hurried in. Their faces and clothes covered in blood and other fleshy parts I didn't want to think about.

"Where's Jon?" My throat was dry.

Will and Leo looked cold.

"They took him," said Leo.

"Who took him?" But I already knew the answer.

"The high priest. The sorcerer."

The ground wavered under my feet. I fought the nausea, and my eyes burned. I wouldn't let them see me cry.

"Is he alive?" My voice trembled.

Will shifted uncomfortably from foot to foot, looking more like a teenager than a man.

"He was, the last I saw of him."

"I heard them say they were taking him to the prison cells," said Leo. "They're keeping him alive."

I rushed over to the desk to steady myself. I was going to be sick.

Why would he keep Jon alive? Why not just kill him like he'd killed Landon?

I couldn't think, and I fought against the sob in my throat.

"So, what are we going to do about Jon?" came Will's tense voice.

The question brought me out of my shock.

I turned and looked up at both men. They were both looking me straight in the face for the first time.

And for the first time in my life, I knew how it felt to be loved. To be loved unconditionally. I'd be damned if I left Jon in the hands of the sorcerers.

"So?" said Will and Leo together. They both trusted me now and looked to me for leadership. That, in itself, was magic.

I lifted my head and looked both men straight in the eyes.

"We're going to get him back," I whispered, "if it's the last thing I ever do."

WITCH QUEEN COMING SOON!

MORE BOOKS BY KIM RICHARDSON

SOUL GUARDIANS SERIES
Marked Book # 1

Elemental Book # 2

Horizon Book # 3

Netherworld Book # 4

Seirs Book # 5

Mortal Book # 6

Reapers # 7

Seals Book # 8

MYSTICS SERIES
The Seventh Sense Book # 1

The Alpha Nation Book # 2

The Nexus Book # 3

DIVIDED REALMS
Steel Maiden Book # 1

ABOUT THE AUTHOR

Kim Richardson is the award-winning author of the bestselling SOUL GUARDIANS series. She lives in the eastern part of Canada with her husband, two dogs and a very old cat. She is the author of the SOUL GUARDIANS series, the MYSTICS series, and the DIVIDED REALMS series. Kim's books are available in print editions, and translations are available in over seven languages.

To learn more about the author, please visit:

Website
www.kimrichardsonbooks.com
Facebook
https://www.facebook.com/KRAuthorPage
Twitter
https://twitter.com/Kim_Richardson_